Restoration

ALSO BY OLAF OLAFSSON

*Valentines*

*Walking into the Night*

*Absolution*

*The Journey Home*

# Restoration

~

OLAF OLAFSSON

ecco

*An Imprint of HarperCollinsPublishers*

*Many thanks to Victoria Cribb for her invaluable assistance when writing this book*

RESTORATION. Copyright © 2012 by Double O Investment Corp. All rights reserved. Printed in the United States of America. No part of this book may be used or reproduced in any manner whatsoever without written permission except in the case of brief quotations embodied in critical articles and reviews. For information address HarperCollins Publishers, 10 East 53rd Street, New York, NY 10022.

HarperCollins books may be purchased for educational, business, or sales promotional use. For information please write: Special Markets Department, HarperCollins Publishers, 10 East 53rd Street, New York, NY 10022.

FIRST EDITION

*Designed by Mary Austin Speaker*
*Map by Chris Costello*

Library of Congress Cataloging-in-Publication Data has been applied for.

ISBN 978-0-06-206565-0

12  13  14  15  16   OV/RRD   10 9 8 7 6 5 4 3 2 1

# Historical Note

At the beginning of 1943, Mussolini lost his hold on Africa. The Allies had taken Tunis, and the Eighth Army, consisting mainly of British troops, reached Libya and headed for Tripoli. In July they used it as a springboard to invade Sicily and proceeded to work their way up the peninsula, while the Germans, coming to the aid of Mussolini and the Fascists, took control of the northern part of Italy, from Rome to the Alps. The Allies pushed north, and the Germans and the Fascists defended their territory. Partisans in support of the Allies sprang up in the Fascist-controlled areas, and the result was a bloody civil war. The partisans were made up of many disparate groups—republicans, communists, monarchists—who sometimes fought among themselves. Other groups who had little interest in politics but were all the more eager to feather their own nests robbed and plundered, following whoever offered the best prospects at the time.

Even in remote areas such as Val d'Orcia in the far south of Tuscany there was no peace. Bands of partisans fled the villages and cities to hide in the countryside. Thousands of soldiers were also on the move, fugitives from the prison camps of the Axis powers—British, Americans, French, Yugoslavs, and Poles.

Some of them threw in their lot with the partisans, others attempted to rejoin their units in the south. They sought food, shelter, and medical attention wherever they could find it. The Germans showed no mercy to those who supported either the Allies or the partisans.

This story takes place at San Martino, a farm in Val d'Orcia, in the summer of 1944.

# I

. . . SHE SITS ON A LOW CHAIR, HER JEWELRY—PEARL necklace, bracelet, and hairpin—laid aside. There is a shaft of light high up on the wall behind her and the brightness calls an answering gleam from her wet hair and delicate shoulders. She is wearing a white shift, and her skin is pale. Her lips are slightly parted, as if she has paused on the point of speaking. She is looking away, one cheek mostly invisible, the other in blue half-shadow. Her hands lie in her lap. Her expression is unfathomable . . .

The picture (oil on canvas, 97.8 x 132.7 cm) is not documented but was probably painted while Caravaggio was living with the Colonna family after fleeing Rome following the death of Ranuccio Tommassoni on May 29, 1606. Although related to his picture of Mary Magdalene, this is a more mature work. The same model, the prostitute Anna Bianchini, may have sat for both, but this is not certain . . .

On behalf of the National Gallery, it is a pleasure and an honor to invite you and a guest to the unveiling of this rare work of art on June 7 at 4 P.M. in the Central Hall. Light refreshments will be served.

From an invitation to the National Gallery
*London, May 1997*

LETTING GO OF THE BOY'S HAND, SHE RUNS INTO THE dim shed to fetch the binoculars. The sun is at its zenith and the air is sultry and still. When it last rained, a month ago, at night, she woke up, climbed out of bed, and opened the window to feel the drops on her arms. But now the leaves of the olive tree are parched and rustle in the light wind. Otherwise all is quiet for the first time in days: no troop movements on the road down in the valley, no gunfire on the mountainsides. She knows it won't last. The birds are silent in the heat but the cicadas are singing. She hears someone calling her name from the main villa but instead of answering, she raises the binoculars and scans the lower part of the turnoff.

The large farm stands on a hillside, with a view of the wide valley. Behind the villa is the central farm, the *fattoria*, which includes the dairy, workshops, laundry, the olive press, and the clinic, and next to it is a small chapel, hidden from the road by a grove of cypress trees. She was coming from the chapel when she decided to survey the roads; the boy had wanted to pray.

She can see no one. The sweat trickles into her eyes; she wipes it from her forehead and tells the boy to stay in the shade. He had just turned four when he arrived at the farm over a month ago with a group of refugee children from Turin.

She immediately learned their names; it is her way, although on this occasion it seemed more of an effort than usual.

The boy whimpers. She hushes him gently.

"Marchesa Orsini," he says, "I'm hungry."

Perhaps she was mistaken, but she thought she saw movement at the bottom of the turnoff, a momentary flash of metal or glass. Now she can see nothing, neither man nor beast. Last week a horse came up this way to the houses, its saddle askew, a riding boot caught in one of the stirrups, and congealed blood staining its flanks. The farmhands washed and fed the animal, then presented it to the partisans.

She catches sight of the young woman when she stands up. She has been sitting behind a rock at the side of the road, but now rises slowly, brushing the dust from her skirt. She's overdressed in the heat and her movements are slow and feeble. She is holding a suitcase and looks first up the slope toward the buildings, then back over her shoulder. She seems lost.

Marchesa Alice Orsini keeps the binoculars focused on the young woman's first steps up the slope. She notices that she is limping but doesn't realize how weak she is until she collapses. Instead of lying down, however, she tries at first to hold herself up, propping both hands on the ground, before eventually giving up.

Alice takes the boy by the hand and hurries over to the villa. He does his best to keep up so that she won't have to drag him along. She starts calling the farmhands before she reaches the house—"Giorgio, Fosco, Melchiorre!"—but they don't hear and she hastens inside, releasing the boy's hand as they enter the cool hall. He watches her dash down the broad passage, past the dining room and the library, until she disappears into the kitchen at the rear.

Soon the three farmhands set off down the road with horse and cart. Following through the binoculars, she watches them halt beside the young woman and lift her onto the cart, placing her suitcase beside her. They make slow progress on their return journey since the slope is steep and the road full of potholes. Dust rises from the horse's hooves as it scrabbles to find its footing, and the men strain to ease the cart forward until the horse manages to get a purchase once more.

The young woman doesn't move. She lies with eyes closed, the dust from the road settling on her sunburnt face. Her mouth is half open, her lips dry. She does not resist when the cart lurches forward; it's as if every muscle in her body is asleep. She did not speak when the men reached her.

They take her into the clinic. She has a deep wound just above her right ankle and both shins are scratched and swollen. The men do not leave, merely retreat a few steps and watch while the nurse removes the dirty dressing and washes the wound. The young woman's mouth twitches and sweat breaks out on her forehead but she does not open her eyes.

There are two other patients in the clinic, both men. The Englishman is asleep, but the Italian is awake and rises up in bed to get a better view.

"Who's that?" he asks.

The nurse doesn't answer. When he repeats the question, one of the farmhands tells him to be quiet. He does as he's told, lies down again, and resumes staring at the cracks in the ceiling over his bed.

The young woman's wound, stitched by an amateur hand, has turned septic. After a moment's indecision, the nurse makes up her mind to remove the woman's dirty clothes and wash her before continuing. Looking up, she says to the farmhands, "You'll have to leave," adding, "except you, Melchiorre."

He's the youngest, not yet twenty. His comrades tease him, saying that he has the eyes of a girl. They are large, round, and bright blue. They say he has the hands of a girl too.

As they leave, the nurse draws a screen around the young woman's bed. Melchiorre helps the nurse remove her clothes and wash the slender body with a damp cloth that he rinses in the white sink by the door. The nurse wrings out the cloth over the sunburnt arms, face, and neck, letting the water cool the young woman's skin. Elsewhere her skin is so pale that it seems almost translucent. Melchiorre gazes at the slender veins branching like meltwater beneath the snow on the mountainside in spring, all the while averting his eyes from her genitals. She reminds him of a statue.

Once the nurse has washed her and cleaned her wound, she covers her with a thin sheet. The wound will need restitching but she decides to wait until the young woman has rested. She is feverish and needs sleep.

The nurse goes to the door, opens it, and waits. Melchiorre is still standing by the bed, gazing at the young woman. When the nurse coughs, he hastily crosses himself and follows her out.

They walk side by side across the small courtyard enclosed by the back of the main villa, the clinic, and the little chapel. Their footsteps echo in the quietness and their shadows lean together. From an upstairs window in the villa, Alice watches them enter through the back door, then turns back to the young woman's suitcase on the table. She has unpacked and repacked it, removing clothes to be washed and replacing a dog-eared book on art conservation and a copy of the Bible next to a pair of shoes and a bar of soap. There were no identity papers in the case but in a side compartment she found a letter in a language she didn't understand. It appeared to be a letter of reference written on the stationery of an academy in Copenhagen, signed by a K. Jensen and concerning one Kristín Jónsdóttir. It was worn and torn along the fold, and after examining it for a while, she replaced it carefully in the side compartment.

She closes the case. A clock in the hall strikes two. If the roads remain open, the priest should arrive by three.

EVERYONE HAS GONE TO BED EXCEPT FOR ALICE AND the priest. They sit at an old wooden table in the kitchen with a candle burning between them. The candlelight illuminates their hands but does not extend much farther, fading out on their arms until the glow on their faces is almost imperceptible.

"It was a beautiful service," she says.

"Thank you."

"Some of them deserved it," she adds.

He smiles.

"I merely perform the rites," he says. "God judges."

"You know what I mean."

"There are some things I'd rather not know."

"There was nothing else they could do," she says. "He put them all in danger."

Silence.

"He wasn't going to sell the Germans information only about the British soldiers we've been sheltering but also about the partisans. His comrades. About the farmers who've taken them in. About us. We couldn't take that risk. What would become of the children?"

He nods, opening and closing his fist, as if trying to grasp the light. His movements are slow, his fingers twisted with arthritis.

"They had no choice," she says quietly. "Yet I feel so awful."

"Then I suppose you want to confess," he says.

She nods. They stand up, he first, then she. There is a piece of cheese left on a plate on the table, and his eyes stray toward it. She notices.

"Won't you finish it?" she asks.

"No," he says. "No. I've eaten too much and now I won't sleep."

He had barely touched his food. A few olives, a thin sliver of ham, a tiny helping of vegetables. That was all. He had eaten slowly, drunk only half a glass of wine, surreptitiously pouring the rest back into the carafe. When offered more food, he declined and passed the bowl or dish to his fellow diners, the nurse and the carpenter.

When he was young, he had trained for the priesthood because it was the obvious choice: he had a head for books and liked to sleep late. The job involved sacrifices, there was no denying that, but his housekeeper had turned out to be both pretty and discreet. He had worried more about the gossip of his parishioners than about the opinion of God, in whom he believed only in moderation. His housekeeper was as sincerely attached to him as he was to her: few marriages were as happy.

Now he sleeps little and has difficulty passing water when he rises at dawn. His housekeeper is dead, and he has failed in his hope of finding God in his old age. In war, God is nowhere to be found.

They walk across the courtyard, she with a lantern in her hand, he a few steps behind her. The moon casts a dim glow on the rooftops. He opens the door to the chapel and goes to light the candles, but she asks him not to. The lantern will suffice.

He takes his seat in the confessional, and she kneels on the other side of the grille. He long ago lost his belief in this ritual but listens anyway, telling himself that it is his duty as long as his flock want to talk. If it gives them comfort, isn't that justification enough?

"I still put vases of flowers in the drawing rooms and in my bedroom," she begins, "and waste time every morning deciding what to wear. I search for new lines on my face and ask the mirror if the shadows under my eyes will ever disappear. I'm abstemious, not to save food for others but because I worry about putting on weight. I notice when men look at me. I don't mind it. I'm vain."

She pauses and he waits. Years ago, when she started coming to confession, she wasn't sure how to conduct herself. He knew she wasn't a Catholic, although they never discussed the fact. He didn't care. He liked the sound of her voice. It reminded him of spring.

"I'm worried about what will become of the garden. I really shouldn't be thinking about things like that when people are dying all around us. I shouldn't worry about rosebushes. Or complain if my head aches."

She is always slow to come to the point; she has to do it in her own time. He is used to this, and listens, opening and closing his fist in the darkness. She draws a deep breath and continues:

"They had no choice. He betrayed them all. They found out that he had made a list of names to sell to the Germans. His girlfriend gave him away. Now she's beside herself with guilt. I tried to console her. I told her there was nothing else she could have done. It didn't help.

"She asked me how he died. I lied that I didn't know. Just before noon yesterday, his comrades asked my permission to bury two of their boys in our cemetery; they'd stepped on land mines outside Chianciano. The Germans are laying them everywhere. I said of course, and asked if they could dig graves at the same time for the British soldiers who died in the clinic last weekend.

"They came up the road just before noon. Fifteen of them. He was in the midst of the group. They sang as they hacked away at the hard ground with picks and shovels, but I could see that he was scared. I wanted to have a word with their leader but decided against it. Perhaps I should have . . . They sang and the blows of their picks carried all the way to the houses. I waited until they had dug the last grave, the fifth. They leant on their shovels and stopped singing. 'Larig,' said Fosco's nephew, 'you know what you've done.' He tried to protest but his words trailed off. Then he ran. He knew it was futile, of course; they had only to reach out and grab him. Two of them led him to the grave, and Fosco's nephew took a gun from his pack and fired a single shot into the back of his head."

She falls silent. The lantern is still alight but the flame is burning low. The leader of the partisans had confessed the day Larig was shot, so none of what she says is new to the priest.

"I knew what was going to happen," she says. "I knew it when I gave them permission to dig the graves. But I made no attempt to talk them out of it."

He has never given her absolution, nor has she requested it, and he is relieved not to make the pretense now. But he senses that she is waiting for him to offer some sort of comfort. Unprepared, he clears his throat several times before speaking.

"I'm old," he says. "I'm still searching for God. In your shoes I would have got rid of Larig too." He adds, "God forgive me."

They remain sitting in the darkness for a while before

making their way out into the dim moonlight. As they cross the courtyard, she stops and looks up at the clinic window. She thought she saw a face there but realizes now that it must have been the moon. Shaking her head, she takes the priest's arm and walks with him into the house.

PERHAPS YOU WILL COME BACK. PERHAPS YOU'LL come back with the dawn, stepping out of the morning like a gift I don't deserve. The tenant farmers will have risen already and welcomed you, showing you what they have done since you left—a new irrigation pipeline or a barn—waiting in suspense for your approval. Because they need it just as much as I do. They've given up asking me when you're coming home; the fattore has forbidden them, so now they ask Pritchett when they think I can't hear.

Do you remember the day we first came here? Do you remember when we arrived at the abandoned villa and you pushed open the old front door, ran up the dark staircase and shouted out of the glassless window in the master bedroom, "This is paradise!" Do you remember? And Pritchett called back, "Hell, more like! There's not a blade of grass on this windblown hill!"

You laughed at him. You never let anything stop you.

I assumed you'd taken nothing with you when you left. More than a month had gone by before I discovered that the picture Giovanni painted for you had vanished. Did you go into his room yourself to fetch it from the shelf where you asked him to keep it for you? I picture you opening the door after a little pause, hurrying in and reaching for it, then leaving just as quickly. You avoid looking at the bed. Keep your eyes straight ahead and lowered. After he died you never went into his room. This would have been the only time.

Or perhaps you didn't hurry? Did you close the door behind you and talk to him for a while in the dwindling light? Did you handle his toys, sit on his bed, and open one of the books you used to read to him before he fell asleep? Did you tell him, perhaps, what you would have liked to tell him while he was alive? I do. I go to his room every day and talk to him. I haven't touched a thing. Everything is just as it was, everything except for the picture that has gone.

I had gone to Montepulciano in the morning for supplies. We hadn't said a word to each other for almost a week, and I had decided to clear the air when I returned from my trip. I asked myself if I was prepared to tell you the truth. The thought alone of confessing made me so sick that I had to ask the driver to pull over. The sun was setting, but the temperature had risen as the wind dropped. I walked away from the car and threw up. I wondered if I should turn back and spend the night in Montepulciano but made up my mind to continue. I had to pretend to be brave despite having no idea what I was going to say to you. I had no way of justifying what I had done.

You were gone when we came home. I wasn't surprised, but it didn't cross my mind that you would not come back. I assumed you had left on one of the solitary riding trips you had started to take. That's what Pritchett thought too when I ran into him outside the chapel.

I stayed in my room for the rest of the evening. The thought of confessing had left me exhausted. Every now and then I heard shooting to the east of the villa but otherwise it was quiet. Pritchett said there had been flare-ups all afternoon, minor skirmishes between the partisans and the Fascists. He had been helping the fattore fix the olive press and spoke about the progress they had made. He was very pleased and maintained that the press had never been in better shape. "Good," I said, "good," and was relieved when he left the room.

I got news of you in St. Moritz just before Christmas but that turned out to be a mistake. Nothing since then. It's been nine months and three days.

I talk to you as I lie in bed in the evenings, just as I used to when you were here and everything was fine. I tell you about the events of the day, now that the war has come to our valley and the Germans and the Fascists watch our every move. I tell you the things that I hesitate to write in this diary for fear that the Germans will find it when they come back. I've received a warning because of the rumors that I help the partisans and shelter Allied soldiers. I don't care about myself, but I can't endanger the children and our people.

I can't trust anyone I don't know. The other day a German came here claiming to be a deserter. He begged for shelter and asked us to burn his uniform. I showed him the door. He was unconvincing. His eyes were shifty and his story didn't ring true.

This morning a young woman appeared at the bottom of the hill and collapsed there. I noticed her by chance; I often find myself scanning the turnoff. Perhaps I'm looking for you. She's injured and has slept all day. There is no identification in her luggage apart from a letter in a language I don't understand, probably Danish. She's pale, Nordic-looking.

Fortunately, the summer days are long. I scurry about from morning to night, trying to be useful. There are twenty-four refugee children staying with us now, most of them from

Genoa and Turin. Schwester Marie, our Swiss nanny, is run off her feet looking after them, and although she has two girls to help her, she takes on so much herself that I worry about her. Giovanni's death affected her just as much as us. I know you will shake your head when I say that but it's true. She spent more time with him than we did during the last year. We're both to blame.

Alice closes her diary, screws the lid on her slender pen and puts it away in the drawer of her dressing table. All is quiet as she gets out of bed, walks barefoot across the floor, and, picking up two loose tiles in the corner, puts the book in the cavity underneath. She replaces the tiles, then takes two steps backward and inspects the floor, making sure no unevenness is visible where Pritchett loosened them.

SHE WAS ENGLISH AND HAD MOVED WHEN SHE WAS five with her mother from London to Florence where she grew up among her countrymen who flocked there in search of novelty. Many of them were wealthy, from good families, and collected art and doted on their cats and dogs, giving them names that she found comic at first, then absurd with the passing of time—Dante, Leonardo, Michelangelo. The English kept to themselves. Their numbers had multiplied after the Great War and the city had an English doctor, a chemist, and even a dentist; English shops that sold tea, tweeds, mackintoshes, and tennis racquets; and two English newspapers, the *Florence Directory* and the *Florence Herald*, which reported the news from home and from their little colony.

Her father was dead, her mother remarried to a nouveau riche Englishman who composed third-rate operas when he wasn't in bed, convinced that he was dying. They were keen for her to find a husband. An Englishman.

He was Italian, the son of a minor landowner but a titled nobleman. He was ten years older. Marchese Claudio Orsini. Her mother said she was heartbroken, and her stepfather took to his bed in the midst of a new opera. They co-opted friends and relatives to try to talk some sense into her and when that didn't work, they asked the vicar at the English church on the Via La Marmora to tell her what God thought of the arrangement.

They were married in the Salone dei Matrimoni in Fiesole. Her mother fell ill just before the ceremony and stayed in her room throughout. Lady Paget, who made shoes of velvet and silk that no one could walk in, gave them a crocodile for a wedding present.

"If you're lucky, he'll eat your husband," she whispered to the bride.

The *Florence Herald* published a picture of the newlyweds, or rather of the bride, as the groom was barely visible, on page two. The piece accompanying the picture reported who had attended the wedding and hinted that Claudio's family was not as wealthy as Alice's.

Claudio was tall and sturdy, with deep-set eyes and a large nose. He had broad, slightly clumsy hands and thick fingers. He was not talkative; the English said he was gauche. He wasted few words on them. At the reception, Alice's stepfather whispered in his ear that Alice had only married him to annoy her mother. Claudio smiled.

They fled on their wedding night. They fled the grandiose English dinner parties, the fancy-dress balls and amateur theatricals. The gossip, the squabbles and feuds. The sleep-drugged mornings, the idle afternoons. The pointlessness. She had tried to overcome it by volunteering at San Domenico where she helped to nurse the poor, but it didn't change a thing. She was twenty-two and saw no prospect of ever doing anything that mattered. They changed clothes in their hotel room, leaving dress and suit on the bed, grabbing the suitcases they had packed earlier and rendezvousing with the driver at the rear entrance as arranged.

They fell asleep in the car once they had cleared the city and did not awake until dawn. By then they were not far from Pienza, and the driver had stopped because he needed directions for the last stretch. Claudio pulled a map from his pocket and they pored over it together while Alice got out of the car to stretch her legs. She walked to the edge of the escarpment a short way from the car and gazed over the valley that opened out beneath her. Mist lay over it. Trees jutted up at the top of the slopes, but down below the mist was like a lake, blue at first, then silver as it began to disperse. Claudio came over and told her that they would have to turn around; the driver had taken a wrong fork several kilometers back. They were heading for a small farm that their friend Cecil Pritchett knew was for sale and thought would suit them. Pritchett lived in Montalcino. He was an architect who had left Florence several months before in search of change and was one of the few members of the English community to accept Claudio when Alice introduced him. The two men had formed an instant rapport. They were similar types and shared an interest in architecture and gardening, both feeling most at home in the countryside. Pritchett had never liked his Christian name, so those who knew him referred to him only by his surname. He was single and some of his countrymen claimed that his tastes did not run to women. But Claudio dismissed such gossip with a laugh.

They had arranged to meet Pritchett at nine. He was going to give them breakfast before taking them to see the farm.

Instead of returning to the car, Alice pointed to a house emerging from the mist on the other side of the valley.

"That's not it," Claudio said, then realized what she meant. "Are you serious?"

"Doesn't it look empty to you?" she asked. "Maybe it's for sale."

"Or maybe not," he replied.

"Come on," she said. "Please. Look, it's so beautiful."

They went to meet Pritchett first.

"Val d'Orcia?" he exclaimed. "Nothing but barren, wind-blasted slopes. The *crete senesi*. No one wants to live there."

She was in such a rush to be off that she barely touched her breakfast.

"Can we go now?" she kept asking, like an impatient child. "Can we go?"

In the end the men gave in, woke the driver who had been napping on a couch in Pritchett's studio, and set off. It was not far, but the journey proved arduous, for the roads deteriorated the closer they came to the house on the hill.

"You see," Pritchett said. "No one drives here unless absolutely necessary."

The driver came to a halt as the road entered a dark forest. Fallen tree trunks lay across the track.

"You'll have to walk from here," he said.

Alice leapt out and almost ran up the slope. Pritchett and Claudio followed behind. When they caught up with her, she was standing outside the villa, at a loss. The roof had partly caved in, the bricks in the walls were cracked, and the garden was a wilderness. The front door turned out to be unlocked, but when Claudio asked her if she wanted to go inside, she shook her head.

"The whole place is falling apart," she said. "I'm sorry I dragged you here."

He pushed the door. It gave way and he entered the dark house, climbed the stone staircase that greeted him in the middle of the hall, and made straight for the glassless window above the front door.

"This is paradise!"

She and Pritchett followed him inside.

"You're only saying that for my sake," she said when they came upstairs. "There's no need."

He put his arms around her and pointed out the window at the unsown fields bathed in sunshine, at the river winding through the valley.

"I'm saying it for our sake. It's perfect. This must be fate."

Pritchett tracked down the owner and they bought the estate two days later, free of all encumbrances apart from those relating to the outlying farms.

The estate covered 3,500 acres of the most inhospitable corner of the province of Siena. There was no vegetation on the hills except the odd fir tree, stunted bushes, and scrub. The soil was clay, and the gray ridges rising one after another away from the buildings resembled the backs of the local oxen. The buildings were all in a tumbledown state; there was no electricity or central heating, no bathroom, and the kitchen was unusable. Everywhere there was a smell of damp. Where the roof was open to the elements, owls had nested in the loft, while mice had even colonized the grand piano in the day room. Grass sprouted between the stones of the courtyard and terraces around the buildings, and reached up under the tips of the sails of the windmill that was crumbling into the ground higher up the slope. The river Orcia flowed through the valley but was running low when they arrived, and the white, sun-baked boulders standing out of the shallow water were visible from far away.

There were twenty-five tenant farms on the property, all in

disrepair. Their roofs leaked, and the tenants—desperately poor peasant families, illiterate and deeply distrustful—had stuffed dirty rags into the window openings where the glass had broken. It was the duty of the landowner to maintain their cottages and pay half the total cost of cultivating the land. In return he received half of the harvest. But here the landowner had neglected his duties for years. The fattore was supposed to look after the tenant farms on the landowner's behalf, but his employer ignored his demands and his clients had lost faith in him. He was in his sixties, a short, sturdy figure, who was overjoyed with Claudio's enthusiasm. For three days they rode from farm to farm, visiting the tenants. Claudio promised improvements, but the farmers were afraid to hope that anything would come of it.

Alice's friends and family warned her against it. "Madness," they said, "you don't have the first clue about farming, brought up with a silver spoon in your mouth. Think what you're doing. There's the fox-trot at Stevens on Saturday night, a new delivery of hats and coats expected in the shops after the weekend, the opening night of your stepfather's opera next week. He'll be hurt if you don't come. He's dedicated the work to you . . ."

It was obvious that they should ask Pritchett to assist them. Before moving to Montalcino, he had restored numerous apartments for the English in Florence, as well as country villas outside the city. He had a reputation for being hardworking and efficient, and they both trusted him implicitly.

Pritchett took care of the buildings, Claudio the farm. Alice withdrew half her patrimony from the bank, her husband most of his savings. They worked tirelessly on the improvements, and gradually San Martino began to take on a new appearance. When the mercury mine at Monte Amiata closed, they employed everyone who had worked there, some two hundred men. They built roads to the tenant farms, restored the buildings, dug wells, constructed dams and bridges. They planted vines and olive trees, cleared fields for wheat, and put in irrigation systems. They blocked the wind erosion with twenty-five tons of gravel and soil dug from the bed of the river Orcia and its tributaries and laid irrigation pipelines up the slopes. Greenhouses rose near the main house and a five-hundred-acre area was planted with cypress trees, dotted with oaks. At first, they had no machines for harvesting. Farmers and field hands gathered at dawn and worked until dusk, forming a long row and walking the fields side by side. The plow was drawn by Maremma oxen, huge light-gray beasts. Years later, workers and oxen were superseded by harvester, tractor, thresher, bulldozer, and steam-powered plow.

After the first six months at San Martino, Alice and Claudio offered Pritchett a share in the farm if he would be willing to dedicate the next few years to its restoration. He didn't have to think long; since he had given up on Florence and moved to Montalcino, business had been slow. Alice and Claudio were ideal clients—rational, thoughtful, and reasonable—and a project like this would perhaps never be offered to him again. He sold his little farm in Montalcino, where he had spent a total of five nights since his work at San Martino had begun, packed up his belongings, and moved for good.

In the summer of 1934, Alice began to keep a diary.

"I live on a farm in the south of Tuscany. Chianciano, the nearest village, is twelve miles away, the railway station six. Our house stands on a hill with a view of a wide valley. On the other side is Monte Amiata, its lower slopes covered with cypresses and beeches but farther up you can see chestnuts attempting to climb toward the top. On this side, however, the land is cultivated. We grow potatoes, wheat, and olives. In the mornings before sunrise the valley is covered by a blue mist; in the evenings it returns . . ."

Silence was banished from the houses, the owls fled the loft, the mice made themselves scarce. Around the main villa they created an English garden, *giardino inglese*, where perfect order reigned, independent of divine caprice. One terrace succeeded another, divided by tall hedges that concealed here and there a grassy dell. Climbing roses and wisteria covered the pergolas between the terraces, and in front of the small conservatory two dolphins spouted water into a fountain, casting a shadow onto the patio in the late afternoon. In the shade next to the villa, Pritchett arranged an old stone bench and table. A lemon tree overhung the bench where Alice would sit and read on hot days.

Claudio and Pritchett toiled from morning to night, earning the trust and respect of the workmen and tenant farmers. But Alice felt that they regarded her as odd. She withdrew, refusing at first to accompany her husband on visits to the farms where she was expected. When she did finally give in to persuasion, she was insecure and anxious. She borrowed some clothes from one of the maids, not wanting to look overdressed, then changed her mind and dressed up as if she were attending a function in Florence.

The tenants stood in a huddle in front of the cottages, staring when she arrived on her horse. She had difficulty finding the right words. They would bring her a chicken or eggs or cheese, as was traditional, but she found it impossible to accept food from such poor people. Perhaps it was obvious? Or did they think she was too haughty to accept a few eggs or the hen that laid them?

She gave up after a few farms and went home. There she shut herself in her room and wouldn't come out until her husband returned from the fields and tapped on her door.

"They were right," she said.

"Who?"

"My mother and the others. I have no business here."

She did not cry; it was not her way.

That autumn, when Claudio had given up hope that his wife would ever get used to living in the countryside, he found her late one morning standing with a group of children in the English garden. They had slipped away without permission from their homes on the farms to see the big villa that they had heard was now like a palace. Alice had spotted them from her bedroom window, stealing into the garden and pausing behind the fountain, watching entranced as the dolphins spouted water at each other.

She had hurried out with cold drinks and fruit and managed to keep the children from running away. They proved to be both hungry and thirsty. Claudio found her as she was herding them off to the kitchen to give them lunch. She read them a story in the library after their meal before sending them home.

"How many children are there on the farms?" she asked him after they had gone.

He didn't know but asked the fattore who guessed that there were around fifty.

"They're illiterate," she said. "We must educate them."

She set to without delay. The outbuildings on the other side of the road were rebuilt, tables and chairs were installed in the newly painted rooms, and maps were pinned to the walls beside the crucifixes and obligatory photographs of the king and Mussolini. The teacher's desk was equipped with globe and gramophone, scissors, ruler, and slide rule. She herself provided the first books for the shelves behind the teacher's desk: *Kidnapped* and *Rob Roy* for the boys, *The Secret Garden* and *Little Women* for the girls, as well as several volumes of fairy tales. She appointed a young man from Pienza to the post and bought him a bicycle. His name was Signor Grandinetti, a short man with delicate features and bright eyes.

The children were collected in the mornings and driven in horse-drawn carts to the school when conditions were good, but when the weather was bad and the roads all but impassable, oxen were harnessed to the wagons. Their route took them down the hill past the main villa and on down the road. Alice used to go out in the mornings to await their arrival. She would hear them long before the carts appeared, their bright, cheerful voices accompanied by the jingling of the harness.

She converted the old barn by the courtyard into a clinic for the usual ailments and injuries and arranged for the nurse who had attended her stepfather when he was ill to move up from Florence. This did nothing to improve relations with her stepfather and mother, but the nurse was delighted at her escape. She was English, a native of Birmingham, Signorina Harris.

In summer we eat outside in the garden under the trees. Just before the sun dips behind the mountains, its last rays are swallowed up by the sea of leaves, the light turns a deep blue, and fireflies come out like little stars among the trees. The nightingale sings and I place my hand in yours under the table.

We live on a farm in the south of Tuscany. I never want to leave.

THE YOUNG WOMAN SAW THE BUILDINGS ON THE hill rise and fall in waves, sometimes disappearing altogether. She stopped, put down her suitcase, and rubbed her eyes, wiping away the sweat and dust as if cleaning an old painting.

The man who gave her directions in the little village just outside Chiusi had said it was less than ten kilometers to the valley where the English lady lived. That was the day before yesterday. He offered her a room for the night, showing her the bed that had belonged to his son who was killed in April when the Germans had surrounded the village and sniffed out the partisans who used it as a base. He said they had shot them in the square and hung their bodies from the lampposts as a warning to others.

"I cut him down when it was dark," he said, "and took him home."

There was a photograph of the boy at the head of the bed where she rested for a while but could not sleep. It was late when she said good-bye to the man and continued on her way. He pressed her to stay the night but she was in a hurry to keep going.

The stitches she had received after the bombing of the train had begun to tear. Sometimes the pain stopped her in her tracks. It was constant now, but she had made it; the buildings undulating on the hill above her fit the description she had been given.

She stopped frequently on this last stretch, putting down her case and wondering if she should leave it behind when she set off again, lighten her load by taking only the essentials. But she never did; she hadn't the energy to open it.

Throughout the journey from Rome she had paid the price for being so badly prepared, and she rebuked herself for her stupidity. Losing her wits, running off like that without thinking, letting panic guide her. She was not accustomed to acting like that. She was not accustomed to behaving as she had done recently.

She had grabbed an empty lemonade bottle before running away from the burning train, and had filled it as she went along, in rivers and streams, in half-ruined houses, from companies of soldiers who took pity on her, and at the field hospital where they stitched up her wound. But now the bottle was empty, and she was too weak to hobble down to the river Orcia, reduced to a mere trickle in its meandering, rocky bed. The buildings faded from view when she looked up and refused to reappear when she rubbed her eyes. Her strength was gone.

She remembered them bringing the cart down the hill. She remembered being lifted onto it and the face of the young man nearest her, his big eyes. The clatter when the horse's hooves slipped on the stones, the snorting, the silence of the men. Then nothing.

The clinic is white: the walls, ceiling, curtains, and the sheet that covers her. The sun shines on a blue water jug by the sink. The window by her bed is open, and when she turns her head she can glimpse an unchanging, cloudless sky. There is a sound of hammering from outside. The screen beside her bed blocks her view of the rest of the room, but she can hear that she is not alone. A man coughs, then heaves a sigh.

She is lying on her back, but when she tries to turn over, the pain in her leg prevents her. She lies back, drawing a deep breath.

She is unprepared when he addresses her.

"Are you awake?"

She is flustered. No matter how she wrestled with the dilemma on the way from Rome, she had been unable to decide what reason to give for her journey. Now she feels she can't say anything until she has worked out a plausible explanation, because one thing leads to another, and words that initially seem harmless can later block off countless avenues of retreat.

"I can tell you're awake," he says. "I can tell from your breathing. I've been waiting for you to wake up. Signorina Harris too—the nurse. And the Marchesa. She came here this morning with Signorina Harris. Then she came back alone. She stood by your bed watching you. She watched you for a long time."

He is a local, she can tell by his accent. Probably in his early twenties, like her. His voice grates on her nerves, perhaps because he is asking questions to which she has no answers.

"I'm Bruno," he says. "Who are you?"

She tries to breathe as she imagines she would if she were asleep. She has no memory of Signorina Harris or the Marchesa. All she can remember is the eyes of the young man who lifted her onto the cart. They pursued her into her dreams, reappearing there in a different face.

The man who sat opposite her in the train compartment on the way from Rome still has his cigarette in the corner of his mouth, but the eyes behind the smoke are those of the boy. They are still there when he is slumped on the floor of the compartment, lifeless. The cigarette has fallen from his mouth and lies burning beside him; his eyes are open, staring at her as if through a thin, watery film. "Out!" she hears someone yelling. "Everyone out!" She sees herself tugging at her suitcase that she has found amidst the wreckage, dragging it behind her out of the burning train. Her leg is heavy, indescribably heavy. She tries to run but can't.

"I don't suppose we'll get any ham today," says the young Italian. "We had ham yesterday. Not you; you were asleep. Not the Englishman; he died just after you arrived. I knew he never had a chance. The Germans shot him when he escaped the camp. I could tell he was dead long before they carried him out. It was a different kind of silence. Just like I can tell now that you're awake. But you needn't talk to me. You needn't say anything. If you die, I'll be able to tell."

She dreamt of a swan flying over a pond. There was cotton grass in the marsh by the pond, white as the swan that left its reflection behind in the water when it flew away. She waded out to catch the reflection, not stopping even when she heard people calling her name.

"Kristín, what are you doing?"

The water reaches up to midthigh. She has hitched up her yellow dress, holding the skirt in her slender little hands. She is eight years old and knows of nothing as beautiful as this pond and the birds that frequent it.

"Kristín!"

She turns around, leaving the image of the swan behind in the water.

AS THE WAR INTENSIFIED, SAN MARTINO BECAME AN ideal refuge for partisans and Allied soldiers who had escaped the prison camps of the Axis powers: self-sufficient and dependent on no one. Marchesa Alice Orsini and her household baked their own bread from wheat grown in their fields, raised sheep, chickens, and geese, and grew their own vegetables; ran their own dairy, gathered honey from their hives, and made jam from fruit picked in their orchards. The ham they ate was cured on the spot, as were the salami and goat cheese. There was abundant kindling to heat the houses, as well as olive kernels that made good fuel. They made soap with the residue of kitchen fats, combined with potato peels and soda. They sewed clothes and made shoes. The clinic stocked essential medicines and surgical instruments, and nothing flustered Signorina Harris, a veteran of the Great War.

An ideal refuge, isolated and remote from the hostilities at first. But of course that would change along with everything else.

Before the partisans and soldiers came the refugee children from Genoa. The vehicle that drove them to San Martino, having gotten lost on the way, rattled up the road as evening fell. There was a nurse sitting next to the driver, but in the back were seven sleeping little creatures, the eldest six, the others younger. All girls except for a shy little boy from Sardinia. He reminded Alice so terribly of her Giovanni that at first she could hardly look at him.

They carried them into the school where a fire was burning in the grate and hot food awaited them. It took them a long time to grow accustomed to the lights; they stood silently in the middle of the room, blinking and rubbing their eyes in the unexpected glare. Their faces were chalk white, their limbs spindly.

The Red Cross had asked her to take them in. Claudio was under the impression that Alice had approached them first, and asked if she thought it was sensible to draw attention to themselves in this way.

"Do you know what repercussions this could have?" he asked. "Don't we have enough on our plates with trying to feed our own people?"

Then he added, "They won't replace him. No one can."

He walked away. It had snowed that morning and she stood for a long time by the window after he had gone, staring at the white-mantled pines in the garden. When the pain finally subsided, she went up to her room and locked the door.

First the refugee children, then the partisans, then the odd escaped prisoner of war. Followed by the children from Turin, more partisans and soldiers. She couldn't turn them away, didn't have the heart despite being fully aware of the risk she was taking.

When she tried to consult Claudio, he told her it was too late.

"Why would you be asking me now? I counted three partisans in the kitchen this morning and two Allied soldiers. In addition to all the children. You've made sure there's no turning back."

She was angry and asked him where his loyalties lay. She regretted it immediately, knowing how unfair that was. An early supporter of Mussolini, Claudio had turned against him and his government as soon as the war broke out.

The winter was cold and wet, and as the Allies pushed north and the Germans retreated, the fighting moved closer. When spring arrived, Alice would sometimes wake up to what she believed was the sound of distant rumbling from the fleet bombarding the Tuscan coast, but gradually the shelling drew nearer, and one day in August the first bombs fell in the valley. It was after dinner; she and Claudio were still sitting at the table in the garden; the others had finished. They had continued their custom of dining with Pritchett, Nurse Harris, Signor Grandinetti, and Schwester Marie, and Alice made it a rule that there was to be no talk of the war during the meal. At first, mealtimes were awkward, but then the household grew accustomed to this eccentric habit and eventually came to welcome it. Pritchett had been telling them about a trip he had made to Rome in May, about the girls sitting on the pavements outside the cafés in their decorative summer hats, the young men strutting past, ogling them, the fountains spraying water into the air, the flowerpots overflowing with irises and roses. It was as if the hostilities had been temporarily suspended, he said. And he spoke of the children in Giardino del Lago, sailing their model boats on the lake, with the swans swimming by. Pritchett was in a good mood—he had completed the annex to the schoolhouse that day—and his story seemed to be building up to a humorous finale. But he never finished it because Claudio suddenly spoke up:

"Yes, Rome's always so entertaining. Isn't it, Alice? So much going on. Too bad the war is now preventing you from spending time there."

Pritchett stopped talking, and the others hastened to finish their meal and leave husband and wife behind with the silence thick between them. When Claudio got up, slowly as if he were physically exhausted, intending to walk away, Alice said in a low voice, "You talk like that in front of them but when we're alone you say nothing."

"I have nothing to say that you want to hear."

"There is nothing worse than your silence."

"Don't be so sure."

She was about to answer him when the first bomb fell. She jumped to her feet and ran onto the veranda, which gave a clear view of the valley. Claudio didn't move. She heard the planes fly away and saw the fire that flared up on the hillside above Campiglia.

"They're here," she said. "The Allies."

He did not answer.

"They're here," she repeated.

At last he rose to his feet. He did not go to her, merely stood by the table and said in a low voice, "Where were you the evening he died? Tell me. Where were you?"

KRISTÍN HAD KNOWN WHAT WOULD HAPPEN THE first time they met. She sensed it the moment he took her hand, adjusted the pencil, and guided it back to the paper. And yet he hadn't uttered a single word.

She had spent four years in Copenhagen at the Royal Academy of Art before coming south. There she had socialized with both students and artists and had chosen lovers from their ranks. These relationships did not last long, but then that had never been her intention. Something had to give way. Artists make sacrifices. Female artists especially. She had no doubt what her fate would be if she let herself be tied down.

She was in her early twenties and sometimes reflected on how young this was as she wandered the streets of Rome, looking back over its centuries. The achievements of the human spirit were all around her—churches and museums, amphitheaters and statues, fountains and colonnades—and from these she sought her inspiration. It was possible to leave behind something that outlived the flesh.

She headed first to Florence, where she rented a cheap little room in a side street near the cathedral and made daily trips to the Uffizi where she sat and sketched one masterpiece after another: the head of Jesus from Verrocchio's baptism scene;

Botticelli's Venus in her shell, blown onto the beach by a balmy west wind; a bowl of fruit from Caravaggio's *Bacchus*. Fragments of countless works. Hands and feet and bellies and shoulders, as her tutors at the Academy had advised her before she set out. Movement. Stasis. Light and shadow. "And don't be afraid of the most famous works," they had said, "don't feel you have to avoid them. Don't say to yourself, 'I don't want to be like everyone else. Everyone knows those paintings. I want to be different.' Michelangelo, Leonardo, Lippi, Raphael, Titian, Caravaggio. Draw as much as you can. You can be different when you have mastered the basics."

It was a tutor at the Academy who had given her Robert Marshall's name. The two men had studied together when they were young and, as the tutor put it, "respected each other." She found his choice of words odd but didn't think much of it.

"He's an Englishman," the tutor had said. "He's lived in Italy for a long time and is regarded as one of the foremost experts on the Renaissance. Author of two books on the period; adviser to Joseph Duveen, the famous art dealer, who will not buy a Renaissance painting without Marshall's blessing."

He wrote his address on a piece of paper: *Signor Robert Marshall, Via Margutta, 118.*

Her funds were running low by the time she reached Rome. Not that her stay in Florence had been expensive, but she had not come away from Copenhagen with much money in the first place. She had worked in a restaurant when she was a student and now found a waitressing job in a café near the Pantheon. The hours were good; she worked nights and was able to concentrate on her art during the day.

When the war broke out, she thought about leaving but quickly put that out of her mind. There was no place for her to call home; her grandparents had both passed away while she was living in Copenhagen. Besides, the war had initially no discernible impact on daily life in Rome: there were no shortages and the fighting was far away.

She looked him up in the summer of 1940, a few days after Italy had declared war on France and Britain. She put her tutor's note in her pocket and walked up and down Via del Babbuino a few times before making up her mind and crossing over to Via Margutta. It was after lunch; the weather was warm and bright, her mind open, her footsteps light.

Via Margutta is a quiet little side street and her knock on the door sounded loud. But then there was silence, and when no one answered, she rapped on the door again, more gently this time, almost with diffidence.

The woman who came to the door listened politely while Kristín explained her business. Then she nodded, asked her to wait, and closed the door again. She returned a few minutes later with the message that Signor Marshall was not available but asked if she would meet him the following day at Babington's Tea Rooms by the Spanish Steps. At three o'clock. Would that be convenient?

She arrived punctually and when she mentioned Marshall's name, she was shown to a table in the front room. There was a painting of a woman on the wall opposite and she took out her sketchpad to pass the time. She was drawing the woman's eyes when he took her hand holding the pencil. She hadn't noticed him and jumped although his touch was gentle. He guided her hand back to the paper and said, "Carry on."

She did so hesitantly, and he stood behind her, watching her in silence. Then he sat down, still watching. She found it hard to concentrate but finished the drawing anyway. He held out his hand and she passed him the pad. He leafed through it, neither quickly nor slowly, stopping at last at the drawing she had just completed.

"Botticelli, Leonardo, the parapet on a bridge, and now this. What do you think of it?"

"I had nothing else to do," she heard herself saying and instantly reproached herself for her apologetic tone.

"Poor Giuseppe," he said. "You've captured him. His mediocrity."

He continued to leaf through, stopping at Raphael's self-portrait, which she had sketched in the Uffizi.

"Mediocrity's easier," he said as if to himself. "But you're on the right track. The neutrality of the master's expression is there. The eyes giving nothing away. The pale, almost feminine cheek. What do you think is missing?"

"I don't know."

Smiling, he closed the pad and handed it to her.

"What news of my friend Jensen? Still as earnest as ever?"

She told him that she had heard that the German occupation of Denmark had had no impact on his job but his previous question continued to echo in her head. She was on the verge of asking him but stopped herself.

"What do you think is missing?"

They drank tea. He told her that eminent Fascists regularly met in the room to the left, while the rumor was that Il Duce's opponents frequented the room to the right. "We're caught between them. In the peaceful zone . . . By Giuseppe's picture."

He did the talking.

"You must draw Botticelli slowly. Lift the pencil regularly and inspect what's there. Try to guess what comes next without looking at the original. Botticelli used to listen to birdsong as he worked. Kept the window open. Can you hear the birds singing when you stand in front of his work?"

"It hadn't occurred to me," she said.

"Not surprising. But it'll come. In time."

Their cups were empty. He fell silent, then looked at her.

"What can I do for you?"

Unprepared for the question, she answered perhaps more bluntly than intended.

"I have been waitressing but . . ."

"But you feel you're wasting your time?"

She didn't feel the right to call herself an artist and blushed.

"You're right," he continued. "You should devote yourself to your art."

She was silent.

"You won't learn anything by being a waitress," he said. "Come to my studio at ten tomorrow morning. We'll see if I can find something for you to do."

Then he was gone. She remained sitting there for a little while longer before rising and putting the sketchpad and pencil in her bag. Before she left, her gaze fell on the painting on the wall. It made her uncomfortable; she suddenly felt responsible for it in some way, as if she were implicated in the artist's inadequacy. She hurried out and before she knew it, she had torn the sketch from her pad and thrown it in a litter bin.

KRISTÍN REMEMBERS THE FIRST TIME SHE SAW ALICE. It was in the autumn of 1940. She and Marshall were standing side by side at the Trevi Fountain, and Alice reached into her bag for a coin to throw into the water. Her movements were slow and unhurried, and she didn't seem to say anything after she had thrown the coin. He did the talking. As always. She saw that Alice was listening as she studied the fountain and the statues above it, of Neptune and Triton and the sea horses. Then she turned to him and communicated something with her eyes before walking away. He stood still, watching her vanish into the crowd.

Kristín had followed Marshall there from the studio. She took care not to let him see her, but it wasn't difficult, as he had no suspicion of being pursued. He went first to the tobacconist's, then straight to the fountain. Alice was waiting for him. Their meeting was brief.

The smell of him still lingered in Kristín's hair, the invisible imprint of his kisses on her breasts and neck. The echo of his voice in her head, the words he had left behind. He talked before they made love and afterward as well, whispering to her what she wanted to hear.

"Kristín, why aren't we alone in the world? Even for a day?"

She had followed him out of curiosity, not suspicion. His kisses were still strange to her, the words that accompanied his caresses still unfamiliar. He had dressed slowly, reaching for the trousers that he had folded and hung over the back of the chair by her worktable, the shirt and jacket that he had laid on top of the trousers. She had watched him putting on his tie in front of a fragment of mirror on the shelf; the long, strong fingers as they adjusted the knot, then reached into his jacket pocket for a comb. He did not speak while he looked in the mirror, but turned to her and gave her a quick smile as he slipped the comb back into his pocket.

"Even for a day."

He kissed her on the cheek, then strode out, down the stairs and outside into the narrow, cobbled street.

"Who are you?" she had asked herself under her breath, and quickly pulled on her clothes and ran out so as not to lose sight of him.

He walked neither quickly nor slowly, glanced once at his watch, and swung the cane that became him so well but was only for show. The day was cloudy but still, with a few puddles on the streets after last night's rain. He picked his way around them, not stopping until he came to the tobacconist's. He did not spend long inside.

He had made her kneel on a bench by the wall, clasping her hips in both hands. She turned her head to look into his eyes, those eyes that saw through time. Saw everything, knew the brushstroke even when it was hidden under dust and dirt, could distinguish countless colors in every shadow, found a ray of light where others saw only darkness. He was her master.

As he dressed, he examined the painting she was cleaning.

A soldier in a breastplate with a sword in his hand, probably mid-eighteenth century.

"He has blue eyes," he said. "And his breastplate's dented on the right-hand side. You'll see that when you've resolved the water damage. A mediocre artist. But the owners don't know that. And there's no need to enlighten them."

She listened with only one ear. She was wondering why he always talked about her work when they had made love. He had done so on the first two occasions as well. She had been restoring an altarpiece. He had talked about the ground layer as he dressed.

Kristín didn't know who Alice was and couldn't tell from her and Marshall's manner how well they knew each other. She tried to guess what had passed between them but soon gave up. She was struck by the grace of Alice's movements. The same thought occurred to her the next time she saw her. Almost three years later.

Now Alice is standing by her bed when she opens her eyes. Signorina Harris is with her. They are discussing her.

"Her leg's in a bad way," the nurse says. "I had to give her morphine."

Kristín closes her eyes again.

"And the wound?"

"I stitched it. It seems to be healing reasonably well."

"Has she said anything?"

"No."

They are silent. She has the feeling that they are looking at her but does not get the sense that Alice recognizes her. And why should she? she says to herself. I was a fool thinking she might.

"I don't understand how she could have walked in that condition," the nurse says.

"When will she be back on her feet?"

"In a few days." She adds, "God willing, and as long as the infection doesn't return."

"We need the bed as soon as possible," Alice says. "We're bound to get more casualties in the next few days."

Alice leaves. The nurse remains.

"When will we have ham again?" asks Bruno.

"Are you hungry?"

"I'm always hungry."

"That's a sign of recovery."

"She's awake some of the time," he says. "I can tell from her breathing. But she doesn't say anything."

In the summer of 1943 Kristín saw Alice the second time at a party at Marshall's home. Kristín had bought herself a yellow dress for the occasion and wore it with a blue scarf knotted around her neck and blue shoes. It was two years since she had been invited to their home, but she remembered the apartment in detail. The room was crowded, and apart from acknowledging her briefly when she arrived, he left her alone. He greeted many people with kisses, but not her. He merely took her hand and said politely, "Welcome, Kristín."

She withdrew and stood by the wall, watching the dancing. He danced first with his wife, who was as beautiful as always. Whenever Kristín had asked him about her, he had always changed the subject, often with a look of disapproval. Now she watched her smiling in his arms.

There were a number of prominent figures at the party, particularly Italians and Germans: Marshall's clients. Some of them she knew by sight, having seen them at the studio. Von Hassel, the German ambassador, greeted her. Others did not recognize her. They were not used to seeing her dressed up like this.

She noticed the woman from the fountain the moment she entered the room. She held her head high but without being haughty. She was wearing a backless dress and Kristín's eyes were immediately drawn to her long, slender neck and her broad but delicate shoulders. Count Ciano, the foreign minister and Mussolini's son-in-law, went straight over to her and kissed her hand. They danced. Her movements were effortless and graceful. Kristín asked a waiter who the woman was. "The Marchesa Orsini," he answered.

Feeling hot, she went into the adjacent room, walked over to the French window and looked out. It was open and faced a square where pigeons fluttered after bread crumbs and young Blackshirts horsed around in the warm evening air. Waiters passed through the room with trays of wineglasses and a young man came over to her, glass in hand, and asked if she was alone. When she said she was, he began to tell her about himself. She did not pretend to be interested at first. But then she noticed her master standing at the door, watching them, and forced herself to turn her attention to the young man. He raised his voice, his gestures becoming more extravagant. She saw out of the corner of her eye that her master was still at the door and couldn't resist the urge to look in his direction.

He was leaning against the doorpost, smirking. He had seen through her and was letting her know it. She was ashamed of her childishness, of her submissiveness and dependence, ashamed of loving this man who she knew would never be hers. She left abruptly, abandoning the young man in midflow, slipping quickly past her master in the doorway, fleeing the scene of her humiliation.

On her way down the stairs she came face-to-face with Marchesa Orsini and another guest, a man she didn't know but assumed was her husband. They were startled and the man quickly let go of Alice's shoulders, but Kristín hurried past them, bumping into Alice, who dropped her bag on the floor. The man bent and picked it up.

"Excuse me," Kristín said, "please excuse me," and hurried into the dusk.

That night she dreamt of her master and his wife. They were dancing in bright sunshine to the sound of gently lapping waves. The sound was clearly audible yet there was no water to be seen. She looked for herself in the dream but in vain. Then she woke up gasping and could not get back to sleep for the rest of the night.

KRISTÍN IS AWAKENED IN THE MIDDLE OF THE NIGHT by a movement in the room. The moon casts a shadow on the wall opposite her bed; it looms larger as the man moves closer. She is in the hinterland between sleep and waking, and the remnants of a dream cling to her for a moment, then vanish. She raises her head from the pillow but cannot see his face until he is right by the bed. She lies back and watches the moon shining on his large, round eyes.

Melchiorre stares at her in silence, then whispers as if to himself.

"You moaned. I thought there was something wrong. But you must just have been dreaming."

He slowly backs away, without waiting for an answer, and resumes his position by the wall. He stands still for a while, then sits down on a chair. His presence does not make her uneasy and soon she closes her eyes again.

She is just about to drop off when she hears a whisper from the other bed.

"Melchiorre, are you in love?"

Melchiorre hushes him.

"Shut up, Bruno. You'll wake her."

"She's not asleep," the other whispers back. "She's awake. She's awake and wondering what you're doing here."

"Shh," Melchiorre says, "let her sleep."

Bruno stops talking. His bed creaks as he turns over and for a while he is quiet.

"Melchiorre," he starts again, "is she the first woman you've ever seen naked?"

Silence.

"I saw how you looked at her when you brought her in. Do you think Signorina Harris noticed?"

She hears Melchiorre shifting on his chair.

"Have you come to try and get another peek at them? Her breasts and . . ."

"Shut up, Bruno!"

Melchiorre tries to whisper but his voice emerges louder than intended, and breaking off at once, he rises to his feet and goes over to the partisan.

"There's nothing wrong with you. You're just pretending so you get proper food and don't have to work. You healed days ago."

"If you'd ever fought, my little friend . . ."

"Call yourselves partisans!" Melchiorre retorts. "You're nothing but thieves. You should be ashamed of yourselves."

"I must say, I'm surprised that you should fall in love with a woman, Melchiorre."

"I know you stole the Englishman's food."

"How am I supposed to have done that? I'm stuck in bed. Just ask your girlfriend who doesn't speak. Why do you think that is? Why do you think she stays mute and pretends to be asleep whenever anyone comes in?"

Kristin knows that Bruno is directing his words at her. She is also aware that he is not afraid she will tell anyone of his getting out of bed and walking around. He peers over the screen but doesn't come any closer, just whispers or rather repeats in a singsong voice: "I know you're not asleep. Open your eyes . . ."

"She was in a bad way," Melchiorre says. "You saw for yourself. She needs rest."

He sits down on the chair. Bruno can't be bothered to tease him anymore.

"Melchiorre, Melchiorre," he says with a sigh. "You're such a puppy."

Just before dawn, Melchiorre gets up, walks over to her bed, and looks at her before leaving. She listens to his footsteps disappear; the sun is rising and light enters the ward, driving the shadows into the corners.

Later, when the nurse arrives, Kristín tries to sit up.

"You're awake."

"I feel better," Kristín hears herself say.

The nurse only asks her about the wound. Kristín tells her that the pain in her leg has settled down and no longer moves about.

"It is just above the ankle," she says.

"A couple more days," says the nurse after examining her.

Bruno wakes up.

"So she can talk?"

"Yes, and you can walk," Signorina Harris replies. "Time for you to go."

He tries to protest.

"Don't listen to Melchiorre. I'm really feeling terrible . . ."

She orders him to get dressed as if she's talking to a child.

"Don't I get breakfast?"

The nurse doesn't bother answering, fetches his clothes, and puts them on his bed. Waits while he puts them on.

"Damn Melchiorre," he says. "Damn idiot . . ."

The nurse opens the door and gestures to him to leave with

her. When she's about to close it behind them, Kristín says, "Thank you."

Signorina Harris stops.

"My name is Kristín. I'm from Iceland."

Signorina Harris nods as she takes hold of the door handle, indicating that this announcement has not escaped her. Then she closes the door and leaves.

ALICE SWITCHES OFF THE WIRELESS IN THE MIDDLE of the news broadcast but then, unable to resist, switches it back on again. The announcer is speaking loudly, but his voice is only faintly audible above the crackle of the static that comes and goes like gusts of wind. She leans toward the set, adjusting the dial a millimeter to the left, listening to the voice fade, then regain its strength as she turns the needle back.

She is alone in the sitting room as usual; she woke up early and watched the sunrise before coming downstairs. All was still and quiet, the smoke from the houses on the other side of the valley standing straight up in the air. She went into her son's room and stood by the empty bed for a while, saying her morning prayer. She felt well and was careful to do nothing that would disturb her peace of mind. She said good morning to the boy, as had been her custom when he was alive, told him it was six o'clock, the sun was up, and the dawn chorus had started. She answered his questions, his voice so clear in her mind.

She carried on talking, afraid that the sense of well-being would vanish. The bad feeling never gives warning but creeps up on her when least expected, even in the midst of a smile. When that happens, she withdraws, shuts herself in her bedroom, and waits for the worst to pass. Afterward she gets up, weak and groggy, and washes her face with cold water in the basin.

The broadcast ends, the BBC announcer falls silent, and the crackling takes over uninterrupted. Her thoughts are elsewhere, and she does not turn it off straightaway. By rights she should be glad, should rush to the kitchen where the nurse, Schwester Marie, and Pritchett are eating breakfast and blurt out the news the moment she opens the door: "The Allies have reached Rome!" But she doesn't. She sits still, staring through the window at the trees in the garden and the dolphins that she can glimpse spouting water between the shrubs. His best friends . . .

She knows what is coming. According to the BBC news, the Germans put up little resistance in the city and are now retreating north toward Bracciano and Viterbo. From there, their route will pass through her valley. She's afraid of what this could mean. In retreat, the Germans have left scorched earth in their wake and executed those they regard as their enemies. That's how it was in January when the Allies landed in Nettuno, fifty kilometers south of Rome. At the time she had rushed to tell everyone the news, dashing into the kitchen before the announcer had finished speaking, only to spend the next few days in the clinic with Signorina Harris after the Germans and Fascists decided to remind the inhabitants of the neighboring villages who was in charge.

She looks worried when she meets Pritchett outside in the courtyard. She has taken a detour so as to avoid the kitchen and is going out to the road to wave to the school-bound children when he sees her.

"What's the matter?" he asks.

She tells him.

"At last," he says. "At last."

She does not reply. He reads her mind.

"Who knows?" he says. "They may not come here. The Allies may manage to drive them east over the Apennines, toward Pescara. That's always been the plan."

They hear the children approaching, their singing arriving before them. It is as if Alice has been touched by an invisible magic wand. She brightens up, pulls herself together, and grabs Pritchett's hand.

"Come on," she says. "Let's wave to them."

They almost run to the road. The horses are picking their way down the stony track, the carts shaking and rattling, as the children, faces beaming, sing loudly.

"Nelle vecchia fattoria, i-a i-a o!"

They shout good morning when they catch sight of the Marchesa and Pritchett, then slowly pass from sight down the slope. They remain standing there as the song fades away. A sharp gust of wind sweeps over the hill, ruffling the trees, then all is quiet again.

"He would be their age," she says. "The cart would have stopped here and I'd have brought him out and lifted him up to join them. Then they'd have carried on down the hill. I can picture it."

They are still holding hands. He squeezes her hand instinctively.

"You mustn't think like that," he says.

"I can't help it," she says. "I just can't."

THE GERMANS DID NOT KEEP THEM WAITING LONG. Two days after the Allies took Rome, a small army truck drove up the hill and stopped in front of the house. The soldiers waited silently in the cab and in the back. Shortly afterward a lieutenant on horseback rode into the yard.

Alice and Pritchett had been watching from an upstairs window as they came up the hill, and they went to the door together.

"Did you hide the wireless?" he asked suddenly.

She nodded.

Back in February, the Fascist government had banned all radio stations apart from the ones it controlled in Rome and Florence. Alice chose the Florence station, which broadcast German news and Viennese concerts. After this, the radio sets in the houses were adjusted to block them from receiving any other channels, but Alice continued to listen to the BBC on a small set that she kept hidden in an old pot in the cellar. She usually went into the sitting room in the mornings, plugged it in, and listened to the news. However, she tended to forget to put it away.

The lieutenant, who was in charge of the hospital in Montepulciano, said he had come to inform them that he needed to requisition the buildings down in the valley for his staff and provisions.

"But that's the school," Alice said. "And the dormitory for the orphans."

The lieutenant was tall, thin, and quite unlike the Germans they were used to; he was soft-spoken and pleasant.

"I have no choice," he said. "We're expecting large casualties when the units get here." Then, lowering his voice, he added, "I'm a doctor. I'm sorry about this."

Alice guessed that "this" referred not only to his demand for the houses in the valley. She nodded; she had no other choice.

"All right then," she said. "How much time do we have?"

"As soon as possible," he replied. "I think it would also be safer for the children to be with you up here on the hill."

The soldiers watched in silence. They were still sitting in the cab and in the back of the truck, and, catching Alice glancing in their direction, the lieutenant explained, "As you probably know, there are rumors that you shelter partisans. I was informed that it would be unwise to come here alone. I see now that there has been a misunderstanding."

He smiled. His smile was weary and implied that he knew more than he was letting on about the partisans and soldiers they hid in the outhouses and tenant farms.

He bowed briefly before remounting his horse and riding away. The truck started up with a loud banging and clattering, then rattled away down the hill after him. The soldiers did not look back.

"I expected him to offer us help with moving the children and the rest of the stuff up here," Pritchett said once they had gone and he and Alice were left standing on the doorstep.

"No," she said, "he knew we wouldn't accept."

The rest of the day was occupied with emptying the guest-rooms upstairs in the main villa and filling them with mattresses from the evacuees' dormitory along with blankets, pillows, and folded clothes. The formal drawing room was converted into a classroom, the library into a dining room; the heavy furniture was carried out to the storehouse beside the chapel, paintings were replaced by the blackboard, the map, and pictures painted by the children. They were excited by the move and eager to help, but Alice asked Signor Grandinetti and Schwester Marie to take them outside and play with them in the garden. Four wagons were required for the move up the hill, two pulled by horses, two by oxen. It was hot and muggy, and Alice felt a growing dread with every step she took. Her nerves were on edge. The drawing room had been emptied and she was standing by the window, watching the children playing outside, when she was suddenly struck by the premonition that she would lose them all.

She braced herself and by the time darkness had begun to fall, the move was complete. The children ate in the new dining room and after the meal Alice read fairy tales to them. Pritchett had ridden from farm to farm that afternoon, spreading the message that they had better put out the lights when it got dark because they could expect Allied air raids any day now. The main villa was lit only by candles, and the children sat in silence as they listened to Alice read. Every now and then she stopped speaking, looked up, and met their eyes, which shone in the semidarkness. Then, taking a deep breath, she carried on.

The moon is bright when she goes out to the cemetery. The sound of vehicles carries up from the road in the valley; they are driving without lights, crawling along painfully slowly, as the road is full of potholes and craters.

She visits him every day. Usually after lunch in winter but in late afternoon in summer when the sun is descending and the heat has become more bearable. She could have rushed over to see him earlier today but there would only have been time for a brief respite, so she decided to wait. She doesn't want any distractions while she is with him.

The grave is by the edge of the wood, farthest from the houses. The wood is thick and dark but there are few trees in the cemetery itself, so nothing hinders the moonlight from spreading its white coverlet over him. Alice kneels, picking up dead leaves and fallen twigs from his grave. The earth is dry and hard, but she doesn't mind. Her shadow moves back and forth over the grave until finally she smooths over the soil, feeling she has disturbed it enough. Then she gets to her feet and fetches a can to water the flowers.

The only flowers on the grave are bluebells, Giovanni's favorite. She moves her lips continually as she waters but doesn't make a sound. When he was dead, she sat beside him and sang a lullaby for him until her husband took her arm and led her out. She was still singing it when they climbed into the car that was waiting for them outside the hospital, and later in their hotel room. She did not stop until, unable to control himself any longer, he screamed at her. He had never done that before. She can still hear the echo of this scream in her bad moments.

The forest breathes. A bewildered hare runs down the path by the grave, dodges past her, and vanishes into the trees. She notices by the light of the moon that she has bloodied her fingertips from rooting in the soil but she does nothing about it, not even brushing the dirt from her hands. The blood has dried and mingled with the soil, black in the dim light.

She sees the girl as she is heading home. She has laid some

flowers on one of the new graves and is now standing quite still, staring into space. Alice remembers her from the funeral: Larig's girlfriend. She pauses, trying to make herself as inconspicuous as possible. The graves have not yet been marked, and Alice sees that the girl is standing not by the grave of her lover but by that of one of the British soldiers who was buried at the same time. She waits till the girl has gone. Then she walks slowly over to the graves, stoops to the flowers, and moves them to the grave where they're supposed to be.

IN THE END KRISTÍN DIDN'T HAVE TO LIE BECAUSE no one really questioned her. Signorina Harris needed the bed and announced, after a thorough examination, that the infection was on the retreat and the stitches would hold despite the bad swelling. She made her stand on her leg before she went to sleep, helped her walk across the floor and back to the bed, asked if she felt faint and wiped the sweat from her brow once she was lying down again.

No, she didn't feel faint.

"Good. You can get up tomorrow morning."

"Tomorrow morning?"

"Rome has fallen. They're heading this way."

"Will I be allowed to stay?"

Signorina Harris studied her.

"You wouldn't get far," she replied.

She was not curt, but her manner implied that she was familiar with death and had witnessed its triumphs. She was a slight, wiry woman. Her hands were a little rough but they inspired confidence; Kristín recognized their touch from the first day when she had sensed them through her half-sleep. She relaxed whenever she felt the nurse's hands and experienced a sense of security, although her touch was inevitably accompanied by pain.

A maid had brought her clothes after Signorina Harris left, laying them on the chair by the wall and departing as quietly as she had come. These were the clothes Kristín had been wearing when she arrived; someone had washed and mended them, and the scent of soap pervaded the room.

Her leg was bandaged up to the knee, the dressing a pristine white except at the bottom where blood had seeped through. She touched the dry bloodstain gently, turning her leg so that the light fell on it. Before she knew it, Marshall's voice was sounding in her head.

"You use pure vermilion to paint blood; you never buy it ready-ground because there's a risk that it will have been adulterated with red lead or brick dust. You grind it yourself, slowly, mixing it with clear water, taking care not to leave it to stand too long, as it darkens when it comes into contact with air. When it is on the canvas, you take red lacca resin, and mix it with tempera. Then you paint this over the vermilion to find the right shade."

He used to watch her work. Sat on the chair where he sometimes made her kneel or lean back with her legs on the arms. There was no couch in the workshop so they had to make do with the chair, the floor, or the worktables. It didn't matter. He was inventive.

From his place in the chair he guided and educated her.

"The red lacca is made by insects on certain kinds of trees: Coccus or Carteria lacca, on trees such as Schleichera, Butea, and Ficus . . ."

He must have known that she would not be able to remember it all and as she could not make notes while she was working, she sometimes wondered what the point of these lectures was. Not that she disliked them. On the contrary, she was grateful to him for taking such an interest in her.

The sky was turning gray when she got up. The outline of the mountain across the valley etched against the dawn, gradually darkening and growing distinct against the awakening sky. Lower down, mist caressed the slopes, catching like tufts of wool on the treetops. She did not wait for assistance but crept to the chair, fetched her clothes, and returned to the bed with them. She moved slowly, examining the garments as if she were seeing them for the first time, then pulled them on one by one, taking care not to catch her wound. Her shirt had been badly torn, her skirt too, but whoever had mended them had known what she was doing. Kristín admired the handiwork and raised each garment in turn to her face to inhale the scent of soap. She was surprised that she was still so weak.

Once she was dressed, she stood up again, limped to the window, and looked out over the courtyard. The sun was shining on the rooftops but remnants of the night lingered in the shadows by the walls. When the nurse appeared at the door of the main villa and set out in her direction, Kristín sat down on the bed again to wait for her.

"You're dressed."

Kristín nodded.

"Let's go then."

"Where's my case?"

"In the house. Do you think you could manage to walk across the courtyard if I help you?"

The nurse held her arm down the stairs and over to the main villa. The day was already hot and Kristín stopped several times to catch her breath. She looked around, at the chapel and the glimpse of hillside between chapel and clinic, where the mist was now evaporating from the trees. Neither said a word but the nurse was patient. She led her into the kitchen, made her sit down at the table, and went out again. There was no one in the kitchen but the cook, who was standing at the stove, and the two scullery maids. They greeted her and one of the maids poured her a cup of coffee. Then they carried on preparing breakfast.

She sat still, watching them work until the nurse returned, this time accompanied by Pritchett. Kristín tried to stand but he introduced himself and told her to sit.

"How are you feeling?"

"Fine. I'm terribly grateful to you . . ."

"You were coming from Rome?"

"Yes."

"The Allies have reached Rome."

She nodded.

"There are no identity papers in your case."

"They must have been left behind on the train. We were hit by a bomb. I told Miss Harris . . ."

"She says you're Icelandic."

"Yes, I am."

He seemed relieved to hear her confirm it.

"Someone thought you were German," he said.

"I'm not German."

"It's probably your accent. And your appearance," he added.

"It's understandable," she said.

"Yes," he said. "Perfectly understandable."

He stood up.

"Well," he said. "Perhaps you could make yourself useful. What can you do?"

"I'm sorry?"

"What's your line of work?"

"Art," she replied, shyly.

"We have a lot of children here," he said. "Evacuees as well as the children from the farms. Perhaps you could teach them drawing. Do you feel up to it?"

"Yes," she said. "I would like that very much."

"You wouldn't need to stand to teach them. You could do that sitting down."

He seemed pleased with his suggestion.

"I'll suggest it to Marchesa Orsini. I think it's a good idea. It's up to her, of course," he added. "But I'll suggest it."

I HAD JUST WOKEN UP AND DIDN'T IMMEDIATELY grasp what I was looking at when I opened the curtains of the window above the front door. A vehicle marked "Red Cross" stood in the drive, a large gray truck with a tarpaulin stretched over its load. The driver was asleep in his seat; there was no one else visible. I met Pritchett on my way down the stairs; he wanted to talk to me about the young woman in the clinic, telling me her name and where she's from, but, beckoning him to follow, I went over to the front door and opened it. The driver did not stir even when the heavy front door opened with a scraping, or when we walked out onto the terrace, our footsteps echoing in the quiet morning. It was not until Pritchett knocked on the door of the cab that the man opened his eyes, but even then he seemed to have difficulty surfacing. Finally he sat up, rubbed his face, and climbed out.

God, he was young. He tried his best to stand up straight but didn't make a very good job of it, and when he saluted us, it was as if he were playing a role that was beyond him. He had a gash on his forehead but it seemed to have stopped bleeding.

He can't have been more than twenty, thin, lanky, quite tall. He introduced himself before coming straight to the point.

The German army had continued its move that night, the

front line creeping north from Rome. The Allies were in pursuit and casualties had been heavy. He had been transporting the wounded near Viterbo when he received orders to get rid of his patients and report immediately to army headquarters in the town. He had not slept for days and explained as much to his superior officers when they told him what was involved, but they would not listen. Soldiers had begun to load boxes and canvas sacks of food into the back of the truck as soon as he drew up. Shortly afterward his passenger had appeared. He wore a uniform but was carrying civilian clothes in his luggage. After some thought he had decided to ride concealed in the back.

Their journey had been uneventful until late yesterday evening. By then the young driver was so exhausted that he fell asleep at the wheel and crashed into a ditch. That was how he had got the wound on his forehead but it was not deep and didn't matter. What did matter was that he had a high-ranking SS officer hidden in the back of his truck.

Pritchett's eyes darted to the back of the vehicle with its tarpaulin covering. The young man shook his head.

"He's not there. He was killed when I drove off the road; he landed under one of the back wheels. I'll be blamed. They'll come looking for me."

"Who's going to tell them?" asked Pritchett.

"I'll be blamed," the young soldier repeated. "I was responsible for him."

I was ready to be convinced by the boy's story but couldn't understand why he had come to us. It worried me.

"What business do you have here?" I asked.

Head drooping, he answered in a low voice, "We were on our way here. I just kept going."

"What?" I exclaimed.

"I just kept going," he repeated. "I couldn't think of anything else to do. I couldn't turn back. I left him behind by the ditch and fled. He hadn't changed out of his uniform yet."

"What do you mean by *here*?" Pritchett asked. "Here in the valley?"

"No, here," he said. "San Martino. I was never told what we were supposed to be collecting but the officer knew. Apparently he had brought it here in the first place."

My blood ran cold. He continued. "May I stay?" Adding with a touch of formality, he said, "I wish to become a deserter."

"I'm afraid you can't stay here," I said. "But we'll give you something to eat."

Pritchett took him to the kitchen, then came and found me in the garden. A porcupine had got into the flower beds in the night and eaten some of the bulbs and rhizomes. Bending down, I picked up some petals and stalks that the animal had left behind and piled them in a little heap by the path.

"It was a mistake," I heard Pritchett say behind me.

I straightened up.

"It was bound to backfire on us," he went on. "What are we to do now? How much does that young man know? How much do other people know about that bloody painting? We must get rid of it as soon as possible."

I had never been able to tell him why I had agreed to Robert Marshall's request. I couldn't now either. Perhaps I never will be able to.

"It's too late," I said.

"But you're such a sensible person," he said. "I don't understand."

"I'm sorry," I said.

He sighed heavily.

"You have to try to get hold of him," he said. "Not even he can expect you to jeopardize everything for a painting."

I didn't reply, although I knew I would not be able to get hold of Robert Marshall. I'd been trying in vain to get messages to him since the Allies took Rome. Nor did I remind Pritchett of what the SS officer had said when he brought the picture: that Marshall's part in it was now over.

Pritchett had the truck moved and parked under a tree where it would not be visible from the air. I went inside and watched the young man wolf down his breakfast before sending him off with a loaf of bread and ham. He didn't say anything and, hearing that the children were awake, I hurried to help get them dressed.

THE GERMANS HAD BROUGHT THE PAINTING AT THE beginning of April.

It had been snowing on and off for weeks and the snow continued to fall after Easter. The boughs of the trees in the garden sagged under the weight and every landmark in the valley was obliterated. The roads to Montepulciano and Chianciano were impassable and the postman had not been seen for days. To make matters worse, there was a power cut, so we had to make do with candlelight and the glow from the fires that burnt all day long in every hearth, for it was bitterly cold and windy. It did not blow incessantly; there would be a lull for a few days, then the wind would suddenly sweep down the valley from Monte Amiata, whirling up the snow and trapping us indoors. The fattore and Signorina Harris were caught in a blizzard on their way back from one of the outlying farms where a woman had been taken ill, and nearly got lost. It was also very difficult to transport food and other necessities down the hill to the children and their minders, but we managed, and some days we were even able to bring the children up to the main villa. They longed to play outside in the snow; they were fed up with being stuck indoors, despite the efforts of Schwester Marie and the teacher to entertain them. We built igloos and snowmen with them and one day the children saw a rabbit hop out of the hedge and across the garden near the buildings. Racing in pursuit, they caught it and took it into the kitchen. Naturally the poor creature was petrified, but we gave it something to eat and decided to keep it as a pet since it gave the children so much pleasure.

On Easter Day, there was a break in the weather. The congregation began to pour into the church early in the morning and the sense of unity in the little building warmed one's heart. The church, a few hundred yards down the road, belongs to chianciano but is close to us. The peasants, many of whom had been sheltering deserters and wounded partisans for months, risking their lives for strangers, brought them along to sit beside them in the pews, among the children, ruddy-cheeked with excitement, and our staff. I took my seat but no one sat beside me in your accustomed place, even though I sensed that everyone knew you were not coming. The church was packed, which made it all the more absurd to leave an empty seat, and no doubt I would have felt uncomfortable if one of the orphans, a little girl from Turin, had not finally clambered up onto the pew and taken your seat. She did not look at me—her eyes were fixed on the candles on the altar and the crucifix above— but slipped her little hand into mine as the priest entered.

After mass, we went home with the children and danced in the drawing room. Pritchett adopted your role as John the Baptist, pasting on a beard and dressing in your fur coat and the Cossack hat that you always dusted off on this day. Caught unprepared, I gave a little cry when I came face-to-face with him in the passage. For a moment I believed it was you. I stood as if turned to stone before him, speechless.

Pritchett grasped the situation at once.

"I'm sorry," he said, "I should have warned you."

I watched the children singing and dancing and tried to join in the festivities, but my mind was distracted. This trivial incident had brought it home to me that when the moment came, I would have nothing to say that could make up for what happened. This realization was a blow, because I had been preparing my speech for months, had written it down, rewritten it, adjusted the wording and punctuation, memorized it and mentally rehearsed it over and over again. What naïveté, I told myself now. What self-deception—thinking I could change anything with words and fine-sounding phrases, however good they looked on paper. Faced with you, the phrases would disintegrate and the words come to nothing. As I had just discovered.

And then the snow began to fall in earnest. It muffled everything, even my anguish. The wind blew away the empty words, and I was never happier than when it was howling around the trees and house, rattling sleet against the windows, presenting immediate problems to solve. It never stopped snowing for long, the clouds always returned and the wind rose, whipping up the drifts and hiding us and the surrounding district from the outside world.

It was during one of these respites that Melchiorre spotted the Germans on his way back from one of the farms on the hill, which had a view right to the mouth of the valley. We didn't believe him at first; he has a fertile imagination that can sometimes lead him astray. But he was right, and for a while we watched their slow progress through the valley, tank first, armored car close behind.

"In this weather," Pritchett said. "Something's up."

As no one dreamed that they were on their way here, we soon tired of watching them and returned to our chores. I remember that someone was chopping firewood outside; the echo carried into the library where I sat with Signor Grandinetti, going over the children's work. The rabbit the children had found was lying under the sofa, peeping out at us from time to time. We had given it a carrot and it seemed perfectly content with its lot. The fattore joked that it was a princess under a spell and tried to persuade Melchiorre to kiss it.

As we pored over the children's exercises, the wind began to howl again. The earth merged with the sky, the windowpanes rattled in their frames, and once again the outside world disappeared.

They had probably been banging on the front door for some considerable time before we heard them. The teacher followed me; I opened the door and found myself looking straight into the black muzzle of a gun. The tank and the armored car were covered with snow, but the gun was pointing straight at the house, a black dot in the blinding whiteness.

An SS officer was walking away from the door, flanked by two soldiers, having abandoned the wait in favor of going around the back of the villa. Now he turned and strode up the steps to where I stood hanging onto the door with both hands so that it would not crash open. Ordering the soldiers to wait outside, he took the door handle himself and closed it. Snow had drifted inside while the door was open and he beat more from his ankle-length leather coat and brushed it from the peak of his cap.

"Who's that?" he said, pointing at the teacher who was standing behind me. "It's not your husband. I know he's not here."

I tried not to show how my heart jolted. Who had been telling this man about my private affairs? I could only think of Robert Marshall.

The SS officer looked around, went to the little room off the hall where I used to arrange the flowers, inspected it, then turned.

"He can leave," he said, jerking his head at Signor Grandinetti. "We will go in here."

Perhaps he had lost his temper while waiting outside, banging on the door, or perhaps he was tired from his journey, I don't know. His manner was sharp throughout our conversation—or rather, while he talked and I listened. I studied him—the harsh face, low brow, pinched nose, and thin lips.

"I believe Mr. Marshall has made it clear what's expected of you."

"He never mentioned German involvement," I said.

The officer ignored this.

"He claims that you have agreed to look after the goods. Has there been some misunderstanding?"

"No," I said.

"Did he tell you what it was?"

"A painting."

"Did he tell you any more than that?"

"No."

"Not the identity of the owner?"

"No."

"Nothing about the painting itself?"

He paused for a moment before using that word. It was the only time. Otherwise he spoke only of "the goods."

"No."

He stopped speaking and scrutinized me as if trying to decide whether I was telling the truth.

"He says you are fully aware of the consequences if anything happens to it."

I waited.

"We know that you harbor our enemies. We have chosen to do nothing about it."

"We've been searched," I said, "and nothing was found. We're peaceable people."

He stared at me in silence before answering.

"You are English. Your husband has left. Marshall is doing you no less a favor than you are doing him."

The officer had closed the door behind him, but now the handle suddenly turned. He spun around but relaxed when Pritchett stuck his head inside.

"It's all right," I told him. "Wait outside."

We finished our conversation. He asked where I intended to keep the goods. I had not considered this, being quite unprepared. All Marshall had said was that he might need me to store an important painting for him because he was afraid for its safety if Rome fell. The conversation had taken place early in March, and he had been uncharacteristically nervous on the phone. When I answered that I had enough on my plate and described the conditions here for him ("We won't escape the hostilities if Rome falls," I remember saying), there was a brief pause at the other end of the line, but then he said quietly, "I think you owe it to me."

He said it smoothly and his tone reminded me of water flowing quietly over stone. I knew what lurked under the smooth surface and my silence was a form of agreement. We ended the conversation, and I remained standing by the phone, trying to get my bearings and recalling the conversation we had had more than three years before by the Trevi Fountain when he put me on notice in such a refined manner that I would have to pay for his discretion.

"Where will you keep it?" the officer barked when he saw that my mind had drifted away.

I had hidden my jewelry in an old underground vault by the mill, where wine had been stored long ago—my jewelry and various personal effects of sentimental value, family photographs and letters, as well as important documents and title deeds. Apart from my husband and me, no one but Pritchett knew of its existence. The trapdoor is hidden under a layer of soil, among bushes and undergrowth. It was only by chance that we found it years ago.

Pritchett was waiting in the hall when we emerged from the flower room, and I told him what was happening.

"Now?" he asked. "In this blizzard? What have you gotten us into?"

"I don't know," I admitted, trying to conceal my growing fear, "but there is nothing I can do."

He shook his head. We put on our coats and went outside with the officer. If anything, the wind had grown stronger. The soldiers were still standing in the same spot by the steps, snow-white and chilled, but of course did not utter a word of complaint. The officer ordered them to fetch the goods and then we walked up the hill toward the mill, Pritchett and I in the lead, the others following a few steps behind.

It was heavy going, as we could hardly open our eyes against the snow, and night was falling. The track up the slope was invisible, the drifts lay deep on the hillside, the wind was pitiless, and the temperature had dropped below freezing, bringing showers of ice pellets. They stung our cheeks and brows, and I had to hold up a hand to shield my eyes. Pritchett kept shooting me glances but I looked away. I had never seen him so bewildered and concerned. I sensed that I was making a terrible mistake.

The opening to the vault was not large, hardly more than a square meter, and after we had dug away the snow from the trapdoor and broken off the ice, it took them a while to ease the painting inside. A packing case had been made for it and the soldiers positioned it foursquare, then one stepped on it and forced it down while the other stood on the stone steps below to receive it. Pritchett and I and the officer were already inside, watching their progress, Pritchett holding a lantern, as there was no light in the vault. When it was finally down, the officer took Pritchett's lantern and peered around before choosing a place for the crate, as far as possible from the entrance. He had already checked the walls for damp and made sure that there was nothing dripping from the ceiling, yet even so he took a tarpaulin that we had draped over some of our belongings and ordered the soldiers to wrap it around the packing case.

They went ahead of us down the slope, the officer in the lead, and did not stop until they were in front of the villa. Two additional soldiers stood there waiting. The officer ordered them to start up the car and the tank.

The officer glanced around. It was as if he enjoyed standing there in the blizzard. He turned to face the wind, letting the icy pellets lash his face. I was careful not to show how cold I was, but Pritchett rubbed his hands together and shifted constantly from foot to foot.

"There is no real winter here," the officer said finally. "A few days, that's all. The people here are soft. They have no backbone. Where I come from, the winters are tough."

The engines of the car and the tank roared and we smelled the fumes from the exhaust. The officer turned to us.

"You will hand over the goods to no one but us. No one.

Whatever happens. Whatever anyone says. Not even Mr. Marshall. His part is over."

I listened in silence. Pritchett looked at me with painful disappointment. The officer regarded us for a moment, then gave a sharp nod and climbed into the car.

We watched them rattle away down the road and vanish into the blizzard.

"Robert Marshall," Pritchett demanded. "Why in the world . . ."

"I had no choice," I interjected. "Please don't ask me why."

The drone of the engines grew fainter and soon there was nothing to be heard but the howling of the wind.

KRISTÍN HAD BEEN WORKING FOR ROBERT MARSHALL for a month when she met his wife for the first time. It was early in the evening and dusk was falling over the city, muting the daytime racket. She was passing through the quarter where they lived and had somehow found herself in their street—to her own surprise, for she did not consider herself curious by nature.

It was not far from the Piazza delle Coppelle; the building was three stories high with a large apartment on each floor; it extended right up to the pavement and towered over the narrow street. There was a café on the next corner with tables on the pavement outside and flickering candles on the tables despite the autumn chill in the air.

Marshall and his wife emerged suddenly just as she was passing the house. They were alone; the children were probably inside. She knew they had two children, a boy of twelve and a girl of seven. Apparently the boy was the spitting image of his father.

"Kristín," he said.

It was only later that she realized he hadn't seemed surprised to see her there. She wasn't sure that a half-smile hadn't played over her lips as he regarded her.

He introduced her to his wife. Her name was Flora and she was younger than he, maybe thirty-five, petite, with a dark complexion. Strikingly beautiful.

"Kristín is helping out at the studio," he told her.

Flora smiled and shook hands with Kristín, saying that she must visit them sometime.

"I'm on my way to meet a friend," Kristín said, realizing immediately that the explanation was superfluous.

Marshall, still smiling his half-smile, looked at his watch.

"We really should be getting a move on," he said. "You go carefully now, Kristín."

"Robert," Flora said merrily, "don't be silly. She's not a child."

They said good-bye. The couple walked away up the street while Kristín hurried in the opposite direction, taking care not to look over her shoulder. She was not surprised that he hadn't told his wife she was working for him.

She went straight home and was agitated for the rest of the evening. Nothing had happened yet, but she knew it was going to happen and she was sure that he knew too. Yet neither of them had said a word, either direct or implicit. She tried to talk some sense into herself, remonstrated with herself, came close more than once to putting an end to the thing that had not yet begun. But she couldn't do it. She waited, and with every day the waiting became more unbearable.

She stayed awake until late, pacing. The room that she rented was in a flat a stone's throw from the studio. The owner, an elderly gentleman, was never there, spending most of his time with his daughter in Florence. The rent was low in return for her watering his flowers and cleaning every other week. Dust sheets covered the heavy furniture in the living room and dining room, where the curtains were drawn. She was happy in the flat but did not spend much time there, often working late and starting early. She rarely cooked for herself, generally eating supper in a nearby canteen, run by a husband and wife.

Eventually she fell asleep but her rest was fitful and Flora appeared before her again and again, smiling and saying that Kristín must come and visit soon. She said nothing in these fragmentary dreams except what she had said when they met, word for word, with a cheerful expression.

"Robert, don't be silly. She's not a child," her eyes on Kristín as she spoke.

Kristín had liked her. No, that wasn't the right word; the feeling had been stronger. When she sat in the semidarkness of her room that evening, she came to the conclusion that she felt warmth toward Marshall's wife. It was a strange thing to feel, but she was forced to acknowledge it. She had always been impressionable, but down-to-earth at the same time, never one to let her emotions lead her astray. She had no desire to hurt this woman whose manner to her had been friendly, sincere, benevolent. It might have been easier if she'd been arrogant and supercilious.

She tried to guess what had passed between the couple after they had said good-bye to her and continued up the street.

"Why didn't you tell me about her?" she imagined Flora asking. "All alone in a new city far from home, knowing no one. We must take the first opportunity to invite her over."

In her imagination he did not answer, merely nodded and changed the subject.

When they met the following morning, he did not refer to their encounter the evening before. He did not arrive at the studio until nearly midday, nor did he stay long. He rarely did, spending more time, when not on business trips, in his office on the floor below with Signorina Pirandello, his secretary. Since Kristín started work at the studio, there had been just the two of them, she and Signor Rosselli, a middle-aged man who had worked for Marshall part-time for a few years.

Signor Rosselli seemed suspicious on Kristín's first morning at the studio, but his attitude improved when he discovered that she had no experience and was expected only to assist him. He was a gaunt, seemingly high-strung little man, and Kristín was immediately aware of the care Marshall took not to offend him. He praised him regularly, stressing the fact that the studio was his domain. Yet at times it was as if Marshall itched to intervene as he watched Rosselli working, as if he had to restrain himself from taking charge.

Initially, Kristín's duty had been to tidy up the studio, go through the pictures awaiting restoration, make sure they were all catalogued, and write a short description of their condition. Some of the paintings were in appalling shape, others required nothing more than cleaning and reframing. Marshall lent her numerous books on restoration and conservation and, being conscientious by nature and eager for his approval, she immersed herself in them, reading into the early hours. She learnt about the effects of time on wood and canvas, paint, glue, and varnish; about the impact of moisture, heat and light, insects, soot, and other kinds of grime. She read about renowned conservators like Madame Helfer in Paris, who worked for the famous dealer William Suhr, as well as reports about paintings that had been saved from oblivion and others that had been ruined by amateur restorers. It surprised her how many great paintings had been touched by hands other than their author's, how extensive these restorations often seemed, and she couldn't help but wonder about the authenticity of some of these works.

She also read articles and features about her master. He did not give them to her himself but there were references to them in the books he had lent her. Later she asked herself if he had assumed that she would search them out. She went to the library at the American Academy on the Janiculum Hill, where she sat for a long time, reading everything she could find about him. An article in the London *Times* claimed that American and British millionaires would not buy a Renaissance painting unless either Robert Marshall or Bernard Berenson had given it his blessing, established the identity of the artist, and removed all doubt of its authenticity. Marshall's expertise was unquestioned, according to the *Times*, and unrivaled, except possibly by Berenson, who had devoted decades to compiling a register of every Italian Renaissance painting held in a museum or private collection. This register was considered the most reliable record of the works, and several books and journals that Kristín had read described his working methods in admiring detail.

Marshall and Berenson were trusted as disinterested scholars. Several newspaper articles also mentioned that Marshall acted as a consultant to well-known dealers, such as Duveen before they fell out, Colnaghi in London and Wildenstein in New York. The *Times* referred in passing to his dispute with Duveen without going into any detail, and she could find no mention of it anywhere else. The article also implied that the dealers paid Marshall a commission, although no more was said of that, the emphasis being on his almost unmatched restoration skills.

There were numerous pictures of him, both alone and in company—with Duveen, Berenson, who was described as his

rival, and Flora. Kristín dwelled longest on the photograph of
the couple. It was not recent and appeared to have been taken
in the studio. There was a painting by Giorgione on the easel
behind them; Marshall was looking directly at the camera,
Flora's eyes were on him. They were both smiling.

Kristín was helping Signor Rosselli remove a small painting by Titian from its stretcher and transfer it to an iron
table when Marshall appeared in the doorway. The picture
was in a bad state of repair; the paint was flaking and had
broken off in places. The white pigment had yellowed where
it could be glimpsed under the surface dirt. They were
holding the picture between them, laying it down carefully before turning on the heating element in the tabletop.
Signor Rosselli's hands were shaking. Kristín had noticed
that he drank quite a bit.

Marshall was wearing a light coat, having come straight in
without visiting his office first. It was as if he had been in a
hurry to see them, yet he said nothing when he appeared at the
door, merely watched in silence as they laid the Titian on the
table. Rosselli grew nervous as always when the master turned
up. Instead of fixing the canvas on the table, he looked in silence toward the door, waiting for Marshall to speak.

The master did not oblige, but walked over to the table and
inspected the picture. Rosselli's eyes shifted between him and
the work.

"Berenson claims it's not a Titian but a Giorgione," Marshall
said finally. "Not for the first time. One would have thought
he'd have learnt from his mistakes by now."

He continued to study the picture without moving, his face
impassive.

"It's not every day you get your hands on a Titian, Piero,"
he said.

Rosselli's voice was unsteady as he answered, "No, but it's not the first time either."

Marshall gave a private smile.

"Pass me a magnifying glass, would you?"

Rosselli went to his desk at the back of the studio and opened the top drawer. Marshall raised his eyes and said quietly to Kristín, "You must keep an eye on him and let me know if he does anything stupid."

She was startled. She didn't say anything but nodded, perhaps a little too eagerly. He came closer to her, gently touching the small of her back on his way out.

When Rosselli returned with the magnifying glass, he was already gone.

KRISTÍN USED TO GET UP AT DAWN AND GO FOR walks before the city awakened. Some days she went down to the Tiber, on others over the Ponte Margherita toward the Vatican, but more often south, into the old part of the city. There she would seat herself by an empty square or on a bench in a small garden and watch the fog lifting and the waiters opening the cafés, rubbing their eyes, spreading white cloths on the tables. She admired the cobbled streets and the magnificent edifices, the statues that came to life as they caught the morning sun. During the first months of working for Robert Marshall she generally took a pen and sketchpad along with her and drew whatever met her eye, but she eventually left the pad at home. It wasn't deliberate, but her mind was now wholly preoccupied by the pictures that awaited her in the studio. For the first few months she only assisted Signor Rosselli with relatively simple tasks, performing them all with precision. She was resourceful and a quick study.

The first time Rosselli gave her a free hand, he ordered her to clean the back of a fairly unremarkable painting by loosening the stretcher and wiping away the dirt that had collected between the stretcher and the canvas and begun to damage the picture, and then to brush the dust off the canvas with a feather and fix the frayed threads. He did not let her touch the picture surface until later, and then only to clean it; he himself saw to the repairs and insisted on being left completely alone when it came to wetting the brush and filling in the gaps. He was always on edge when there was a lot at stake; his hands had a tendency to shake and beads of sweat would form on his forehead. He didn't like her to watch, and would send her out, often on some pointless errand. She learnt to behave as if she were taking no notice, and would focus instead on her duties, however dull they seemed in comparison to his work. If Marshall turned up, Rosselli would stop working and wait for him to leave.

As the winter passed, Signor Rosselli's drinking became more serious. He kept a bottle in a locked drawer in his desk, and would use it either for Dutch courage or to reward himself for a job well done. By February there would be two or three occasions a week when he did not turn up for work in the morning. When he did finally appear at midday or later, he drifted around the studio like a ghost or sat at his desk, staring into space. Kristín used the opportunity to take over his work because he was too lethargic to forbid her, too depressed to give thought to her chores, which she sensed must be insignificant in comparison with his own private demons.

"Signor Rosselli," she would say at such times, "would it be all right if I carried on with what you were doing yesterday? Sewing. Making a new stretcher. Cleaning. Gluing. Patching . . ."

He did not have the strength to drink for two days in a row, so he would turn up the following morning as if nothing had happened, continuing the work where it had been left off. He never commented on Kristín's contribution, neither criticizing nor praising it. She did not refer to it either, merely stepped back and assisted him as required.

One day toward evening, after Rosselli had gone home early, Marshall appeared unexpectedly at the studio. He had been away on business for the last week. She did not hear him enter, and was not aware of him until he was standing behind her. This time she was not startled, but stopped working and lifted her hands from the table.

He said nothing at first, merely examined the painting. It was a work by a little-known sixteenth-century artist, *Virgin and Child with Musical Angels*. She had cleaned the back and had just begun to loosen a patch that was distorting the canvas. She had dealt with this kind of damage before; when the glue pulled at the threads in the canvas, cracks would form in the picture and the paint would eventually flake off.

He touched her hand in silence, taking the fine cutting blade from her and poking it carefully into the patch that she had begun to loosen. He freed a few threads, moistened his right index finger on his lip and used it to lift the dried crumbs of glue from the canvas. After examining them for a moment, he raised his finger to his mouth and bit the crumbs with his front teeth.

"Wheat glue," he said. "Always trouble. What's more, the patch is not made from the right material. It's fine. The canvas is coarse. The patch needs to be similar to the canvas, preferably identical."

She nodded.

"Is he hungover today?"

The question took her by surprise.

"He's gone home," she said.

"You can't protect him," he said, "no one can. Not I, not

even he, because he can't help himself. He's an assistant by nature and can't stand the pressure that comes from being in charge. That's true of many—perhaps most—people, but it's not an easy thing to face up to. The pawn aspires to be a knight, the knight a rook, the rook a king. His ambition has brought him nothing but misery."

Falling silent, he walked over to the window and watched the last rays of the sun catching the rooftops across the street.

"It's essential to know your own limitations, Kristín, and be satisfied with your lot—whatever that is, because no job is without value. We're all guided by providence."

He turned from the window and studied her as she stood by the worktable.

"Take you, for example. You know you're more talented than your boss. You can tell. You've probably known it from the first day, although you've never said as much, not even to yourself. You've performed every task impeccably but you want more. He's holding you back, standing in your way. You watch him work and sense his failings. Even though you don't yet know all the techniques, you still know that you could do better. A strange feeling, isn't it? This certainty—and the power that goes with it. You watch and wait, because you know your time will come. And little by little he cracks, becoming ever more despairing; his drinking gets worse, he loses his grip on his work. You seize the chance to offer your services. He accepts—in silence, I suspect—because he has no other choice. And your motives are pure. No one could accuse you of anything else. It's not your fault that he has overreached himself. You're doing him a favor. And providence is doing the same for you."

No one had ever spoken to her like that before. She couldn't respond but sensed that he did not expect an answer.

He walked toward the door, stopping halfway.

"Are you still drawing?" he asked.

She hesitated.

"Not as much lately," she said.

He smiled.

"That doesn't surprise me."

He left. She stood still, unable to understand why she suddenly felt crushed.

"     . . . KRISTÍN JÓNSDÓTTIR HAS GRADUATED FROM
the Royal Academy with a favorable report. She has mastered
composition and the handling of color and light, has a good
sense of form and a firm grasp of anatomy. She understands
perspective and ambience, and possesses the patience that is
such a necessary quality for those who practice art . . .

"However, it is above all in the technical area that Kristín
excels. Her technique is almost faultless, and the present
writer, who has taught at this institution for well-nigh thirty
years, cannot remember a single student who possessed such
a strong feel for materials and their processing as Kristín . . .

"As regards her capacity for originality, time will tell where
Kristín's requirements and talents lie. At present her strength
appears to be principally in the area of technique and dexter-
ity, although it should be noted that her graduation picture of
an Icelandic landscape was both outstanding and unexpected,
in terms of composition and the handling of color and light—
the radiance from the glacier lending the barren waste an aura
of tranquil sanctity. It is to be hoped that the talent Kristín
evinces in this picture is a sign that she is maturing from a first-
rate technician into a promising artist . . ."

She folds up the report and lays it aside. The document

shows signs of having been read often, sometimes daily, some-times many times a day. She has come within an inch of throw-ing it away but has never been able to take the irrevocable step. Sometimes she tries to convince herself that she is seeking encouragement from it, but she does not succeed. Reading it never makes her happy.

" . . . a sign that she is maturing from a first-rate technician into a promising artist . . ."

Jensen was well disposed toward her, had been from the first day. He was warm and friendly to his students, and actu-ally seemed relieved when she handed in her graduation piece, an oil painting of the Vatnajökull glacier.

"This is good," he had said, "this is . . . very good. Kristín, you've taken me by surprise. This is a real improvement. To tell the truth, I was beginning to think you didn't have it in you . . ."

She listened in silence and when her reaction was not what he had expected, he patted her shoulder and said, "I didn't mean to offend you but I wasn't expecting this. The radiance from the glacier, Kristín; it comes from within."

What she had meant to paint was the picture that she has been carrying around in her head ever since she was a child. It's of a swan, raising itself in flight from a small pond. It is early winter, the grass has withered. The swan leaves its reflection behind in the pond for a little girl who has run down the slope and is now wading into the water to catch it. She is wearing a yellow dress and has just emerged from the church on the hill. The church is not visible in the picture. Nor is the funeral procession that has stopped and is looking from the girl to her mother who is dressed in black like the six men bearing the coffin. She calls after the girl who hears nothing but the distant echo of her father's voice saying, "You must show reverence for God's creation, Kristín dear, for the fishes and birds, the mountains and winds. The waves on the sea . . ."

She can hear nothing else as she snatches up the skirt of her dress and wades into the water. Can see nothing but the reflection, neither the people outside the church nor her mother on her way down the slope nor the horses grazing on the faded grass under the darkening sky. Can smell nothing but the meadowsweet that she had meant to give her father when he returned to land.

The water is icy but she doesn't let that stop her. When she reaches out for the reflection, everything becomes still.

That was the picture she had intended to paint but she couldn't do it. It was vivid in her imagination yet she couldn't fix it on canvas however hard she tried. A comprehensive knowledge of anatomy, of light and color, materials and their processing was no use. She tried again and again, only giving up when she had lost all hope. By then she was in danger of missing her deadline, and so she painted the picture of the glacier. She knew where the radiance came from. It was not from within.

"A ONE-PICTURE ARTIST. YOU'RE FAMILIAR WITH THE concept, I assume?"

She is still lying in bed, with the sheet pulled up around her shoulders. He is standing beside her, fastening his belt as he talks.

They have started to meet at her flat, sometimes during the lunch hour, but more often toward evening when the light is fading, since he is afraid that someone might spot him in daylight. She goes on ahead, he follows ten or twenty minutes later, coming straight in since she leaves the door open for him. He wants her to wait for him naked. He looked her straight in the eye when he told her that. He looks her straight in the eye when they make love as well. Tells her to turn her head so they can see each other when he is taking her from behind.

He is a patient and considerate lover. His movements are fluid and uninterrupted; he has them perfectly under control. He never comes too soon, never too late. His hands are always hot, even on cold days when she has to crawl under her quilt for warmth while waiting for him. The flat is chilly, and the draft makes matters even worse. But he is always hot and sometimes puts his arms around her and pulls her against him before they start, to warm her.

She's under his spell. She knows it but doesn't resist. She waits impatiently for him to give her the sign to leave the studio, and then counts the minutes until he appears at the flat. At first, she had the feeling he was playing a game with her by deliberately making her wait, but when he stopped she suspected it was because he couldn't wait to see her.

"A one-picture artist."

She drew the sheet up to her neck because it was cold. A few snowflakes had fallen in the morning but later the weather had cleared and the temperature had dropped. They had gone to the flat at twilight.

"They do exist. Painters who appear only once to have risen above mediocrity, only once to have exceeded their own limitations to paint a picture that is in no way consistent with their ability. I've made a study of them because they interest me. There are not many of them, and few are household names: Jean Bourdichon, Ugo da Carpi, Jan Mostaert, Giorgio Vasari . . . You won't have heard of them. Except Vasari, of course, for his writings about other artists, although his *Lives* are not as remarkable as some may think. It's not that he lacks talent; on the contrary, he's very perceptive. But his writing is ruined by a pervasive undercurrent of disappointment. The observant reader will pick up on it and think of the *Entombment* that Vasari painted as a young man. Did he himself know that it surpassed all his other work? Was it invariably on his mind when he took up his brush and mixed his colors? Did he always know in advance that the picture he was embarking on was doomed to be inferior to the *Entombment*? If so, what a torment that must have been. Over fifty, wealthy and respected, adviser to the elite, architect, art critic, a man who passes judgment on others. But who no longer dares to pick up a brush himself because he knows he is a one-picture artist and that any new attempt will do nothing but confirm the fact. So he stops painting, turns instead to writing and architecture, to worldly matters. Gives no explanation, doesn't need to, is held in high esteem during his lifetime. He lives a life of luxury, erects a monument to himself—a palazzo in his birthplace, Arezzo. But time is not kind. His paintings are forgotten as he foresaw—even the *Entombment*—buried among the mediocrity."

He pauses a moment, fastening the last button on his shirt, then glances in the mirror and runs a comb through his hair. There is no need as his hair has not been disarranged by their lovemaking, but he is a man of routine.

"What is it that happens on that one occasion? What is it that transforms these men for a few weeks or months, elevating them above themselves? And then abandons them, leaving them empty and forlorn. Is it divine intervention? Not if we believe that the Lord is well-disposed toward us, because that fleeting pleasure proves nothing but a curse."

He puts on his jacket, goes over to the bed, kisses her on the brow and says in parting, "Most mediocrities are content, Kristín, because they don't understand greatness. We both know that this doesn't apply to you. You're critical; you spare neither yourself nor others."

He left and she sat up in bed. Doves cooed in the eaves but otherwise all was quiet. He had found her that morning painting a hand with rings on two of the fingers. There was a red stone in one ring, a green one in the other. It was a male hand, small and stubby, with short, pudgy fingers, a right hand that was missing from a painting she was restoring. There was a hole in the canvas that she had to patch before filling in the gap and painting the hand from scratch. The left hand was visible in the picture, so she was able to use it as a guide, but even so the task was not easy.

When he had brought the painting, she had asked for his guidance, concerned about how extensive the damage was and unsure how far she could go when fixing it. He had responded firmly:

"Our job is to fight the ravages of time, Kristín. It requires not only technique and skill, but also judgment and intuition. No canvas lasts more than two centuries. If left alone, they all turn into dust. Those who think that art restoration is simply dusting and cleaning exhibit incredible naiveté. Interpreters, Kristín. That's what we are."

The rings were her idea. She felt they suited the owner of the hand, a wealthy seventeenth-century landowner, a corpulent figure with a low brow and slack jowls. Rather than painting directly onto the patch that she had glued to the back of the canvas, she decided to do a few trials first. Having prepared a small stretcher, she placed it on the easel beside the portrait of the landowner, then got down to work.

He came in just as she was finishing. She did not put down her brush but continued working. He stood behind her. She could hear his breathing. At last he said, "I can't suggest any improvements."

It felt like ages since she had painted for herself. The days at the studio were long and her master kept her busy. Rosselli did not show up again after Marshall took him to task over his drinking. They met in the office, so she didn't know what had passed between them, but Rosselli disappeared after their conversation. He stopped by the studio to fetch his coat but did not say a word and left in haste. When she asked Marshall when Rosselli could be expected back, he did not answer, merely shook his head with a look of chagrin as if he didn't know, and repeated what he had said before about Rosselli's failings. She pitied her colleague, but her joy proved stronger than her sympathy. Pure joy at being able now to learn from her master and show him what she was capable of. She hoped, deep down, that Rosselli would never return.

She painted not only the hand but the arm as well and part of the body, the red sleeve, the gilt buttons on the robe, because she wanted to be sure that her hand would fit seamlessly into the picture. She would have painted more of the land-owner if the canvas had been larger, because she was enjoying the work and felt there was nothing standing in her way—no doubts about her own ability, no feeling of apprehension—and her eyes seized each square centimeter, transferring it instinctively from the original to the canvas she had strung on the little stretcher. The brush obeyed her every command and she did not hesitate once; it was as if she had always been meant to paint this picture and it was only by coincidence that Guercino had done so three centuries before.

Although she knows that her work has come off well, his praise takes her by surprise, since he has always been sparing with it. A smile steals across her face and, turning, she tells him how much she has missed painting, how she longs more than anything else to paint the entire picture again from scratch but that there is no room on the canvas; she should have used a larger piece. And then the shutters come down. She notices where others might not; his eyes darken but he says nothing at first. He is thinking. Then he seems to come to himself and says in the gentle, paternal tone that she has come to know so well, "The last thing I want is to hold you back, Kristín. It would be a pity if you felt you hadn't done what you wanted. In the long run, I mean. If you want to paint, you must paint. I can find someone else. Someone more experienced so I wouldn't need to spend as much time here as I have recently. Not that I haven't enjoyed it. But it's been for your sake. I wouldn't have done it otherwise. Because you have potential in this field, Kristín. Rare potential."

She opens her mouth to say something but he continues, "You must paint if you feel the need to. Perhaps it would be for the best. Of course I should have employed someone to replace Rosselli years ago. I'll employ someone else. Then you can come and give him a hand if you need to eke out your money. Unless you'd prefer a waitressing job, as I think you mentioned the first time we met."

Beginning to shake now, she flings her arms round his neck.

"No, I don't want to leave. You're so good to me. I only said it because I so enjoyed painting this hand, creating something. I felt at last I'd achieved what I'd set out to do. I don't miss anything, I've never been happier."

"Kristín, I don't want to stand in your way . . ."

"I don't want to go. Really I don't . . ."

She presses herself against him, kissing him, but he frees himself gently, saying quietly, "Not here . . . Not now."

He goes and she is left standing by the picture with the patched hole and the little canvas on the easel beside it on which she has painted the right hand; bewildered and trembling as if she had received a physical blow. Yet he could not have been more considerate, his voice could not have been gentler, his eyes kinder.

She stands by the easel, waiting for her heart to cease its pounding in her chest.

FLORA INVITED HER. SHE TURNED UP AT THE STUDIO
one Friday morning just before eleven and was halfway across the
room before Kristín noticed her. She was wearing a light-colored
coat with a yellow scarf around her neck and a yellow bag over her
shoulder, and looked about as if remembering something. Kristín
was startled; they hadn't seen each other since she bumped into
the couple outside their house the previous autumn.

"So this is where he hides you."

Kristín did not answer but put down her tools and wiped
the paint from her hands with a damp cloth.

"I decided to invite you myself, as he still hasn't managed to
get you to accept an invitation to pay us a visit. Eight o'clock
tomorrow evening. Clients mostly."

It came as no surprise that he hadn't mentioned these invitations to her. They didn't discuss his family, Flora or the
children. He expressly forbade it and she didn't go against his
wishes, although she sometimes found it hard.

"Thank you."

"So you're not otherwise engaged?"

"No," she says.

"I'd forgotten how peaceful it is here. And how good the
smell of canvas and paint is. It must be nice working here."

"Yes."

"I know he's demanding but he thinks very highly of you. He says you're talented. I wanted you to know that, because he doesn't say that about many people."

She smiles and Kristín tries to smile back.

"Tomorrow evening. Eight o'clock."

"Eight o'clock."

"See you then."

She left. Kristín went to the window, opened it, and watched her walking away down the street. It was as if she had brought the summer with her, that cheerful brightness that seemed to float over the city on cloudless mornings before the temperature rose and it was oppressed by the sultry heat. Those light footsteps. That warm smile. Why was he unfaithful to her?

They are in the living room; he had wanted a change of scene. The door is locked and she hands him the key that she keeps in one of the kitchen drawers. He folds his clothes as usual, laying them over the piano stool; there are white dust sheets draped over the furniture. The sunlight, entering through a crack between the curtains, trembles in the air between them. Everything is quiet.

He kisses her on the forehead and throat, breasts and belly. She stands in the shaft of light from the window, and he kneels and continues to kiss her. It is then that she says, "She came to the studio this morning."

He says nothing but stops kissing her and releases his hold on her thighs.

"She invited me to your house tomorrow evening."

He stands up.

"There was nothing I could do but accept the invitation."

He studies her. Unable to endure his gaze, she looks away.

"What did you talk about?"

"Nothing."

He turns away from her and reaches for his clothes on the piano stool.

"Why?" she asks.

"I must go."

"Why are you here with me? She's so . . ."

She doesn't finish the sentence, she can't go on. He stops buttoning his shirt and looks up. She is sure that he will say it now, use the word that she has never heard him utter:

"Because I love you."

But he doesn't say it; he opens his mouth only to close it again and hastily does up the last few buttons.

She hears the front door close, his footsteps descending the stairs, then silence.

The afternoon sun shines on her nakedness. She feels the imprint of his dried kisses on her body and lifting her hand, unconsciously runs her fingers over them one by one before stepping out of the sunbeam to be enfolded by the gloomy silence.

Their apartment is large and bright, with paintings on the walls, sculptures on the floor and shelves—a torso here, a bust there. Everything is expertly placed, every object arranged with thoughtful precision, even the books on the shelves, which either lie piled one on top of the other or stand on end, the colors of their spines perfectly matched. There is nothing lacking, nothing superfluous; it is neither too heavily nor too sparsely furnished; the Persian rugs on the polished wooden floor are suitably large, their colors muted so as not to distract from the paintings on the walls. The windows are floor-length, letting in the sun by day and the streetlights by night; when open, they let the city inside.

She pauses in the middle of the room and looks around. The party is crowded but she recognizes no one. Outside, the dusk has begun to deepen in the streets, the shadows are merging, evening bringing its calm. Inside, lights twinkle on the silver trays that the waiters carry among the guests and on the crystal glasses that they leave behind in their hands. There is a steady hum of voices but instead of listening or entering into conversation with the other guests, she sticks to the walls, reading the spines of the books, examining the ornaments on the shelves, the photographs and paintings. She stops in front of the Guercino, her eyes on the ringed hand, moving close to the work to smell the freshly applied paint. When she steps back again, she nearly collides with another guest.

She had not noticed him before. A middle-aged man, hair graying at the temples and combed back, a high forehead and slightly jutting chin. He is tall and lean, and the hand he offers her is pale and elegant.

"Excuse me," he says and introduces himself. "Prince Philipp of Hesse."

She has heard Marshall talk of him as a prospective client. He is married to Mafalda, daughter of King Vittorio Emanuele III of Italy. A German of aristocratic birth, who could pass as English with his dark-blue double-breasted Savile Row suit, starched white shirt, and gold cuff links. There is a gold pin too in his blue-striped tie.

"He's a genius. I saw this picture when it had a hole in the middle the size of my palm. Unbelievable how he does it. It's like a new picture."

She sees her master out of the corner of her eye. He has spotted them and is heading their way.

"We were just admiring your work," the prince says. "This young lady . . ."

Kristín introduces herself, having had no opportunity before.

"My assistant," Marshall adds.

"So you have observed this miracle in the making. I envy you. The rings . . . the colors in them . . . What is it that's reflected in the red one?"

The prince steps closer to the picture, bending and inspecting the red ring. She looks at Marshall. He coughs.

"Guercino means 'the squinting one,'" he says. "His real name was Giovanni Francesco Barbieri; he worked mainly in Rome and Bologna. Some put him on a par with Caracci, others with Guido Reni or Caravaggio. It's worth taking a trip to Piacenza to see the fresco he painted in the cathedral. It's one of four and transcends the others by Caracci, Procaccini, and Morazzone. They're all first-class but can't compare to the Guercino."

The prince turns to Kristín.

"I'm trying to persuade him to sell me this picture," he says, smiling. "Can you put in a word for me? He seems suddenly reluctant to part with it."

Can it be true? she asks herself. Is it possible that he's keen to hold on to it because of me? Does he feel that I am near when he looks at it?

"Apparently he had a dreadful squint, but it doesn't show in his self-portraits," Marshall continues, "where his eyes appear normal. Vanity? I don't know. Who can blame him? Wouldn't we all have been tempted to do the same?"

The guests take their places for dinner. They are Italian or German, apart from an American who represents the Wildenstein gallery in New York. Kristín didn't know much about Marshall's business dealings and he never discussed them with her. Every now and then Signorina Pirandello, his secretary, would mention a customer or a sale, but she mostly complained that Marshall had had to stop doing business with his countrymen after Italy had declared war on them. His finances had suffered initially, she said, but he had bounced back thanks to interest from other parts of the world, as she put it. Kristín didn't ask her to elaborate, it was not her place and, frankly, she wasn't that interested.

Marshall stands up once the first course has been served and addresses his guests. His words sound familiar to her—"In the face of great art we are all equal; it unites us, its sublime intent raises us above petty squabbles, its pure and unadulterated claim on a higher purpose, its universal quality, independent of nationality, of longitude or latitude, of the soil from which we are sprung, of the vagaries of our times." His guests nod, some hesitantly, others enthusiastically, and applaud when he sits down after concluding his speech. Smiling at him, Flora takes his hand. "Bon appétit."

The American is sitting next to Kristín. He has visited the studio more than once and knows her from there. Now he whispers to her, "The prince is angling for the Guercino. So are we. You don't happen to know what he's offered for it?"

No, she doesn't know.

"I gather it was so badly damaged that Marshall got it for a song?"

She says it is correct that the picture had been in bad shape.

"He's going to make a buck or two," the American says.

"And he deserves to, though I'm not exactly thrilled seeing the Germans buy up all these masterpieces."

"But the prince is married to the king's daughter," she says. "Isn't he buying for himself and his wife?"

"He's a middleman," he replies. "The paintings he acquires end up with Hitler for his planned museum in Linz."

She must have looked skeptical, for he continues, "The prince works with Hans Posse, the director of the Führermuseum. Posse uses the prince's social connections to find the best pieces and his political influence to circumvent the export restrictions. They've made some great purchases, I'm afraid to say. But they do have competition."

"You, I assume?"

He smiles.

"I do my best but that's usually not good enough these days. No, Hitler's competition is Göring. Both ravenous collectors with full-fledged buying operations here in Italy. Göring's agent is Walter Hofer. Has he come to visit?"

"I don't know," she answers after a brief hesitation.

"Here, they're at least paying. In the occupied territories, they don't bother. There they just take what they want. We hear there is massive confiscation of art going on in France and the Low Countries. Massive. Greater than anyone could imagine."

A waiter pours wine into their glasses.

"Cheers," the American adds. "Your boss has class. Can't take that away from him. Pitting us against the Germans over quail and Brunello di Montalcino."

And that is how she realized that she was present at an auction. It should not have come as a surprise, which may have been why she was so upset. It was as if a veil had suddenly been stripped from her eyes, and she felt she had been stupid and pathetically naïve; she who had let herself dream that he wouldn't sell the Guercino because of the hand she had painted. What childishness, what self-delusion. She was ashamed.

Later, when she lay in the clinic at San Martino, listening to the cicadas singing outside the window and watching Melchiorre's shadow by the door, it occurred to her that she had begun to change that evening. It took a long time; there was more than one veil over her eyes, and they were not stripped away all at once but little by little, until she finally saw Robert Marshall in a cold, pitiless light. And that was when she committed the crime, in the light that spared no one and was devoid of all beauty or forgiveness.

YESTERDAY MORNING THE COOK CAME TO SEE ME and reported that there had been a theft from the pantry in the night. It has never happened before, and I asked her twice if there was any way she could have been mistaken. She stuck to her story, listing with characteristic precision what was missing—a loaf of bread, a piece of ham, two jars of fruit, some nuts, and a bottle of red wine. I accompanied her to the pantry and she showed me where the provisions had been stored—ham at the back, bread at the front, tins on the top shelf—and I said (more to myself than her), "How can you remember all this?"

She was deeply attached to you and although it may be my imagination, I get the impression that she knows your absence is somehow my fault. Instead of giving me a direct answer, she said that the least she could hope for was that her kitchen would be left in peace. I nodded and made myself scarce. I always have the feeling she is accusing me. "The least I can hope for . . ."

I didn't have a clue who the culprit might be and neither did anyone else. It was awful having to speculate whether this or that person might be guilty, about people who are all dear to me. So I avoided naming any names, although I admit I ran over a mental list.

"It can hardly be the children. What would they want with red wine?" Pritchett said finally. "Anyway, they get enough to eat like the rest of the household, so whoever the thieves are they can't be stealing for themselves. But for someone else? Could that be it?"

I cut short this speculation, as it was futile and would do nothing but sow suspicion in our minds.

"She may be mistaken," I said, and he nodded, although he didn't believe it any more than I did.

However, he did not let things rest there but ordered Melchiorre to stand guard in the kitchen last night. That proved to be the right decision: the thief appeared after everyone had gone to bed, creeping indoors with the moonlight on his heels, and would no doubt have made a beeline for the pantry if Melchiorre hadn't started up in the rocking chair in the corner. The thief ran for his life, with Melchiorre in hot pursuit, but he was too slow and lost sight of him. Nevertheless, he insisted that he had recognized the culprit; it was the young German who turned up here the other day in the truck marked with the Red Cross.

I had forgotten him as soon as he had driven away down the road but Pritchett claims that his concerns had not disappeared with the boy.

"Where could he have gone? We should have seen this coming."

The fattore and the farmhands found the truck this morning. The young man had hidden it in the woods a couple of miles down the road and set fire to it. They looked for him for hours but couldn't find him. Pritchett told the fattore to send word to the people on the outlying farms to keep a lookout and let us know if he was spotted. This bore fruit within hours when the farmer from Pietraporciana, at the top of our hill, caught sight of him at the edge of the forest.

"What are you going to do with him?" I asked.

"We'll decide that when we've caught him," Pritchett replied.

He took the fattore and two workmen with him. I watched them leave in the rain, feeling terribly nervous. The weather doesn't help as leaves rain down in the mud outside. The temperature has dropped sharply and the rooms are so cold and dank that we decided to light a fire in the big hearth in the drawing room, which is now being used as a classroom. The children huddle in front of the blaze where Kristín is reading them a story. I'm cold too; this damp pierces one to the marrow. It's even worse than the winter chill since we are unprepared for it in the middle of summer. It is dark, even in the middle of the day, and I have difficulty picking out the road down in the valley. Earlier I thought I heard the roar of a plane but realized when I looked out and saw lightning in the distance that it was probably nothing but thunder. What I'd really like is to wrap myself in a blanket and curl up in the rocking chair in the kitchen, but I'm too restless.

They are soaked to the skin when they return. The horses hang their heads in the downpour, their hooves sinking into the mud. Pritchett dismounts slowly, shaking his head, and follows me inside. He takes off his boots in the hall and I help him out of his raincoat before he goes into the drying room to change his clothes. We sit down by the fire in the kitchen. He rubs his hands together.

"We found where he's been sleeping in the forest," he says, "but he'd gone. We looked everywhere."

"We'll survive even if he does pilfer the odd loaf," I say.

He looks up and stops rubbing his hands.

"We both know this is not about loaves of bread, Alice. How long do you think it will be before he tells someone that we're hiding something of great value for the Germans? The partisans, if they find him. The Allies, if he ends up in their hands."

"He said he didn't know what was hidden here."

"He knows it's important. Otherwise he wouldn't have been sent here with a high-ranking officer. In the middle of a battle. Here . . ."

"What are you going to do with him if you find him?"

"I don't know."

"Hold him hostage?"

"Maybe."

"Where?"

"He could jeopardize everything, Alice. Everything."

I hear a slight noise at the door. It is Melchiorre. He has obviously been standing there for some time, listening to us.

"Melchiorre," I say. "Why don't you come in?"

"I didn't want to disturb."

"You're drenched. Go into the drying room and change your clothes."

"I'm sorry," he says. "It was my fault he got away. I was careless."

"Nonsense," Pritchett retorts. "Go and put on some dry clothes."

"His horse slipped in the mud as we were approaching the forest and made a lot of noise," he says after Melchiorre has gone. "He thinks the German must have heard him. Of course it's only his imagination."

The day grows darker and the thunder intensifies in the

afternoon. Lightning illuminates the countryside and Monte Amiata appears from time to time, bathed in violet light, before vanishing into the rainy gloom. The fattore has kept up his search for the boy, going around to some of the other farms to ask for news of him. He returns toward evening and tells us that the Germans have taken control of the towns at the mouth of the valley and that their numbers are increasing. They have been joined by reinforcements from the north and are now preparing for fierce fighting with the Allies, who are rapidly approaching from the south.

"We'll end up on the front line," he says. "It's just a question of time."

The fattore has a tendency to worry unnecessarily but in this case we all know he's right. We eat in silence, staring into the fire that has been burning since morning. From time to time Pritchett gets up and adds more wood. After dinner, he goes out alone to check for signs that anyone has been searching for the underground vault by the mill and is gone a long time. Growing uneasy, I put on my raincoat and follow him. The rain is cold on my face and the courtyard is covered in leaves and twigs that the wind has torn from the trees. I can't find him by the mill but stay away from the trapdoor for fear of leaving footprints in the mud.

On the way back I stop and survey the buildings—the *fattoria* with its silent olive press and cold baking ovens, the chapel, the clinic, the main villa. I gaze at their outlines in the rain and darkness and all at once I feel as if this world is slipping from my grasp and I have only myself to blame, not the war or the political turmoil but myself.

I go to bed early, utterly worn-out. Pritchett is reading in his study. I can tell that his mind is not on his book and we exchange a few words before saying good night. He tells me that Melchiorre is insisting on guarding the kitchen tonight, though there is no likelihood that the German will return.

"From now on we'll lock the doors at night," he says.

"If you like," I say.

I am awakened by a commotion outside in the courtyard. It is two o'clock. When I look out the window, I see shadows moving in the darkness. I hear Pritchett's voice. His agitation is plain, although I can't distinguish a word he says. I hurriedly pull on a dressing gown and head downstairs.

They are in the courtyard by the chapel—Pritchett, Melchiorre, and Kristín. The door is wide open and I can see a candle burning by the altar. Outside a man is lying facedown on the ground. Pritchett looks over at me, then at the man.

I do not need to see his face to know that this is the young German we have been searching for. He is motionless, his arms by his sides, his right cheek pressed to the cold stone. Pritchett has a torch and when he flashes it on the ground I see that the pool around the boy's head is red. The blood is thinning in the rain but I can follow the trail over the threshold and into the chapel.

Pritchett and Kristín stand still and Melchiorre is staring at the young man on the ground, scrutinizing him with single-minded absorption as if looking for something, perhaps waiting for him to open his eyes and sit up. I'm too shocked to speak. Finally Pritchett takes my arm and leads me into the chapel.

I take care not to step in the trail of blood. It glistens in the feeble candlelight, a slender, intermittent trail, ending in a pool before the altar. We stop and Pritchett says in a low voice:

"He must have come in here to pray—the boy, I mean."

I gaze at the pool before automatically glancing out at the

rain. I can glimpse the shapes of Melchiorre and Kristín outside; they are still standing in the same place, with the body between them, as if guarding it.

"Melchiorre found him kneeling by the font," Pritchett says. "He panicked when the boy jumped to his feet and he shot him. You can't blame the poor wretch."

"No, you can't," I manage to say. "Poor Melchiorre."

"He'd dragged him outside before I arrived," he says. "Couldn't bear watching him on the floor in here."

Pritchett suggests that he wake up the fattore to help him take the body to the quarry on the hillside to the east because it would be too risky to bury him in our cemetery.

"We must bury him in consecrated ground," I reply, adding quietly, "how would they ever know? There are so many new graves . . ."

He looks at me and sighs, then goes to get the fattore. I take Melchiorre inside. He's crying. I do my best to console him and give him a glass of wine to calm his nerves before I tell him to go to bed.

Lifting the body between them, Pritchett and the fattore carry it to the cemetery. I give Kristín a broom, a bucket, and cloths and leave her behind in the chapel while I fetch the priest, who has been in Montepulciano for the past two weeks but is now staying with us for a few days. I'm surprised to find him awake.

"I don't sleep much these days," he says.

Pritchett and the fattore have already dug the grave when I arrive with the priest. The fattore climbs back down into it and receives the body as Pritchett lowers it to him.

In the rain and darkness, the priest's movements seem even slower than usual. His words merge into the noise of the rain and disappear with it into the ground. We stand in the mud, eyes straight ahead. When the priest stops speaking, Pritchett fills in the grave over the body.

Kristín has cleaned the chapel by the time we return. I tell her she is not to discuss the events of the night with anyone. She nods but I feel compelled to repeat myself.

The candle on the altar has gone out and I feel how cold it is inside. The priest takes my hand and we stand there in silence for what seems like a very long time.

KRISTÍN WAS AWAKE WHEN SHE HEARD THE SHOT. Her room was upstairs in a small building beside the main villa. Signorina Harris and Schwester Marie slept on the ground floor, Signor Grandinetti in the room next to hers. The teacher had moved there from Pienza when the roads were no longer safe for him to travel on his bicycle. He was quiet and unobtrusive, missing his girlfriend back home. Sometimes he played his guitar in his room and sang in a very low voice.

Her leg ached but she didn't mention this to Signorina Harris. It generally began to ache in late afternoon or evening when she had been on her feet for a long time. That day it had been unusually bad. She was sitting with her leg up on the table, trying not to let her thoughts stray to Robert Marshall, trying not to think about anything, listening to the infinitesimal changes in the rhythm of the rain on the glass.

She wouldn't have heard the shot if she hadn't been paying attention. She knew about the theft from the kitchen and had heard Schwester Marie telling the teacher that Melchiorre was going to stand guard that night. Clasping her leg, she lifted it down from the table, grimacing involuntarily as the pain returned, then stood up as quickly as she could and put on her shoes. There was no one in the kitchen, but the door to the courtyard was ajar. Grabbing a raincoat from the peg next to it, she went outside.

Melchiorre was dragging the body out of the chapel when she found him. He stopped when he saw her but did not let go of the German's legs. The shot had hit the young man in the neck and a small pool quickly formed on the floor around the boy's head. Glancing at the pool, Melchiorre started to stammer.

"I don't know what happened . . . I thought he . . ." And then, echoing Pritchett: "He could have jeopardized everything."

The German lay on his back, his eyes open, staring up at the chapel ceiling.

"Jeopardized what?" Kristín asked.

Melchiorre hesitated, as if trying to remember what exactly Pritchett had said to Alice. Befuddled, he continued to drag the corpse toward the door.

"He could have told someone . . ."

"What?"

"That we're hiding something for the Germans. Something of great value."

As he was dragging the corpse over the threshold, Pritchett loomed out of the darkness. He was wearing a hat and rain was dripping from the brim. His face was in shadow until he raised the lantern he held in his right hand.

Kristín began cleaning when Alice had gone to fetch the priest. Listening to Melchiorre's words echoing in her head, she tried to concentrate on her task but her mind was racing. Finally she had her confirmation. The painting was here. They hadn't changed their minds, hadn't taken it elsewhere as she had begun to imagine. Where could they have hidden it? Where should she start looking? And when? There was always someone around. She thought about Alice. Would she be held accountable if Kristín destroyed the painting? By now Kristín knew that Alice's husband was gone. Not that anyone spoke about it but she had seen pictures of him in the house and asked a maid about him. She also knew that this was not the man she had seen with Alice in Rome. Who was that man who had so hastily let go of Alice's shoulders when Kristín came running down the stairs?

Kristín's legs were bare and the stone was cold to the touch when she knelt to scrub the floor. The blood had begun to congeal but the trail was thin except where it had pooled. The rain had washed away most of the blood outside but nonetheless she rubbed the cloth repeatedly over the patch where he had bled the most.

After she was finally done, she decided to go to the cemetery. Her leg was sore but she was able to limp along. She spotted them as she neared the gate: four shadows in the faint glow of the lantern that Pritchett had hung from a branch by the grave.

She paused and although she had not intended to hide, she stepped instinctively behind the stone wall by the entrance. From there she watched as Pritchett lowered the body into the grave, the fattore climbed out, and the priest stepped forward to the edge. She was soaked to the skin and cold but stood without moving until the priest had fallen silent and Pritchett had refilled the grave. Afterward she turned and picked her way back along the path through the darkness between the cypresses that had begun to sway again in the wind, step by step, and had just reached the courtyard when Alice arrived.

"Not a word to anyone," she said, and Kristín nodded more eagerly than was necessary, feeling a kind of shiver of frightened relief and anticipation go through her.

IT DOESN'T TAKE MUCH TO TURN ONE'S THOUGHTS to the past, not when one longs for a respite from the here and now—a word, a movement, a shard of light in a mirror, the echo of a voice through a half-open window.

The rain has eased, and the view from the window is autumnal; there is a gray film over the fields and the meadows are colorless; the flowers seem to be hibernating. Yesterday I had the lemon trees moved into the greenhouse, and Pritchett did not object as the farmhands had nothing more pressing to do; it was impossible to work in the downpour, and I was on edge and had to find myself some employment. I tried to be of use to the farmhands, not leaving their side while they worked, holding the reins of the horse as they lifted the trees from the cart and carried them inside. I remained behind after they had gone; it was cool and damp in the greenhouse and I stood still, listening to the quiet and looking out through the glass at the English garden where all is neat and orderly and there is nothing to show that the world is going up in flames.

The farmhands went straight from the greenhouse to the cemetery to dig fresh graves. The Fascists and the partisans clashed in the forest last night, fighting in the rain and the dark. Near Fontalgozzo and Chiarentana, our two most outly-

ing farms, there were many casualties. The farmers brought
the bodies down the steep slope on a cart, which was no easy
undertaking in the mud, but they were in a hurry to see them
buried. They drank coffee in the kitchen while Pritchett supervised the laying of the bodies in the simple coffins that the
carpenter started making this morning. They were all young
men and of course there was no way of telling which faction
they had belonged to—in death they were all alike, peasant
lads snatched by fate.

It doesn't take much . . . Concentration, a few sentences,
or perhaps the drawing I found after the burial when I was
rooting through the papers that were cleared out of the library
when we converted it into a dining room for the children. It is
Pritchett's drawing of the fountain in the garden, with its two
dolphins spouting water, dated May 14, 1935. I smooth it out
on the table and think of those days when all was well and we
were cheerfully busy from morning to night, when suddenly I
hear his voice in the emptiness: "Mummy, the dolphins are my
frog's best friends." Putting down my pen, I shove the drawing
back into the pile of papers where I found it. But his voice, still
so clear, persists. We are sitting out in the garden, listening to
the tinkling of the fountain, and I'm reading him *Pinocchio*.
The sun is shining but we are in the shade of the pergolas; he's
sitting on my lap.

"Mummy, why did Pinocchio's nose grow so long?"

"Because he told lies."

He scrambles down to the ground, turns and looks me in
the eye.

"Mummy, look at me."

"All right."

"Ready?"

"Yes."

"I can fly. I can talk to the dolphins," he says, waits a moment, then asks, "did my nose grow?"

I smile at the memory and am about to answer him as I did then but the words won't come. His voice fades, the echo grows distant and with it his face. I can no longer see it in my mind's eye, can no longer picture it, no matter how I try. I start to panic and quickly reach for a picture of him, staring at it for a long time, engraving it in my brain.

When I sat singing to him after he died, I told him I would never forget him. Not his voice, not his fingers, his eyes, his lips, his hair . . . I don't believe I stopped singing for the whole time I was talking to him in my head and stroking his cold brow and cheeks before they took him away. It was a lullaby that I sang over and over again, ceaselessly, until we were back at the hotel and you yelled at me. I hadn't realized I was still humming it.

I started to cry uncontrollably. I didn't have the strength to get up on my feet but reached out to you where you were standing in the middle of the room. For a moment I thought you were going to take me in your arms, for a moment I believed you were going to put everything aside but our sorrow. But you didn't. You turned and, hiding your face with one hand, you reached for the doorknob with the other.

I sat on the unmade bed all night, without undressing or turning on the light. The pills I had in my purse might have helped but I didn't want to take them. I hoped I would die. Not only that night but long after.

KRISTÍN THINKS BACK TO THAT DAY EARLY IN NO-
vember. It was cold, but her father's hands were warm when
he caressed her cheek before he cast off the boat. They were
always warm, those big, thick hands.

The farm stood at the head of the fjord where it narrowed
and the mountains retreated from the sea, making room for a
small area of lowland. The river cascaded down a deep ravine
at the head of the fjord, then meandered in a shallow course
over the sands before deepening and flowing down to the ocean
through the meadow by the farm. Farther down the fjord a village stood by a small cove, sheltered from the open sea, home
to some two hundred people.

She watched the boat moving away down the fjord. It had
one set of oars, and her father and her uncle shared the rowing.
She waved to them as usual, watching them grow distant until
finally they were nothing but a black speck at the mouth of the
fjord. There the expanse of water widened, the mountains rose
high, sheer and black against the sky, and birds swarmed along
the cliffs. Beyond lay the open sea.

She dawdled up the river. There was a hoarfrost on the
marsh, a thin film of ice, pierced here and there by a head of
cotton grass, nodding gently in the light breeze. In the west,

above the cliffs at the fjord's mouth, the pale winter sun dipped in and out of the clouds.

Her mother, who had been making pancakes, came to the door to check on her. Kristín waved to her and she waved back, holding her arm aloft for a long time before going back inside.

She didn't feel the cold and continued to walk up the river as far as she was allowed, to the big rock that was shaped like a troll. She was not allowed to go any farther to the east, and no farther south than to the patch of marsh, absolutely no farther, and only as far as the sheepfolds to the north. These were her boundaries, and she had once been spanked for forgetting herself and walking up to the waterfall alone. Her mother undertook the task, as her father had begged to be excused. Kristín heard them talking; he said, "Oh, couldn't you do it, love?" Her mother did not hit her hard but Kristín wept long and bitterly over the shame.

She threw stones into the marsh, the film of ice broke, and the stones disappeared with a hollow sound into the bog. Her mother came to the door and called her. She went inside.

So passed many an afternoon. She sat on a chair in the kitchen, reading a book or coloring, while her mother knitted. Her mother hummed a tune, time passed, and darkness fell over the fjord. Every now and then her mother glanced at the clock, and when it was dark she went out and lit the little beacon that her father had built. There was a larger lighthouse in the village but they had their own beacon, too; there was safety in that.

At six o'clock her mother began to prepare supper. She laid the table, scrubbed the potatoes, and sliced the bread she had baked that day. Her father and uncle rarely came ashore later than seven, unless they made a big haul or were caught in a storm, in which case they would sometimes row to the village and wait out the weather with Kristín's maternal grandparents.

Her mother attended to the embers and looked out of the window. The wind was picking up; they listened to it beating on the windows, a cold westerly, blowing straight in from the sea. The chimney whined and the blue flame flickered but did not go out. Her mother was not anxious, she was used to the wind, yet she glanced out of the window and absentmindedly stroked Kristín's cheek as she returned to the fire. The pot was ready, waiting for fresh fish. Kristín pictured them coming in to land, dragging the boat up the beach, hurrying inside. She saw them so clearly: her uncle first, as he came in and gave her a hug, slipping a cold finger down the back of her neck to tease her, her father following with the fish for supper—"There you are, girls." They took off their wet clothes and thawed out by the fire while the fish simmered on the stove. The evening stretched out before them, with cards or reading and the jokes of her uncle who did not get on with his father and preferred to live with them. That's how it was: idyllic, the four of them in that little house on the limits of the inhabitable world, at the bottom of a deep fjord with the mountains overhead, the winter and the night, and the sea outside, the sea that both gives and takes away.

Seven o'clock passed, then eight o'clock. A blizzard had blown up; wet snow plastered the windowpanes and the house shivered. She followed her mother to the door but was told to wait inside while her mother went out to look for the boat. She came straight back in because it was impossible to stand upright in the wind. The snow blew in with her and she shut the door hastily, brushing off the wet flakes, then said, "They'll have gone to the village. Let's eat."

Despite making sure that Kristín ate well, she hardly touched her own meal; her fingers trembled and kept flying to her face to push aside a lock of hair. She got Kristín ready for bed and said her prayers with her, then sat still beside her while she was falling asleep. But Kristín couldn't get to sleep right away, although she closed her eyes, and when she heard her mother saying her prayers again she almost opened them to remind her that she had already done that. But she didn't because she liked hearing them again and feeling her mother's presence. Finally she fell asleep and dreamed that they had come home and her father was sitting beside her, stroking her cheek as he always did when he had had to wait out the storm in the village until late at night or next morning. She heard their footsteps in the kitchen and their voices through her sleep, and waited to feel the hand on her cheek, cold from the sea. When it didn't come, she woke up and got out of bed. They were standing in the kitchen, her grandfather and two other men, cold and plastered with snow, still wearing their outer clothing. Her grandfather was hugging her mother who looked like a sparrow in his arms, so small and weak that Kristín hardly recognized her.

The church stands on a mound outside the village. From there one can see over the roofs of the village to the farm at the head of the fjord. The church is white with a red roof, a small porch, five rows of pews, and a cross over the altar. Kristín was christened there.

Her mother insisted that they conduct the funeral as if the bodies were there and bury the men in coffins. Kristín's grandfather tried to dissuade her but she would not budge. Kristín heard him mention his concern to the minister.

"Perhaps you could make her change her mind?" he said. "Empty coffins . . ."

The minister shook his head: "It's up to her to decide."

It is cold in the church during the closing of the coffins, which takes place two days before the funeral. When the minister speaks of her father and uncle, Kristín averts her eyes and puts her hands over her ears.

"Dear," her mother says, trying to pry her hands from her ears, then abandons the attempt. "Dear . . ."

Kristín is the last to leave the church, deliberately lagging behind, making herself as inconspicuous as possible. The minister leads her mother by the hand. Her grandfather has been keeping an eye on her but now forgets himself and goes out with the others. Once she is the only one left she turns back and goes over to the coffins.

She pushes aside the lid of her father's coffin. There is nothing inside, nothing but his Sunday suit and a copy of the Bible. She climbs into the coffin, lies down on her back, and closes her eyes.

She hears them come in. They seem agitated, then approach the coffin. She senses their presence as they look at her but she does not move or open her eyes. She is dead. Surely they must understand that and leave her alone.

She refused to wear anything but her yellow dress. Her mother did not have the strength to argue with her and no one else tried. It was as if the grown-ups did not know how to handle her, not even her grandparents; they were kind to her, of course, cuddled her and patted her on the head but said little. But no one seemed to know what to say, not even her mother, who moved like a shadow, weeping for the first few days, then stopping, too drained even to cry.

During the funeral Kristín's mind was on the pond below the mound. She had seen inside the coffins and knew that her father and uncle were not there. So she thought about the pond where she used to play when she came to see her grandparents, and the birds that visited the pond. There was a swan there when they arrived at the church and her thoughts were on the swan the entire time the minister was speaking. The church was packed to overflowing. The wind had dropped abruptly; now an easterly breeze freshened the air and the sun laid a blue film over the fjord where harmless ripples tossed the sunbeams to and fro. She was impatient to go outside and see if the swan was still there, and she wriggled in the pew, turning around, trying to see out the open door. But the church was too crowded and she encountered too many eyes that did not know how to meet her gaze, so she looked away and waited for the service to be over.

The moment they were outside, she let go of her mother's hand and set off at a run down the slope. Everyone stopped but it was a moment before her mother reacted. Perhaps it was only a few seconds but it seemed much longer and the congregation stood rooted to the spot, watching the child wade out into the pond as if her life depended on it. And then the swan took off, slowly and smoothly as if wishing to leave behind its reflection intact on the surface of the water, rose majestically into the air and soared away over the fjord. Kristín was left standing in the water, not moving until her mother's voice split the cold silence.

Shortly after the funeral, she and her mother moved to the village to live with her grandparents. Her mother had never been talkative but now she grew even more distant. The house at the head of the fjord stood empty until the following spring when a young couple moved there from the village.

As soon as she was old enough, she went to study in Reykjavík, and from there to Copenhagen. Her mother passed away when she was a teenager, drifted away quietly on a summer morning. Her grandparents supported her but they were not rich, so she worked alongside her studies.

She never went back to the head of the fjord after she and her mother moved into the village. She didn't even look in that direction, not in daylight. But sometimes in the evenings she would climb up the mound by the church and watch the beacon in the darkness, wondering if they had seen its light as they drowned.

THE REHEARSALS WERE PROGRESSING SLOWLY. NO one wanted to be a dwarf whereas competition was fierce for the part of Snow White. Negotiations were tricky, but Kristín proved a model of patience. She reasoned with the children, skillfully averting acrimony by distracting the attention of enough of them to the work that needed to be done behind the scenes. By the time she had finished, three wanted to be responsible for the costumes, five for the creation of the back-drop, and four offered to rewrite the story to give the dwarfs a more prominent role. It fell to Signor Grandinetti to guide the children in writing the script, while Kristín took responsibility for the set and costumes, and Schwester Marie and I for the actors. I had been the one to suggest that the play should be performed in the greenhouse where the lemon trees were stored. They were still there, although the storm appeared to be abating, the temperature was gradually rising, there were glimpses of sunshine, the wind had fallen silent, and the colors had been revived in the garden and fields.

The teacher and scriptwriters got down to work in the class-room while Kristín led her charges outside to the greenhouse. Their work progressed well, and once they had drawn the stage design on paper, they went inside to find props and costumes and to paint the backdrop—an old canvas that I had found in a shed below the house—before sweeping the floor and tidying up while the script editors finished their work.

The rehearsals got off to a good start until the wicked step-mother forgot herself so far as to eat the apple that she was supposed to give Snow White, and felt so ashamed that she tried to hide the evidence. But of course she was found out—as, she was reminded, is always the case—at which point the other children started complaining that it was unfair and they wanted apples too. By then it was past three o'clock and time to feed them anyway, so I decided to go inside and ask the kitchen staff to bring some fruit, bread, and drinks out to the greenhouse.

I did not hurry back. My spirits were higher than they had been for a long while; the shadows had disappeared with the rain and the sunshine penetrated right into my soul, shooting the odd shaft of light into the corners where darkness had taken up its abode. Perhaps it was the change of weather, perhaps it was the children and this project, the play, which, while not exactly heaving rocks, nevertheless required work and concentration and prevented my thoughts from wandering. I knew that what I had to avoid was inactivity, empty hours—they were like holes in a sheet of already thin ice.

Such were my thoughts as I emerged from the kitchen after giving the staff orders for afternoon tea, and my footsteps became even lighter, for I felt I had solved some puzzle that had been troubling me. Of course I know that nothing was more important than having something to do from morning to night, chores with a clear beginning and foreseeable end, which taxes my powers of organization and resourcefulness, but to a manageable degree. I had often told myself so before, but never as clearly and bluntly as on that day.

I decided not to return directly to the greenhouse but instead to walk down below the villa to the English garden where flower beds alternate with strips of lawn, separated by neatly clipped hedges, some at right angles, others curved or crescent-shaped, because I wanted to savor this weather change in my soul for a few minutes before returning to the children. Pritchett has kept up the garden as far as possible, clipping the hedges himself and making sure that the flower beds do not become overrun with weeds, but it's naturally not looking its best; it's a heroic feat to keep it in check. The valley was tranquil; smoke rose from a farm on the lower slopes of Monte Amiata, ascending in a straight column before dispersing into thin air. No aircraft, no roar of engines, although I knew this could change at any moment.

Quickening my pace, I left the garden, heading up the path that leads to the forge and the *fattoria*, before descending the slope and sweeping around to the greenhouse. The sound of the children's voices carried to me and I couldn't help smiling to myself; they were clear and full of infectious enthusiasm now that most of the actors had memorized their lines.

I saw you as I was turning off the path to take a shortcut to the greenhouse. You were standing on the slope above, among the cypresses that concealed the rose garden, your back turned to me, looking toward the main villa, motionless at first, but then you withdrew farther into the shade under the trees. The sun was in my eyes and I raised a hand to my brow to get a better view as I set off at a run toward you. I wanted to call out to you, but my voice failed and so did my legs after a short distance, when in my heedlessness I tripped over a projecting root. I had not taken my eyes off you while I ran and now frantically tried to locate you again as I scrambled to my feet, wiping the sweat from my eyes and the tears that had begun pouring down my face. But you had gone and there was nothing under the trees but the shade that had hidden you—yet I kept going, running as fast as I could, careless of being struck by branches or losing my footing, repeatedly shouting your name, without realizing I was doing so, during the last stretch up the slope.

You were gone. I looked everywhere but couldn't find you. There's no path over this slope; above are thick woods, to the west the cemetery and the cluster of buildings. The view of the main villa could not be better—the drive in front of the house, the courtyard between chapel and clinic, the kitchen door from which Pritchett was just this moment emerging. I turned in a circle, peering into the forest thickets but could see nothing but the birds that fluttered from bough to bough, shaking the leaves. I had been prepared to give chase but now felt the strength draining from my body. My arms fell to my sides and my legs stopped working; the air was stifling, the sunlight blinding. What had appeared to be within reach a moment before now seemed impossibly remote; I saw the buildings as if in a mirage, could no longer distinguish Pritchett or the horses that were tethered in the courtyard outside the kitchen door. Yet they were there, I knew it, though I could not see them. There was a ringing in my ears but gradually it faded and I heard the voices of the children, first singly, then all raised in unison in the song that accompanied Snow White's wedding to the prince.

Just as I was about to start picking my way down the slope, I saw two maids coming along the path to the greenhouse with baskets of food. Not wanting them to see me in such a state, I withdrew into the shadow under the cypresses and hid where you had stood, perhaps in your very footsteps.

I dried my eyes, tidied my hair, and brushed the dirt off my skirt. I felt duty-bound to go to the children, feed them, and help Schwester Marie, Kristín, and Signor Grandinetti with the finishing touches, as the premiere was imminent. I was on the point of setting off to join them but, not trusting myself, changed my mind at the last minute. I had to be strong for the children. Turning around, I went home by the shortest route, looking neither right nor left until I reached my room.

"He's here," I said to Pritchett when he came to see me.

"Who?"

"Where's he hiding?"

"Who are you talking about?"

"I know how close you two are but I'm shocked you're prepared to go behind my back like this."

"Alice," he said, "what are you talking about? Would you like me to bring you a drink of water?"

He fetched a glass and held it out to me but I didn't take it.

"He was wearing his green sweater."

"Alice," he said, "you should rest."

"Claudio's here. Don't try to deny it. I saw him."

He stared at me in silence. I had to look away.

"Alice," he said eventually, "you know how much I care for you both. You know I would never lie to you."

Was he lying to me or was I losing my mind? I wasn't sure.

The premiere exceeded all expectations. Schwester Marie persuaded some of the staff to attend so the greenhouse was packed to overflowing. I watched the play in a daze from the doorway. The sun hung low in the sky; in the garden dusk fell, the lower lawns and flower beds lay in blue shadow while above daylight still lingered. Unable to sit still, I got up between the second and third acts and slipped away quietly.

I hadn't walked more than a few meters from the greenhouse when I spotted you. You were standing where you had stood before, half hidden by the cypresses, holding a pair of binoculars and scanning the valley. This time I was able to call your name, this time I was able to tell my feet to run, this time I was not going to let you get away.

I didn't see Pritchett following me nor did I pay attention when you dropped the binoculars and turned toward me. Your face was so clear in my mind's eye, your voice so bright when I heard you say, "Alice, I'm back," that I didn't realize my mistake until it was too late.

"What are you doing here, Bruno?" I heard Pritchett say as he gently pulled me away from the troublemaking partisan who looked even more confused than I was.

"One of our men is missing."

"Where did you get that sweater?"

Bruno looked at me first, then at Pritchett.

"The sweater?"

"Where did you get it?"

"He gave it to me, Marchese Orsini. Last year."

Pritchett quickly ended the conversation.

"We don't want any trouble here, Bruno," he said, pointing to the rifle at the partisan's feet. "Do you hear me? No trouble here."

I don't know if he answered or whether he was still trying to comprehend what was happening. Pritchett led me away, taking me in his arms when we were out of sight. By then I was so deflated that all I could do was close my eyes to prevent the tears from coming and me from making even a bigger fool of myself.

IT'S TOO EASY TO BLAME IT ON SOME DEMONS IN MY head, too convenient to claim that you drove me to it, and wrong to call it love.

I had begun to miss Florence terribly. The parties that began with splendid dinners and lasted till the early hours, the fancy-dress balls on Fridays, the amateur dramatics on Saturdays. I missed the lazy mornings after the parties, late lunches, idle afternoons with a book in my hand, sunset over the rooftops. The visits of the woman who gave me manicures and pedicures and anointed me with luxurious creams and potions. The gossip, the dogs Dante, Leonardo, and Michelangelo, and their owners who were each more eccentric than the other but whom I found easy to understand because they were my countrymen. I missed the English tearooms and the shops selling tweed and tennis rackets, and the local English newspapers. We hadn't been living in the country for long when I started receiving them by post but canceled the subscription when I saw your reaction. I had left a copy of one of the papers on the table in the library and you stopped in your tracks when you saw it, giving the table a quick glance before leaving the room. You didn't say a word. You didn't need to.

I missed the very things I had fled, even my mother, whom I

had been determined never to speak to again after she had boy-cotted our wedding. We began corresponding again and when she broke her leg and asked me to come and visit, I didn't hesi-tate. This was in 1936, more than three years after we moved to San Martino. I was careful not to let you sense how much I looked forward to going, saying merely that I couldn't really refuse my mother's request given the state she was in; everyone has their cross to bear. I went to great lengths to convince you of my sincerity, putting on a martyred expression and saying I hoped I wouldn't have to be away too long. You didn't say much, you seldom did, and I wondered if you actually cared at all. You were more preoccupied with the farm than ever and with the improvements that were progressing slowly at the time.

"I've worked out the total distance of the roads we need to build," you remarked while watching me pack. "Fifty kilome-ters. We've built twenty so far."

I didn't know how to answer. Was this some sort of accusa-tion?

"I've also worked out how much land we need to cultivate for the farm to become a going concern. Five hundred acres. Maybe more. And for that we need water. Not just from the river. That's not enough."

I remember moving slowly, taking a long time to pack a blouse into my suitcase, then saying, "I won't be away long."

"We'll have to see if we can find water up in the hills," you said. "We'll have to dig deeper, in more sites."

Shortly before this, the fattore had told me about a man from Chianciano who knew how to divine for water. I was fairly sure why he had imparted the information to me rather than to you. Now, suddenly, I found myself talking about this man, quoting the fattore. You appeared to be listening, though you were looking not at me but out the window, at the barren, gray wind-blasted hills. When I fell silent, the muscles of your face tautened slightly, then you turned to me and said, "It won't do the people who rely on us any good if we indulge their superstitious nonsense."

Of course you were right, but once again I felt completely inadequate and convinced myself that you were doing everything you could to fuel my insecurity.

You went to the door, saying before you left the room, "The car will be here any minute. You'd better hurry if you want to get there before dark."

What had happened to us? Why had we drifted so far apart? I felt you were more concerned about the goats than about me. You felt I was a spoiled child. And neither of us had the courage to speak our minds.

I had expected to find the house quiet, my mother in bed with her leg in plaster, my stepfather in a fret. I'd said I would be there by six but my departure had been delayed and it was seven before we drove into the city. I opened the window and breathed in the smell of the Arno as we passed the Ponte Vecchio; it was late spring, the dusk was warm, and the sound of the river was restful.

There were lights in all the windows when we drew up at the house. The front door was open and a maid could be seen receiving guests in the hall. Familiar music flooded out, a composition of my stepfather's. Once this music would have caused me to wince but now I welcomed it.

When the maid caught sight of the car, she started and called into the house. A moment later my mother appeared with arms outstretched in the doorway.

"At last! I was beginning to get worried. What took you so long?"

I looked her up and down. Neither of her legs was in plaster and she wasn't even limping as she came down the stairs.

"Mother," I said, "I thought you'd broken your leg?"

"Alice, my darling, let me give you a hug."

She embraced me and instead of resisting I hugged her tight in return.

"It's been such an age! You're not still cross with me, are you?"

We both laughed, wiping our eyes and sniffing a little.

"No, I'm not cross with you," I said. "But what's this about your leg?"

"Come inside, darling, they're waiting for you. My leg got better the moment you said you'd come and see us."

"Mother!"

"Don't be angry with me. What else could I do? That awful husband of yours won't let me see you."

I didn't tell her how unfair that was, didn't bother to defend you who had so often encouraged me to make peace with my family. Instead I just laughed at her outrageousness, encouraging her in the process.

"Just awful," she repeated. "Beauty and the beast . . ."

The drawing room was full of people and a noisy welcome broke out as I entered. I wasn't shy—being the center of attention was all of a sudden refreshing. My stepfather had tears in his eyes.

"Now don't you start blubbing," my mother said to him.

"This calls for singing!" he declared.

We sang and drank toasts and they filled me in on all the latest gossip. I enjoyed hearing it, even though nothing much had changed since I'd been gone. No one inquired after you and I didn't really think about you at all until late in the evening when, after a long dinner with numerous courses and uneven speeches, I went out onto the veranda to get some fresh air. There was nothing in the evening's conversations that should have made me start brooding over the discussion we had had a few weeks earlier about having children, nothing at all. But there I stood, remembering every word, justifying my reluctance and accusing you of pushing me too hard, when I heard someone approach. I turned around and tried to shake off my thoughts when I saw Connor MacKenzie's youthful smile.

"The rebel is back."

I laughed.

"Hardly a rebel."

He gave me a big hug, kissing me on both cheeks.

"Sorry I'm late. I just got off the train from Rome. It's so good to see you."

He hadn't changed. Always mischievous. Sensitive. We used to play together as children and I had been very fond of him. He studied in England and had been abroad when we got married. I hadn't seen him for a long time.

There was a cheerful din from inside the house. The darkness was warm.

"I've often wondered how you'd look now," he said. "You have a tan. And your hair's lighter."

"Life in the country," I said.

"Well, it obviously suits you."

I didn't answer but, lowering my eyes, slowly clasped, then unclasped my fingers.

"And you?" I asked eventually. "What news of you?"

It was then that he reached for my hand, slowly and carefully, as if taking hold of something fragile. I did not withdraw it and he let it lie in his own, raising it to his face for a better look. Then, apparently finding what he was looking for, he released it and smiled.

"What?" I asked.

"Do you remember cutting yourself on that piece of glass?"

"Yes. That was a long time ago."

"But you still have the scar. I always blamed myself. I got you to keep it for me."

"We were children."

"I told you it was treasure. I wouldn't trust it to anyone but you."

We smiled at the memory as we gazed at the outlines of trees and bushes in the blue dusk. I asked him about his work and he asked me about life in the country, and it was as if no time had passed since we last met, no time at all. Then out of the blue, he said, "I hope you don't mind me saying so, but you're more beautiful than ever."

I blushed but managed to smile.

"Thank you. You were always able to lift my spirits."

He took my hand again, but the touch was different from before.

"It's so good to see you again," he said, then quickly added, "we should go inside before I'll be accused of monopolizing you."

We met there every day that week. It was so easy talking to him but just as comfortable being silent with him. Some mornings he came over for a late breakfast (how nice it was to sleep in!) and read to me from the paper, and we discussed the news, gossiped and reminisced about old times. Other days we took long walks around the city, always ending up by the river. He found everything I said interesting, and I was so encouraged that I spoke more than I had for months. He seized every opportunity to touch my arm or shoulder, pointing out something he thought I should pay attention to, leading me through a crowd. He never asked me about you and I didn't talk about you or the country, didn't talk about anything that would disturb my peace of mind.

Of course I sensed that he was falling in love with me, but I managed initially to tell myself that his interest was purely that of a dear old friend. It was not until my mother remarked one night over dinner (after too much wine, with obvious glee in her eyes) how nice it was to see Connor again that I stopped lying to myself.

Did that cause me to pull back and come to my senses? No, quite the contrary. I encouraged him even more than before, bathing in his admiration, loving his love for me.

Vanity, childishness, irresponsibility, I say to myself now, but that doesn't help.

After a week we rented a hotel room and spent the afternoon there together. He was so gentle and kind, so concerned that I wouldn't feel rushed or compromised in any way. In an attempt to justify my betrayal, I contrasted his behavior and my resulting calm to how tense and uncertain I had felt with you recently. And of course I blamed you: it had to be your fault since with Connor I felt exactly the opposite.

After making love, we lay in bed side by side, listening to the silence, finding each other's hands. We kept the window open, barely exchanging a word.

After ten days I could extend my visit no longer. We decided to meet again as soon as possible, either in Florence or in Rome, where he was about to start a job at a small law firm.

I had only talked to you once on the phone during my visit. You had asked about my mother and I had said, "She's better." I omitted to tell you that the broken leg had been a fabrication, having no desire to cut my visit short.

I FELT SICK IN THE CAR FROM FLORENCE, TORMENTED by mingled loss and guilt. I tried to commit everything about Connor to memory, afraid I would forget some essential quality—his eyes or the movement of his hands, or his voice, whispering so delightfully in my ear as we lay watching the breeze stirring the curtains in the hotel room. I dreaded my homecoming, terrified that you would be able to tell what I'd done, and had to ask the driver to stop more than once so that I could get some fresh air. But I calmed down eventually, and as we drove up the valley and I saw the cloud of dust rising from the quarry at the eastern end of the hill, I felt I had recovered my composure.

As strange as it may sound, our relationship improved after my return from Florence. I am not saying it in an attempt to excuse myself; it just happened that way. I made an effort and you responded in kind; we became warmer toward each other, trying to nip all disagreements in the bud, sometimes touching for no reason. We hadn't slept together for a while but this now changed when, the day after I came back, you and I made love as tenderly as when we first met. It was as if months or even years of strain and disappointments had been wiped away. You held me in your arms all night, wouldn't even let go in your sleep. When we awoke, you didn't say anything but looked at me with a smile that almost broke my heart.

That morning I sat down at the desk in my bedroom and wrote Connor a letter, telling him that I had made a terrible mistake, apologizing profusely, wishing him well. It was poorly written, but wanting to get it out of the house as soon as possible, I didn't take time to improve it. He didn't respond for a long time, and I did everything I could to stop thinking about him.

I achieved a great deal that summer. I planted wisteria and many varieties of roses, and helped Pritchett clip the new hedge in the English garden. It had been a cold, windy spring, mice had eaten the carpets, and the damp had made it impossible to tune the piano, but summer arrived with the most glorious weather imaginable: hot, sunny days and warm nights.

When I discovered at the beginning of November that I was pregnant, we were both happy, you not least. You behaved like an excited little boy, laying your ear to my stomach when we got into bed in the evenings and forever ordering me to be careful, not to bump into anything, not to overdo it, and to make sure I didn't trip. We had tried in the past, most recently a year before, and when nothing happened, it was as if we had failed. At least that's how I felt, and although you never admitted it, I could tell that you felt that way too. After that we seemed incapable of bringing ourselves to make love; the passion had gone and the act had become a mechanical chore with a specific aim—just like the improvements on the hills, the construction of roads, dams, and bridges.

I chose an obstetrician in Rome for reasons that had nothing to do with Connor. Dr. Lombardi had looked after your cousin during a difficult pregnancy and was widely respected.

I thought the local doctor was good enough but you wouldn't hear of it.

Connor's letter arrived three days before my first appointment with Dr. Lombardi. While it was short, I could sense that he had rewritten it a thousand times, not knowing what tone to strike. At the end of it, he begged me to meet him one last time, if only to properly say good-bye. I decided to call him that afternoon and arrange a meeting in Rome. I told him to meet me at three o'clock the following Wednesday in the lobby of my hotel and asked that he follow me discreetly up to my room since I didn't want to be seen with him in public. I would explain everything and that would be it. We would part friends; he would go on with his life, I with mine.

On the train to Rome, I scripted my speech to him, even writing down parts of it. By the time I was done, I felt pleased with it, convinced that within hours I would be putting this episode behind me in a careful and responsible manner.

It was therefore surprising how nervous I felt when I disembarked and hurried from the station into the city. Dr. Lombardi noticed my agitation but naturally could not guess the reason for it.

"You've no need to worry," he said. "Everything looks fine. You're a fit young lady and really don't need any special care."

I had left my suitcase behind at the hotel on Via Veneto, next door to René's hair salon which would later become popular with the wives and mistresses of German officers. It was before three o'clock when I returned from the doctor but Connor was already waiting for me at the bar in the lobby and must have been watching the door, as he noticed me the moment I entered. Without making any sign, he followed me at a little distance to the lift and waited there with me, not saying a word. We were not alone and he stood behind me on the way up. My room was at the end of the corridor and I made for it without looking back. I could hear his footsteps behind me and slowed down when I realized how much I missed him and wanted to be with him, almost coming to a halt. He slowed down too. But then I continued, opening the door to the room, leaving it ajar, taking a few steps inside. The curtains were drawn back and the sun shone on the blue wallpaper and an opalescent vase of yellow flowers that stood on the mahogany table by the window. As I stood there in the silence, I heard him close the door.

He didn't say anything but took me in his arms and kissed me on my neck.

"Connor," I started but failed to continue when I felt his hands on my shoulders and breasts.

After making love, we lay as we had done in the hotel room in Florence, side by side, listening to the din from the street.

"Why don't you leave him?"

His question caught me unawares.

"You know how much I love you."

I reached for his hand, stroking it with my thumb.

"There's nothing to hold you," he continued. "While you don't have any children."

I hadn't yet told him I was pregnant. I had meant to but couldn't find the words.

"Shh," I said. "Let's not talk."

He was quiet, but I could sense from the tension in his hand that the same question remained on his lips. I sensed it as I caressed his hand with my thumb and when I took hold of his long, lean fingers. His hand lay still; he did not caress me in return but neither did he pull it away.

As the light faded and the rumble from the street died down, my eyelids drooped. When I woke up, he had gone.

I hadn't unpacked my suitcase when I checked into the hotel. It stood on the floor in front of the wardrobe and I contemplated it in the dusk as I grasped the fact that Connor was no longer with me. Sitting up in bed, I switched on the lamp to see if he had written me a note. I was surprised when I saw that he hadn't.

It was only just past seven o'clock, yet it seemed much later. Feeling uneasy, I went into the bathroom where I washed my face with cold water. I was drying it when I heard the chambermaid knock at the door to inform me that there was a phone call for me down in reception.

I hurried down, convinced it was Connor ringing to explain or apologize for his disappearance. So I was unprepared for the sound of your voice and my reaction gave me away.

"You didn't call after seeing the doctor. Is everything all right?"

"Yes," I said. "Yes, it's all right."

All of a sudden I found that I was shaking.

"I've been waiting for you to call."

"I'm sorry."

"Is everything all right? What did the doctor say?"

"That it all looks normal," I reassured you.

"Thank God. I was starting to worry."

"I'm sorry," I said.

"Alice, what's the matter?"

Realizing that my voice was about to break, I had to put an end to the conversation.

"I want to come home," I said. "Tonight."

I hadn't intended to return until the following day and had

missed the last train. But I couldn't bear to stay; I felt that everything I held dear was slipping from my grasp. When I went up to my room and looked in the bathroom mirror, I saw that I was deathly pale. You're despicable, a voice whispered in my head. Despicable.

Suddenly weak at the knees, I slumped to the floor and sat there as if paralyzed until there was a knock at the door. It took me a long time to get to my feet and answer it, and the chambermaid was clearly startled when I opened the door.

"Your husband rang," she said, avoiding my eye. "He's found you a car."

We set off at nine o'clock. The driver was a young man whose father owned the car but as he was getting on, his son had largely taken over the job. He told me this, as well as a number of other things that I've forgotten. He was chatty but I sat silently in the back, trying to get a grip on myself. It wasn't easy; the voice in my head persisted and was unsparing, yet not as merciless as it was to become later. I pictured you at the train station when I left, calling after me: "Take good care! Don't carry your case yourself!"—still standing on the platform as the train had pulled away.

"I'm sorry," I heard the driver say when I didn't answer one of his questions. "I talk too much."

He was a nice young man. The sound of his gentle, cheery voice made me feel better, and I told him so.

Gradually I calmed down, and by the time we were well on the way home, I had begun to see my life in a clearer light than before. I had made a terrible mistake, but it was not irrevocable. Connor had done me a favor by leaving; we had no future. I didn't blame him. He had said he loved me but I had been unable to return the words, knowing it wouldn't do any good.

I've behaved like a spoiled child, I told myself in the darkness on the journey home. I've jeopardized everything with my selfish irresponsibility. Thank God I've come to my senses.

It was late at night by the time we drove up the road to the house. The odd bird, awakened by our passing, flew into the beam of the headlights; otherwise all was quiet. You were waiting for me in front of the house and came over to the car the moment it stopped. You looked anxious but this changed when you bent down and saw my face. You hugged me and I began to sob.

"I'm sorry," I said, "I'm so sorry."

"It's okay," you said, stroking my cheek. "It's okay. I'm glad you came back tonight."

As we walked into the house hand in hand, the moon lit up the hillside and the ribbons of mist down in the valley.

I live on a farm in the south of Tuscany, I wrote in my diary the following morning. Twelve miles from the nearest railway station and five from the nearest village. I never want to leave.

WHEN THE FRONT LINE REACHES US, THE VIOLENCE we have witnessed so far—partisan skirmishing, the odd air raid, random executions by Germans and Fascists—will seem like a mere rehearsal.

There is fighting around Orvieto and on the roads north, and we can hear the rumble of guns from beyond Radicofani, which presumably means that the Allies have reached Acquapendente. They are advancing fast; it's only four days since they took Bracciano. The traffic in the valley was heavy during the night as the Germans prepared for battle. They have set up antiaircraft guns by the city gates, according to the plumber who came from Montepulciano yesterday to repair a broken pump, and from tomorrow will embark on a house-to-house search for partisans and other hostile elements. This may only be a rumor but we can't take any chances and have told the farmers to make sure that any partisans they may be sheltering will be gone by sunset. Signorina Harris has been attending to a Brit and a partisan in the clinic; two of the farmhands are taking them into the woods where they can hide.

Meanwhile, I ask Melchiorre to get ready to take me to Montepulciano. We're running short of medicines and I blame myself for not having gone earlier. Pritchett is not pleased that

I'm making this trip but knows that there is no way around it. I don't expect it will be easy to convince the officer—or doctor, rather—to part with even a small portion of his valuable supplies, but I'm relying on my belief that he's a sensible man. I may also ask him if we can have back the buildings that he requisitioned but hasn't yet made use of for purposes other than storage.

Before we leave, Pritchett hands Melchiorre a revolver. He hesitates before taking it, and I can see him thinking back to the night in chapel.

"It's all right," I tell him. "I trust you with it. We all do."

He finally takes it and quickly shoves it under his seat.

The road is in a bad state and our progress is slow. Everything is quiet at first; there's no traffic because the Germans avoid the road in daylight and the country people don't take unnecessary risks. We notice two German military trucks in a clearing halfway between San Martino and Montepulciano; they are camouflaged with branches and leaves and the soldiers are sitting on the hood of one and the roof of the other, scanning the sky for aircraft. But there are no planes to be seen, not until we approach Montepulciano; then one heads straight for us, abruptly lowering its trajectory. We leap out of the cart and take cover in a ditch beside the road but there is no need, since the plane climbs again and vanishes behind Monte Amiata.

As we approach Montepulciano, I see the antiaircraft guns by the city gates. It is a chilling feeling to look down their barrels, and Melchiorre tightens the reins a little before he recovers. A soldier stops us when we reach the gate and walks around the cart. He does not speak and after a short pause waves us on. I sense that Melchiorre is jumpy and say to him, "You're doing well."

The horse is tired and plods slowly across the piazza inside the gate. The sun gleams on its sweaty neck, but disappears as we climb the cobbled street that opens off the square. The buildings cast a cool shade and it is so quiet that we can hear nothing but the rattling of the wheels and the echo of hooves. The houses are shuttered, all the shops closed, and for a moment I feel as if we have entered a ghost town. Then I see a woman with a basket on her arm appear at the end of the street and later a crowd in the Piazza Grande in front of the cathedral with its unfinished campanile. The hospital stands on the other side of the hill, the northern side, and silence envelops our journey there, deadening the hoofbeats and filling me with misgiving. I tell myself that there is no reason to be afraid; the inhabitants are sensible to keep a low profile, and anyway the sun is at its noontide zenith, the hour of the siesta. Yet I jump when the church clock strikes one. My heart pounds in my chest and takes a long time to slow down.

I wonder if I should take Melchiorre in with me but decide against it. He drives into the shade beside the entrance, climbs down from the cart and fetches water for the horse. I watch him walk away up the street, holding a bucket in his right hand, its handle squeaking as it swings to and fro.

Outside the hospital two soldiers are sitting in chairs, smoking. One of them makes as if to stand up when I enter, but changes his mind. Inside the cool lobby I ask after the doctor and am kept waiting for quite some time. When he eventually appears, he says, "You shouldn't be here."

His manner is not curt but I'm taken aback nonetheless.

"We need medicines," I say, giving him the list of what Signorina Harris has requested. He hurriedly runs his eyes down it.

"You couldn't have come at a worse time," he says, handing the list back.

Beckoning me to follow, he strides quickly down the corridor, without looking left or right. I see into two small wards where staff are tending to patients, then a large room where one bed after another is being made up. There are two long rows of them against the walls and there is a window at the end of the ward; everything is white and orderly and the floor gleams with polish. All the beds are empty. From the window the dome of the church of Madonna di San Biagio can be seen on the hillside below the city wall, dazzlingly white in the sunshine. I slow down and the girls and boy who are making up the beds, clearly all locals, look up in my direction. I quicken my pace again, as the doctor is now far ahead.

He is already gathering the medicines together by the time I catch up with him at the medicine store in a room off the end of the corridor. Assuming that he won't be able to remember the list, I hesitantly hold it out to him. But he doesn't give it a glance, just hastily takes bottles and jars from the cupboard and tells me to open my bag. I obey and together we arrange the medicines inside it; those there is no room for—two small bottles—I stick in the pockets of my dress.

On my way here I had worked out how I was going to ask him to assist us and the people we are sheltering when the front line comes our way. But I was given no opportunity to raise the issue because he glanced at his watch, shook his head, and said, "You shouldn't have come. Get off home as fast as you can. Hopefully you'll escape."

"What do you mean?" I finally had the presence of mind to ask but he didn't answer, simply steered me into the corridor and led me to the entrance.

"On such a beautiful day too," he said when we emerged. "Signora Orsini, get out of here as fast as you can."

The soldiers who had been sitting by the door smoking when we arrived were now nowhere to be seen. Melchiorre had watered the horse and was waiting by the cart. He helped me up and the doctor stood in the doorway, watching us with a look of impatience. He did not say good-bye as we slowly set off but his eyes followed our progress up the street.

I remember what I was thinking when we set off from the hospital. I remember it clearly because it was in no way related to the doctor's behavior or the sense of foreboding that accompanied the treacherous silence. It suddenly struck me what a beautiful little town Montepulciano was. Here it has towered on its chalk escarpment for centuries, I said to myself, poised between heaven and earth, like some covenant between God and man, the work of both, enjoying the blue of the sky and the scent of the earth. Here it has stood, through war and catastrophe, representative of eternity in our little district.

Such were my thoughts as we retraced our steps along the cobbled streets, into the shade between the houses and out into the squares, a white, fair-weather cloud floating sedately overhead and Melchiorre rocking in the seat in front of me, his shoulders relaxed. Such were my thoughts when the silence exploded.

The soldiers seemed to spring up out of the street. First they came running but a moment later there was a roar of motor vehicles speeding up the hill, gray open-backed trucks that could drive up the main street but not through the narrower side streets and so halted in the squares. The soldiers sitting in the back leapt out and joined their comrades in storming one house after another, dragging out the people they had been looking for and throwing them into the waiting trucks. Melchiorre and I watched as we cowered together in an alley a short distance from the cathedral, unable to do anything but hope they would leave us alone.

Within minutes, bursts of firing were coming from every direction. The horse took fright and bolted with the cart and there was nothing we could do but watch it go. A troop of soldiers moved to a house down the street, and several of them forced their way into the building with yells that I didn't understand, although my German is not bad. A frenzy had taken hold of them and when they came out with two teenage boys and threw them in the street I almost rose to my feet, but Melchiorre seized my arm and held it tight. A woman ran out after them, the boys' mother I presume, and tearfully pleaded with the soldiers to let them go. They waved her away at first but when she wouldn't stop, one of them struck her. Blood gushed from her face and the boys yelled at her to go inside, everything would be all right. In the end she obeyed and the soldiers disappeared up the street with the boys.

The firing continued. It had moved farther away and was now coming from lower down the hill. Finally daring to get to our feet, we began to inch our way along the street, back the way we had come, toward the hospital. We hugged the walls, Melchiorre in front, I on his heels, limping because I had twisted my ankle when we ran for cover. But it was nothing to complain about and neither was the mist that had suddenly descended over my eyes and that I couldn't rub away.

For the first stretch we met no one and everything was

eerily quiet but that changed as we approached the hospital. One vehicle after another pulled up, the square in front was in chaos, and there was a crowd in the hospital lobby where the staff couldn't keep up with the stream of the dead and injured, both soldiers and civilians. Neither of us had wounds that required attention, so we did not really have any business being at the hospital, yet we hurried there because there was no other place of refuge. Our horse and cart were nowhere in sight but when Melchiorre said he was going to look for them, I stopped him. We walked into the crush outside the hospital and were borne to the doors with the stretchers. Only a hundred meters away they are fighting each other, I thought, yet here the wounded and the dead come together, lying side by side on stretchers or in the arms of their friends and loved ones, to these doors where everyone is equal. Perhaps a time is coming when it will be like that everywhere, when the war will end and the hatred will give way to common sense and goodness, I thought, suddenly glimpsing a ray of hope in this chaos of tears, blood, and despair. But this feeling did not last long; it was extinguished by four storm troopers who charged in, their officer in the lead. The doctor was standing in the corridor, examining the injured and issuing orders about what should be done with them, when I saw the officer move in his direction. He began yelling but when the doctor looked up, I saw that his eyes were without fear. He carried on with his work; there was a young man on the stretcher, a partisan, his chest soaked in blood, yet still conscious. The doctor was peeling off his shirt when the officer reached him and gripped his arm.

"What the hell do you think you're doing?"

A silence fell on the crowd; everyone stopped moving. I

could hear the labored, rattling breath of the boy on the stretcher. A whole eternity seemed to pass before the doctor took the officer's wrist in his free hand, loosened his grip, and said, "I give the orders here."

He did not speak loudly yet his words filled the lobby. They grew in magnitude after he stopped speaking, spreading out until they had driven all other words from the building, all shouts, whimpers, and sobs.

"I give the orders here."

The officer was momentarily thrown and I thought I could read his mind in his flickering gaze: I can't kill him because if I did, who would tend to my injured men? But then something seemed to occur to him, something that lightened his load, some solution to his problem. He turned on his heel and did not look back until he reached the door.

"You may give the orders in here," he said, "but outside I'm in charge."

He walked over to the wounded partisans waiting to come inside and shot them, one after another. Walked up to them, whether they were lying on stretchers or being supported by friends or relatives, aimed his gun at their temples and fired. It may not have taken long to kill them all, perhaps only a few minutes, but it seemed a whole lifetime to me. No one in the lobby moved, not even the doctor who stood motionless by the stretcher, watching through the door. I looked at him, saw the despair in his face and the hand that lifted slightly, only to fall back to his side.

When they had finished the executions, the officer and his four troopers drove away. We listened to the car recede into the distance, then walked out into the silence.

Melchiorre found the horse by the city wall. The sun had

begun to set when we left but it was still hot. We didn't speak on the journey home. Night fell on the countryside and the stars came out as if nothing had happened. I watched the darkness settle on Melchiorre's shoulders and the outline of his head disappear and only then did I finally allow the tears I had been holding back to fall.

MARSHALL'S BUSINESS BECAME MORE DIFFICULT AS the war intensified. After Italy declared war on the United States in the wake of Japan's attack on Pearl Harbor in December 1941, Wildenstein and Marshall's other buyers in America disappeared, as had his British clients the previous year. The Germans, on the other hand, became increasingly active, easily bypassing the laws and regulations intended to limit the export of national treasures. Not only did the Italian government bend the rules for them, but the Germans also employed agents who had local connections and were energetic in pursuing their interests, foremost among them Prince Philipp of Hesse and Count Contini Bonacossi. While the Prince and the Count did look to Marshall now and then to restore pictures or establish their provenance, the remuneration was slight in comparison with the business he had gotten used to, restoring paintings he had bought himself and selling them for a profit. He lacked these men's connections and found it hard to hide his envy, though he managed to disguise it behind a show of politeness.

Nevertheless, Marshall kept up his custom of throwing dinner parties when he had something to sell. It was not he but Signorina Pirandello who told Kristín of these gatherings so she was surprised when he handed her an invitation out of the blue one day, with the comment that she might want to come by.

"It's been a long time since you last visited."

The city lay under a thin covering of white. The snow continued to fall during dinner and she watched the flakes against the lights outside, forgetting to listen to her master when he got to his feet to describe the painting that was hanging on the wall where the Guercino had last hung. He had restored this picture, a painting of the Virgin Mary, himself and she thought it beautiful. However, the artist, Bicci di Lorenzo, was little known and failed to capture the guests' interest, although they were polite. They said little as they stood before the picture after dinner; indeed, they didn't get much of a chance, so voluble was Marshall in his praise of both painting and artist. Kristín felt uncomfortable; she had never found her master pitiable before. She was glad he didn't notice her when she heard Flora whisper to him that Prince Philipp had sent his regrets.

"Why?" he kept asking, trying to keep his voice down. "Why?"

"The snow," Flora whispered, but he shook his head, repeating sarcastically, "the snow . . ."

Two days later he told her he had sold the painting, making the announcement the moment he walked into the studio. Kristín had been so absorbed in her work that she didn't hear him enter and so failed to hide her look of disbelief. By the time she realized, it was too late. He stood still, looking her up and down, then walked over to the easel and remarked without any particular emphasis, "You're capable of this."

That was all. He left and she felt her stomach disappearing, a sense of inadequacy welling up inside her. She tried in vain to take herself to task. Her teacher Jensen's words echoed in her head as so often before when she was filled with self-doubt: "It is to be hoped that . . . she is maturing from a first-rate technician into a promising artist . . ." The glacier appeared before her mind's eye, the radiance "lending the barren waste an aura of tranquil sanctity."

Marshall knew. He didn't need to define what she could not do. His praise was like a blow.

For Christmas, he sent her a present via Signorina Pirandello: a book about Caravaggio. The accompanying card wished her a merry Christmas and a happy New Year from him and his wife, in Flora's handwriting.

The studio was closed between Christmas Day and New Year's, and Kristín set up an easel in the living room, having decided to use the holiday to draw and paint for herself. She spread a canvas over the floor and drew back the curtains to let in the meager light which was all that was available at this time of year.

She rose early, made coffee, and watched the gray, watery sunrise. The living room was cold, so she put on a sweater before arranging a vase, a book, and a magnifying glass on a table by the window. It took her a long time; she kept moving the vase, changing the book, repositioning the magnifying glass until it reflected the gray light from the clouds outside. Then she began to draw, tentatively at first, trying to drive his words from her ears: "You're capable of this."

She was not displeased with her progress but proceeded cautiously nonetheless. It was like walking on ice, not knowing if it was safe, inching slowly forward, stepping lightly. But the ice held, and as her courage grew, her tense muscles relaxed. She worked tirelessly at the easel till noon, continuing later in the day after a break for a walk and a light meal at a café. She did not lay down her brush until the light began to fail, and she spent a long time clearing up after herself, happy to stand in the living room with her work before her eyes—the cloth on the table, the red spine of the book, the half-painted handle of the magnifying glass, ivory with a black diamond pattern.

She finished the picture on New Year's Day. But instead of taking it off the easel, she covered it and decided not to look at it for a week or two, knowing that she would not be able to see it objectively until then. She pulled the curtains, locked the door, and put the key in the kitchen drawer.

Two days later Flora turned up at the studio. She had come to see Signorina Pirandello but looked in to wish Kristín a happy New Year before she left.

"We missed you over the holiday," she said. "I hope you enjoyed your trip. Florence is always lovely, even in winter."

Smiling, she added, "Especially when one's in love. Perhaps you'll introduce him to us some time."

When Kristín looked away, Flora said, "I'm sorry. Perhaps I wasn't supposed to know?"

He avoided her. She knew when he was in the building and was on edge, ready for him to appear in the doorway any minute. But he did not show his face, not until a week into January.

It was cold that morning and Kristín hurried inside and up the stairs, failing to notice him until she had shut the door behind her. He had neither turned on the light nor taken off his coat but was sitting on a stool in front of the easel, his eyes lowered. He did not look at her when she came in but said quietly, "I've decided to leave her."

She stood motionless in the middle of the room, feeling

the strength leave her body together with the contempt that had been growing inside her since Flora's visit. Did she believe him? She didn't stop to wonder about this, not until later. Now she merely stood without moving, aware of how much she wanted him and needed him in spite of everything. That's what she said to herself as she stood there in the half-light: in spite of everything.

A long moment passed; she standing in the middle of the room, he sitting on the stool, both silent, not looking at each other, until he stood up and came to her. He did not put his arms around her immediately, not until she turned her head and looked him in the eye. Then, receiving the confirmation he needed, he pulled her against him and said quietly, "I'm sorry. I thought I could live without you."

Later that day, after they had made love at her flat and he was dressing, he suddenly asked, "Where's that smell of paint coming from?"

She answered evasively but he went out into the corridor and took hold of the door handle to the living room.

"What are you hiding?"

"Nothing," she said.

"Don't be silly. Let me see. You've not set up in competition with me?"

He smiled. Neither his words nor his smile contained the slightest hint of accusation; he was joking.

She had not entered the living room since covering up the still life; she hadn't had the courage. But now suddenly she decided to take the key from the kitchen drawer and unveil the painting with him at her side, perhaps from a sense of anticipation, perhaps to see how he would react.

She didn't want to turn on the light but there was no avoiding it. She walked slowly over to the easel, hesitating halfway, perhaps waiting for him to take the initiative. But he took care not to preempt her and stood behind her, waiting.

"It's really nothing," she said, "only a still life."

She tried to appear nonchalant as she removed the white sheet from the picture and placed it on the table where the vase, the book, and the magnifying glass still stood untouched. She folded the cloth before looking at the picture, as if in no hurry. He moved closer to the easel, bent forward and eventually said, "It's a fine picture, Kristín."

Her heart lurched. Did he mean it? She turned and asked him.

"Of course. A beautiful picture, Kristín."

The verdict was delivered without any caveats, even minor ones. She wanted to fling her arms around his neck but, restraining the impulse, merely took his hand and squeezed it. He looked at his watch, kissed her quickly on the cheek, and said, "It's past five, I must be going."

After he had gone, she stood for a long time in front of the still life. First, she studied it as if she had never seen it before, then, closing her eyes, she continued to view it like that. And suddenly, without warning, the doubts set in. She retreated, hurriedly turning out the light and locking the door behind her.

SHE HAD ALWAYS ASSUMED THAT SHE WOULD change with age and that the aspects of her character that troubled her would disappear. Since childhood she had waited for this to happen, picturing herself older and free from her weaknesses. Then she would look like the daughter of the couple who lived in the house next door to her grandparents; she wore a blue coat, had fair, wavy shoulder-length hair, and smiled, full of self-confidence, when she said farewell to the village, waving to friends and family before climbing onto the Reykjavík bus. That's what she herself would be like when she was older—full of self-confidence, free from fear.

She didn't stop to consider that the world might change. In her imagination it stood still—the mountains remained where they had always been, the sky above them, the sea below. And the waves that sucked to and fro, came and went and came back again.

When she herself moved to Reykjavík, she acquired a blue coat. Although she persuaded herself that it was a coincidence, she sometimes thought about the girl next door to her grandparents. She didn't know what had become of her, never saw her again, yet she pictured her turning around in front of the bus to smile and wave good-bye to the people at home. No hesitation, no doubts, all roads open to her.

Did he see that girl when he looked at her? Did he see the village and the mountain above it, the waves that had caressed her father's cheek on his voyage into the depths, then whispered messages from him to her as she stood on the beach? He encouraged her. When she mentioned to him that she didn't think much of the still life, he told her she was wrong.

"Paint more," he said, "anything you like. Keep at it."

She had the leisure for this now because he was spending more time on restoration work himself since business had started to fall off. He offered her the chance to work part-time, in the afternoons.

"Mornings are the most productive time," he said, "use them for your own painting."

He had never paid her much, no more than was customary for an apprentice, and now that her hours had been reduced, her wages dropped correspondingly. But she was thrifty, so it didn't matter. She gathered from Signorina Pirandello that he was in a tight spot financially and, unwilling to be a burden to him, felt only relief when her wages were cut.

His words gave her the courage to paint. That was the most important thing. For that, she would have done anything for him.

She painted every day. When spring came, she rose at dawn to make the most of her time. And as the weather grew gradually warmer, she started opening the windows in the living room. The breeze stirred the curtains, bringing in wafts of birdsong.

She felt she was making progress and Marshall agreed, offering her steady encouragement. He was gentler than he had been for a long time, and she couldn't help concluding that financial success had confused him.

He did not say anything more about leaving his wife and she did not raise the subject, believing there was no need. He was moving toward her, every day he came closer. She sensed it as much in his eyes as in his caresses, in his words, and in the silences between them. She had never been happier.

As summer passed, he started traveling again. His trips frequently took him to Florence, more specifically to I Tatti, Bernard Berenson's villa outside the city. He was not very communicative about these visits, not at first, but they came as a surprise to Kristín, who had never heard him say anything complimentary about Berenson. He used to make fun of his methods and had more than once implied that his opinion could be bought.

These trips usually took him away for three to four days at a time. She did not ask him any questions when he returned but was pleased to have him back and told him so. She knew from experience that he disliked this kind of talk, but she couldn't help herself. He never answered; at best he would smile thinly and change the subject. At the beginning of July he reacted to her confession with these words: "He's a Jew, you know."

She waited and he continued, telling her that Berenson was a prisoner in his own home; he had often contemplated fleeing the country after the war broke out but had never gone ahead with the plan. He walked around the gardens in the mornings and evenings but wouldn't risk going beyond the borders of his property and, not daring to make himself conspicuous, could no longer do any business.

He added, as if in answer to her unspoken question:

"There was never any bad blood between us, only slight professional disagreement from time to time. All that's forgotten now. He's taken to his bed and would probably be dead by now if he didn't have an assistant to look after him day and night. I feel I have a duty to help him."

In August a *Christ* by Verrocchio unexpectedly came into her hands. There was a knock on the door late one afternoon and after opening it to the visitor, a young man with a van, Signorina Pirandello called up to Kristín. She introduced them; he was her nephew who worked for the post office. He gave his aunt a basket of fruit, two chickens, and the painting, wrapped in a blanket. He had fetched it for her—or rather for Marshall—from Berenson's villa and used the opportunity to stock up on food on the way. Signorina Pirandello had mentioned her nephew to Kristín; he was a member of the Fascist Party and had a bright future, as she put it. After saying good-bye and watching the van drive away, they went upstairs, Signorina Pirandello carrying the food and Kristín the painting.

It was accompanied by a report from Berenson, which Kristín read carefully. The handwriting, in blue ink on yellowing paper, was almost effeminate. Signorina Pirandello couldn't hide her pleasure: the lean months were behind them. Marshall and Berenson had joined forces: Berenson would find the pictures, Marshall would procure them and see to the restoration and sales. They would share the profits. She made a point of emphasizing that they would not sell the works of art to the Germans; that was agreed, neither would dream of it.

"What about the Guercino?" Kristín asked. "Wasn't it the Prince who bought that?"

"No," the Signorina said firmly, "it was his wife, Princess Mafalda. Signor Marshall would never have sold that picture to the Germans."

The *Christ* was so badly damaged that she had to repaint a good part of it; the canvas was moth-eaten and the strainer warped and rotting. She wasn't surprised that Marshall had asked her to restore it; by now he always did when substantial repainting was involved.

"That's where you excel," he told her. "That's where your capabilities are unique."

The restoration took four months and she postponed her own painting, as Marshall said the job was urgent. He didn't ask her to sacrifice her mornings; he didn't need to, she did so willingly. When she finished the restoration, he was immensely grateful and urged her to return to her own work. She had completed eight pictures and had just embarked on the ninth when the Verrocchio turned up.

It was not long before another masterpiece came into Berenson and Marshall's hands, a picture of a boy playing a flute by Giorgione. It was in no better state of repair than the *Christ* and Kristín let slip to Marshall that she wondered how he and Berenson could be so sure that it was a Giorgione. Hadn't Berenson been mistaken before, attributing work to him that turned out to be by Titian?

She had only asked from curiosity, but her heart missed a beat when Marshall's face hardened and his mouth twitched. She hadn't seen that expression for a long time. He delayed his answer, staring at her in silence, then cleared his throat and said slowly and quietly, "Don't worry about that. I have established that it is by Giorgione. Your job is to restore it."

She sensed that he wanted to say more, but he restrained himself and left. Next day, however, he was affable and made no reference to the exchange. But she was unhappy and the fact did not escape him. That was when he said, "You should hold an exhibition of your own pictures, Kristín. I'll arrange the gallery for you. It's not large but the pictures will be displayed to their advantage there. You'll only need twelve paint-ings. How would you like that?"

She didn't answer and he patted her shoulder, saying she was ready and had nothing to be afraid of; he would book the space, that would be best, and she could always change her mind. After that he went, leaving her with the moth-eaten masterpiece on the easel and doubt gnawing at her soul.

HE WAS BORN AT THE BEGINNING OF JULY. I BROUGHT him home two weeks later on a hot, sunny day with a haze lying over the valley. It was past one o'clock; I remember we were running slightly late because I had been delayed that morning, unused as I was to traveling with a baby. Schwester Marie, whom I had hired at the beginning of summer, came with me in the car and you were there to meet us, having set off two days earlier from Florence to prepare our homecoming. I hadn't seen Dr. Lombardi in Rome apart from that one occasion, telling you that since the pregnancy gave every sign of being normal, the English doctor in Florence would be perfectly adequate. Giovanni had slept most of the way but woke up as we climbed the hill and a wild boar ran into the road, causing the driver to brake suddenly. He had been driving slowly, so we were not badly shaken, although the shock was enough to wake Giovanni who grimaced and began to cry when the sun shone in his eyes. I picked him up and held him against me, breathing in the sweet smell of his soft head.

You had been waiting for us and were standing in front of the house with a welcoming committee. A great feast was being prepared in the garden to celebrate the imminent completion of the threshing; they would usually have held the celebra-

tion the following day, but it was brought forward to coincide
with my bringing Giovanni home. I had seen the stacks of corn
from the road and the steam-powered threshing machines,
the dust golden in the sunshine and the farmhands, stripped
to the waist and sweating in the heat. But now all abandoned
their work and flocked to greet us, and Giovanni began to cry
again when the faces crowded around him with the inevita-
ble exclamations. I took him inside via the kitchen where the
women from the tenant farms were busy with the cook and
the scullery maids, tending to pots and pans, dishes and bowls,
and there we were given another welcome and he continued
to cry, though not with quite the same conviction as before.
Schwester Marie and I took him up to his room where everything was as it should be and the window was open with the
curtain drawn to prevent the flies from entering. There was a
comforting murmur of voices from outside and gradually he
calmed down, eventually falling asleep in his cradle. Schwester
Marie reminded me that everyone was waiting for me and I
tidied myself up in the bathroom before going downstairs. She
remained with him, sitting in a rocking chair by the cradle,
and I paused in the doorway to watch the shaft of sunlight that
illuminated her shoulder whenever the breeze stirred the curtains. I lingered there longer than intended, savoring the sense
of well-being that had suddenly enveloped me. It was deep and
pure and I can still remember it because I'm sure I've never in
my life been as happy as I was at that moment.

The celebration lasted into the evening. We had soup
first, followed by smoked shoulder of pork and pasta, then
*l'ocio*—goose that had been fattening for weeks, followed by
sheep's cheese and finally gelato. A great deal of red wine was
drunk, there was laughter and dancing, and the sun shone on

the valley, now pale yellow from the threshing. The children
played among the corn stacks, climbing up and jumping off,
and their excitement grew as the light faded and the chirrup-
ing of the cicadas intensified. I told myself it wouldn't be many
years before my own son would be climbing the corn stacks
with them. I believe I smiled to myself at the thought. You had
been holding my hand under the table and now accompanied
me when I went to feed Giovanni, gazing at my breasts as if
witnessing a miracle.

Over the following days we received countless gifts and
congratulations from friends and family. The women from the
outlying farms brought sweaters, hats, and mittens they had
knitted, as well as a variety of items designed to bring my son
good luck—a pebble, a rabbit's foot, a bird's feather. The days
were hot and so were the nights, but I had cut my hair short
that spring to be prepared. Now I cut it even shorter and you
enjoyed running your fingers through it; you said I was turning into a proper country girl. We laughed and my thoughts
were only of you and our son; they did not stray and I had no
need to discipline them. Everything was as good as it could be
and I woke up every morning happy and carefree. We went
out into the garden after ten and I read under a tree while
Giovanni slept in his pram at my side. Schwester Marie was
always nearby so I could slip away when I needed to, though
that was not often, as I lacked for nothing.

I don't know when the restlessness began. The summer
of our son's second birthday had passed more quickly than I
would have liked; without warning, harvesttime was upon us
and I took a more active part in it than before, supervising the
grapes being picked from the vines and carried to the *fattoria*
in wooden tubs drawn by the oxen in big carts; watching the

workers crushing the grapes in the tubs with long wooden poles before the wine was poured into barrels and left to ferment over the winter. I enjoyed this process more than ever before, as well as the sowing after the fields had been plowed. I attended mass in the chapel when the priest led the congregation in a prayer for rain, and celebrated with the peasants when our prayer was answered and clouds gathered over the valley, bringing the gentle showers. At last I had become part of this world and, though you said nothing, I could tell how much this pleased you.

He wrote me a letter after Giovanni was born. It took me by surprise, as we hadn't had any contact since he disappeared from my hotel room in Rome. It was a short letter containing polite congratulations and nothing more. I read it only once before placing it on the pile of other letters we had received after Giovanni's birth. You read it too and asked who Connor was; an old family friend, I explained, truthfully enough, and didn't even have to remind myself how fortunate I was.

Then just before Christmas of '39 I received a package from him. It was a little book, a special illustrated edition of Chekhov's *The Lady with the Dog*. I knew what it meant, it wasn't hard to guess, and this time I didn't leave the accompanying card lying around for all to see but placed it inside the book, which I then locked in a drawer. Yet it contained nothing that I couldn't have explained, nothing that wouldn't have stood up to scrutiny. All the same, I couldn't help dwelling on the story of Anna Sergeyevna, the lady with the dog, and her forbidden love for Dmitri Dmitritch Gurov, and tried to remember how it had ended. I couldn't, but stopped myself nevertheless from fetching the book from the drawer to find out.

Christmas passed quickly, to be succeeded by a cold, gray, uneventful January. I stayed indoors for the most part, reading or just letting my thoughts wander. While Giovanni was very attached to me, he did not complain when Schwester Marie attended to him. I began to take long walks in the afternoon, knowing that he was in good hands. When I was a child, I had been much closer to my nanny than to my mother, which may very well have been her intention. I did not want that to happen to our son.

It was on one of my walks that I saw you ride up one of the steeper hills on the western part of the property. You were alone and seemed to be in a hurry. There is only a single farm over there, one of three or four we should probably not have bothered restoring when we purchased San Martino. It was small and unproductive, supporting only one family: a young couple living with the husband's mother and two farmhands. You had taken a liking to the young man from the start; he was hardworking and dedicated, and you said there was no one as skillful with horses as he. It had been a terrible shock when he died in an accident in the quarry two years earlier, crushed by an avalanche of rocks. With help, the widow had carried on, a remarkably determined and good-natured young woman. Or so I thought.

I watched you go inside and the farmhands come out minutes later. They went into a shed adjacent to the farm and started chopping wood. I listened to the echo as I waited for you to come out, never even thinking of crossing over to the farm myself or making my presence known in another way. It was cold and damp, the earth hard under my feet, a pale moon rising over Monte Amiata. When you finally appeared, more than a half hour had passed. You said something to the farmhands who stopped chopping and watched you in silence as you mounted the horse and rode down the hill before going back inside.

I kept to myself for the next few days. You asked if I wasn't feeling well but I ignored you instead of confronting you. You were perplexed but shook it off, concentrating on your many responsibilities, saying to yourself: this too shall pass. At least, that was the impression I got. When Pritchett asked me what was bothering me, I told him. He quickly came to your defense, first reminding me that you had been keeping a close eye on the farm's operations ever since the husband had passed away, then offhandedly talking about the "complicated" relationships many landowners have with their female tenants, citing examples and making light of it all. Seeing my reaction, he quickly added, "But that's not what's happening here. You should talk to him if you don't believe me."

But I decided not to, telling myself that nothing good would come of it and conveniently concluding that you were as guilty as I.

I did continue my walks but I never saw you again near the farm. Sometimes I stopped and waited, hiding at the edge of the forest, watching the smoke rise from the chimney. I often wonder, when I'm prosecuting myself, whether I was relieved or disappointed when you didn't show.

So January passed and February arrived with the *tramontane*, the cold north wind that sweeps down from the hills and holds the valley in an icy grip for weeks at a time. When my mother announced that she wanted to come for a visit, I didn't know what to do. I couldn't face all the hullabaloo that would accompany her stay, but at the same time I wanted to see her. I told you about my dilemma. One could no doubt argue about your incentives; perhaps you just wanted to get rid of me—I wouldn't be surprised, given how distant I had been lately. Anyway, you suggested I go on a trip with her, perhaps somewhere to the south. It would do me good, you said. I said, "I don't want to leave Giovanni." And you replied, "It's only a couple of weeks. Schwester Marie and I can manage." Our conversation continued along these lines for a while; my telling you that I found the idea of leaving difficult and your encouraging me to go, but eventually it was decided, and I called my mother, who was overjoyed. We resolved to go to Sicily for a week and then for a few days to Rome where my mother wanted to celebrate a friend's sixtieth birthday. When she let it slip that she knew that Connor would be at the party, I didn't bother responding. Never subtle and not ready to let the subject drop, she then added, "He's been in love with you since I remember. Poor boy. You were never particularly nice to him."

I was taken aback and had to stop myself from asking what she meant. Maybe she knew how much her statement would bother me, maybe she was pleased with herself when I cut the conversation short and hung up the phone.

Later that day I retrieved *The Lady with the Dog* and the card that had accompanied the book. I read it in one sitting and decided it was time for me to thank him not only for the book but also for the note he had sent us when Giovanni was born. My letter was short and warm but neutral in tone. In closing I mentioned that I was on my way to Sicily and would be stopping off in Rome on my way home.

And so it started again. With that short letter, and the trip to Sicily with its restorative blue skies and landscape festooned with almond blossom. With my stopover in Rome and our trysts under cover of dusk and self-deception, with cautious words at first and hesitant touch. So it started, with his promise never to ask me to leave you and Giovanni but to settle for the secret hours we snatched together, to tell no one of our meetings and deny them if pressed. Deny them, whatever happened, whoever asked. So it started and did not end until too late.

I STARTED TRAVELING REGULARLY TO ROME, STAY-ing there for a few days each time. The English doctor in Florence had retired and I didn't care for his replacement, so I seized the opportunity of consulting Dr. Lombardi again. I sometimes suspected that you did not mind my absences, yet our life together was generally harmonious, and we made an effort to treat each other with courtesy. Although I was usually the one to initiate anything more intimate, I don't blame you for the lack of excitement in our love life—far from it. I am no less at fault since I showed you affection only when my conscience was plaguing me, which was usually before and after my trips to Rome.

I was admitted into the English social circle in Rome. They had always been cliquey and grew even more so after war broke out. Francis Goad and Harold Troye were the leaders of their little society, along with Miriam and Christopher Jones, who were diligent hosts and would invite both Italians and Germans to their dinner parties, such as Ambassador von Hassel and Foreign Minister Ciano. They had always done so and probably found it difficult to abandon the habit; anyway, in Rome the war was still little more than newspaper reports. Connor belonged to this circle of expats, though it was not he who put me on the guest list but Miriam Jones, who knew my parents.

At first Connor and I were very nervous at these gatherings. We greeted each other politely but tended not to talk—rather too conspicuously, as he pointed out when we were alone together. I knew he was probably right but saw no other solution; I couldn't bring myself to put on an act with him.

It was at one of Harold Troye's parties that I met Robert Marshall and his wife, Flora, for the first time in more than ten years. I had been too young to remember much about them when they lived in Florence but Pritchett certainly did. They had had many of the same clients, wealthy Englishmen who relied on them for good advice, and Pritchett felt that Marshall took advantage of them at every opportunity. At one point Pritchett apparently confronted Marshall who, forced to lower the price of a painting, retaliated by undermining Pritchett, criticizing his work behind his back and recommending other architects to his clientele. Or so I was told, not by Pritchett, but by my mother. At any rate, here was Marshall with his beautiful wife at Harold Troye's party, affable and jovial. This was in the autumn of 1940—in October, if I remember right. I had traveled down by train from Chianciano earlier that day; it was late so I didn't arrive at the party until nearly eight. I hadn't seen Connor since the summer and remember how impatient I was and how difficult I found it to do no more than shake his hand. But that's all I did, I simply greeted him as I greeted everyone, taking care that our handshake should be no longer or shorter, firmer or looser than any other. Then I waited for the evening to pass and for us to leave—he first, then I. The party was no different from any other. Perhaps our eyes strayed to each other more often than usual, that's possible, but otherwise nothing was any different. So it's always been a mystery to me how Robert Marshall guessed the nature of my relationship with Connor. I have often gone over that evening in my mind—the conversation before dinner when we were drinking champagne in the library, the long meal, the farewells—but I cannot remember a single moment that can have given him pause for thought. Yet even so, he noticed something that no one else did and was quick to grasp the situation.

He got in touch with me the following day and asked me to meet him. I was nervous, although I had no reason to be, and I didn't ask him what it was about when he suggested we meet by the Trevi Fountain. I arrived before him and was watching a group of young Fascists in black shirts throwing coins in the fountain when he touched me on the shoulder. I jumped slightly and he apologized, then came straight to the point.

He had known my late father, he said, and always felt he owed him a debt of gratitude for assisting him when he first arrived in Italy.

"It was a pleasant evening," he then said. "Troye's parties always are. But you should be careful."

I said nothing, waiting for him to continue.

"It's nobody's business how you live your life, not mine or anyone else's, but you'll both have to be more careful if you want to keep your affair with Connor under wraps."

He broke off and looked at me as if to gauge my reaction. I was too shocked to respond, too devastated to look him in the eye. What does he want? I asked myself. Why is he telling me that he can ruin my life in this almost fatherly manner, his voice so smooth, his smile so carefully cultivated?

I reached into my purse for a handkerchief but my fingers

came up with a coin instead which I somehow managed to throw into the fountain.

"Connor's a good chap," he said, "but a little sensitive. That's why I decided to speak to you instead, though we don't know each other."

Smiling, he added, "Though I'm not sure that this is how your father would have wanted me to repay his kindness."

That was it, and I said nothing more before we parted, though I looked at him for a moment, at those deep-set eyes that saw what others missed.

Over the next three years, we met at numerous social gatherings, but never again in private. He didn't refer to what had passed between us and nor did I, though I always sensed that it was very much on his mind. I didn't tell Connor either; it would only have caused him unbearable anxiety. He was sensitive as Marshall had said, often unnecessarily so.

Of course I realized at once that something more than kind concern had motivated his meeting with me. Yet I knew he would tell no one about his discovery, whether from a slip of the tongue or deliberately, because if he did, he would no longer have any hold over me. I think I must always have known that he would eventually demand repayment.

From this time on he behaved toward me as if we were old friends. I received several invitations from him and his wife; their dinner parties used to be lively affairs. When Marshall invited Connor to these dinner parties, I felt as if he had us under a microscope. On one occasion he sat us side by side at dinner, the next time we could not have been placed farther apart. On the first occasion he said to Connor, "You know each other, don't you?" And smiled when Connor stammered, "Yes, since we were children in Florence." "Of course," he said, "silly me."

By the time I attended my last dinner party at the Marshalls', Giovanni was already ill. It had started with vomiting, mouth ulcers, and a high temperature. The doctor from Chianciano thought at first that he had food poisoning but when Giovanni did not improve over the next few days, he retracted this diagnosis. I had a long-scheduled appointment in Rome with my mother who was staying there with friends for a week, but I postponed the trip and sat with my son for the next few days. Little by little he improved and began to recover his appetite, and I remember my relief when the fever left his eyes and he started sitting up in bed and talking to me. By the time I finally left for Rome, his temperature had returned to normal.

I sat on the edge of his bed to say good-bye.

"What shall I buy you in Rome?" I asked, stroking his forehead. "What do you want more than anything?"

He looked at me for a long time before answering. I assumed he was trying to make up his mind.

"Don't go, Mummy," he said at last.

The car was waiting for me outside; I had my coat on and my bag on my lap. At that moment Schwester Marie came into the room.

"Look who's here," I said.

He didn't answer, just laid his head back on the pillow and looked away. I put my arms around him and kissed him again and again, telling him I wouldn't be away for long.

"I'll bring you back a lovely surprise," I said.

I felt awful during the drive to Chianciano and even worse on the train to Rome. I phoned home as soon as I got there and was relieved when you reported that Giovanni had eaten his supper and was asleep. He's better, I assured myself. Thank

God, he's better. Shortly afterward I was at the Piazza Tor San-guigna.

The Marshalls' dinner party was the following evening. I had phoned home that morning and talked to Schwester Marie, who said that Giovanni was still improving, but I was on edge all day and when I arrived at the party, I suddenly felt over-come. I was about to turn back when Marshall, who was stand-ing on the landing in front of the apartment, seized me by the hand and led me inside to where people were dancing. Count Ciano invited me to dance the moment he spotted me, and I tried to hold my head high as we floated around the floor, fo-cusing on stopping my knees from buckling. The Count began to whisper in my ear about the painting Marshall had for sale, which was hanging on the wall in the dining room, but I did not respond. I looked over at Connor and tried to signal my distress to him, but he didn't pick up on it.

I escaped as soon as I could. The party was crowded and I managed to disappear without anyone but Connor noticing. He followed me and we stopped at the bottom of the stairs. There was no one in sight so I put my arms around him and held him tight.

"What's the matter?" he asked.

I was about to answer when a young woman suddenly came running down the stairs. She was wearing a yellow dress and must have been at the party, though I hadn't noticed her. I released Connor immediately and must have inadvertently moved farther away than I meant to because she bumped into me on her way past. My bag fell to the floor, and Connor bent down to pick it up. As she begged my pardon and hurried out, I saw that she was crying.

That evening we broke our rules and went back to his

apartment together. We made love and stayed awake all night, but I felt the whole time as if I was saying good-bye to him. I had convinced myself that Giovanni's illness was a punishment for my behavior and that I had no choice. I didn't tell this to Connor because I knew how foolish it sounded. I sensed that the illness was serious. I think I had sensed it from the first day.

At dawn we took a walk, crossing the Tiber to the Vatican. When we saw a group of monks intoning their matins in an open square, we stopped and listened. It started to rain and we sought shelter by a wall while they continued their prayers. Their voices merged with the hissing of the rain and gradually they disappeared from sight into the grayness, together with the buildings on the other side of the square, and it was as though we were standing outside everything, isolated, with no hope of receiving grace.

HOW STRANGE IT WAS TO COME HOME ON THAT beautiful day and see the roses reaching up to the sun and the dolphins sending a jet of water into the fountain and to hear the laughter of the children as they came down the drive with their teacher. Everything was so at odds with the darkness in my soul. And then to go into his room where death had already set its mark on him, though we wouldn't let ourselves admit it, and to see that the fever had returned to those eyes that I had expected to brighten on seeing me, but that did not.

I stayed with him from morning to night. I had bought him a canary in Rome and we set up the cage on the bookcase where he could easily see it. I was pleased at the way he instantly took to the bird, and we spent a long time debating what to call it. The final decision was Petro and he asked me to make up stories about his new friend; they all began with his escaping from the cage, whereupon he got into all kinds of scrapes before returning to Giovanni, who was waiting for him.

The first specialist diagnosed paratyphoid fever. You didn't trust him, however, and the doctor you got to call a week later wondered if it could be appendicitis. We took him to Montepulciano for an X-ray and his condition deteriorated during the journey. He whimpered all the way home, crying that he

missed his canary. Over the next few days he had spells of de-
lirium during which he was convinced that the bird had flown
away and was now in danger. I regretted having made up the
stories and you couldn't restrain yourself from muttering that I
should stop telling them. I reacted badly to this remark and we
didn't speak again that day.

We started giving him oxygen every two hours and with
that he perked up and recovered his appetite. We were overjoyed, and he slept better and woke up hungry. I saw that he
was growing stronger and one morning he woke up and asked if
he could get out of bed. We were of two minds about whether
this was a good idea and hastily phoned the doctor to make
sure it was safe. We helped him out of bed together and led
him to the window and all I could think about was how wasted
his body was from the illness. He was like a little sparrow and
I bent and took him in my arms and held him by the open
window. He was so light and his flesh so emaciated that I felt as
if the heart that pounded in his chest was no more than a hairs-
breadth beneath the skin. He held out a thin arm and pointed
at the hillside with his finger.

"That's where Petro flies when he's having an adventure,"
he said. "Over there and then up to the stars."

"Yes," I said, "but he always comes back to you."

By the next day, one side of his face was paralyzed and he
could no longer sit up in bed. We took him to Rome where he
was admitted to hospital. The doctor quickly diagnosed men-
ingitis but stressed that it would have been harder to identify
the disease in its early stages.

We kept vigil over him during those last days. He slept for
the most part and when he woke up he turned his head and
stared at us in silence. I held his hand; his fingers were limp and

I stroked them constantly as if I thought I could massage some strength into them. He liked the feeling and gave a low moan every time I let them go. I didn't stop until his eyes closed once more and he drifted off to sleep.

When he was asleep, you and I took turns getting fresh air or something to eat. We were never away for long. The days were warm with cloudless skies, and I found it hard to adjust to the glare of the sunlight when I emerged into the street where life carried on as usual and everyone seemed so oddly cheerful. There was a small public garden across the street with a fountain and a bench by the fountain, where I sat and watched the water, my mind empty. Never for long, ten minutes at most.

I had just crossed the road when I saw Connor. He had been waiting a little way off and did not follow me into the garden until he was sure I was alone. It was growing dark and I nearly jumped out of my skin when he put his hand on my shoulder.

"Sorry," he said. "Your mother told me."

I'd been fighting to keep my feelings under control but now I began to shake all over, and the tears came without my being able to do anything to stop them. He put his arms around me and led me farther into the garden where we would not be seen. We said nothing, nothing I remember, but he held me, waiting for me to calm down. We must have stood there for quite a while. It was late in the day; darkness fell in the garden, the streetlights came on and the noise of the city grew muffled. He asked me how Giovanni was and I told him. He kissed me on the brow in parting and I clasped his hands before I left.

I had no sooner entered the lobby than one of the nurses who had been caring for Giovanni hurried up to me.

"We've been looking for you," she said. "I hope it's not too late."

I ran up the stairs and along the corridor to Giovanni's room. I couldn't feel my feet, couldn't feel anything, it was as if the corridor was rushing toward me while I stood still.

Someone had turned on the overhead light and the brightness hurt my eyes. The doctor was standing by the door. You knelt by the bed, holding Giovanni's hand. You didn't look at me. Bowing his head, the doctor left the room.

Giovanni's eyes were closed and when I sat down on the bed, took him in my arms and pressed him against me, it was like holding a small sack of flour. I groped for where his heart used to pound just under his skin but could feel nothing.

I sat with him in my arms, humming a lullaby to him in farewell. Ran my fingers through his hair, stroked his cheeks as they grew cold. You did not move, until eventually you stood up, very slowly, and said, "He asked where you were. Again and again."

Then you left the room and I sat on with our son in my arms in the merciless glare of the overhead light.

HE WAS DRESSED IN WHITE BEFORE BEING LAID IN HIS coffin. Signorina Harris and I dressed him together; at first I didn't think I could do it but then I pulled myself together, fetched the clothes from his cupboard and slid his arms into the sleeves while she held him up. I picked white tulips and Canary Bird Roses in the garden and arranged them by the coffin along with the bluebells that he used to think so pretty. The coffin stood open all day in the chapel and I sat beside him while the local people came to pay their respects. They started arriving just after ten o'clock and from then on there was a steady stream of mourners until dusk. The priest stayed with me for most of the morning but left when, seeing how tired he was, I suggested he take a nap. Everyone needed comforting, children and adults, men and women, and I did my best. It gave me strength to repeat my words of consolation again and again, "He'll always be with us . . ."

The priest returned after everyone had gone. We lit candles and he said a prayer before closing the coffin. You and I were alone with him and stood on either side of the coffin, looking at the candlelight on his face but not at each other. In the soft glow he looked as if he were sleeping, with color in his cheeks after a long day of running around in the hot sunshine. I said it aloud;

I said: "He looks as if he's sleeping," and only then noticed that you had started to cry. You wept in silence and did not try to stop the tears from running down your cheeks until I held out my hand to you. Then you wiped your eyes rather than take it.

The funeral was held in the church because the chapel was too small. Friends and family came from Florence and Rome and the country people turned up to a man, the children too, which meant the most to me. You complained about the sea of flowers—gardenias, lilies, and roses inside, wreaths of lavender and cypress around the grave—not to me but to Pritchett. To me you said little. It was a beautiful service and when it was over, you, Pritchett, Melchiorre, and the fattore carried the coffin to the cemetery.

That evening you came into my room when I was getting ready for bed. You had taken to sleeping in another room when Giovanni was ill and continued to do so after we returned from Rome. I had spent a long time in Giovanni's room before going to bed, touching one object after another, talking to him as I used to before he went to sleep. The strength I had been able to summon was gone and my words of consolation sounded hollow when I tried to repeat them to myself. I crouched down in the corner, holding his pillow, shaking with unbearable pain.

I don't know how long this lasted. I tried to get up a few times but couldn't. I heard footsteps outside in the passage and sensed more than once that someone was outside the door, about to come in. I assumed it was you but had neither the will nor the energy to find out.

Eventually I managed to get up and go back to my room. It was almost midnight. I drew the curtains and sat down on my bed. Minutes later, you tapped on my door and opened it without waiting for an answer.

You did not speak. I still had Giovanni's pillow in my hands and for whatever reason suddenly felt guilty about it.

"I'll put it back," I heard myself say.

You looked at me.

"Where were you?"

I clasped the pillow and began to shake.

"Where were you when he died?"

"Please," I managed to say. "Please . . ."

"We looked for you everywhere. One of the nurses said she saw you go into the garden across the road. With a man. Who was he?"

Was there anger underneath that pained look? I couldn't tell. After all these years, I couldn't tell.

"Who was he?"

"No one," I said. "There was no one."

You looked at me. I didn't look away.

"I went into the garden to look for you," you said. "I went to the fountain. You weren't there."

"I went farther in," I was going to say but stopped myself because I didn't feel I could keep this up any longer.

"Come and sit down beside me," I said.

This seemed to take you by surprise and you hesitated a little before saying in a low voice, "Pritchett's waiting for me. I must go."

I heard your footsteps recede down the stairs and, going to the window, watched you cross the courtyard in the direction of the stables.

Would I have confessed everything if you hadn't left? I hope not. I hope I would have spared you the pain.

During the next weeks and months you did not speak again of the day Giovanni died. I withdrew, spent most days in my room, unable to participate in daily life. You made sure you were constantly occupied and sometimes you left for days at a time, riding aimlessly in the hills, sleeping under the stars.

The priest tried to be helpful but there was nothing anybody could do. I sank deeper and deeper and I don't know what would have happened if the evacuee children hadn't arrived.

It was the priest who had brought the request from the Red Cross to my attention a month earlier. I had agreed but had not given it much thought. But one night they were here, after a twelve-hour journey from Genoa, tired and hungry, with white, pasty faces. "Mamma, mamma!" I heard them cry as the car drew up, and I ran downstairs as if touched by a magic wand.

They saved me. They gave me purpose and strength, these scared little creatures whom fate had dealt such a terrible hand.

Your attitude toward me didn't improve with the arrival of the evacuee children. You became increasingly irritated, implying that I had taken in the children to compensate for the loss of our son. I chose to ignore this, telling myself that at least you were no longer interrogating me about the night our son died. In this I turned out to be deluding myself, as I discovered the evening the first bombs fell in the valley.

"Where were you?" you asked as I watched the lights of the planes in the night sky and the fire that flared up on the hillside above Campiglia.

"Where were you?"

A week later you disappeared.

# II

KRISTÍN WAS WALKING ALONG THE VIA DEL CORSO when she caught sight of Flora Marshall. Unsure at first, she crossed the road and followed her. She was walking slowly, keeping in the shade of the buildings, swapping her shopping bag from left hand to right, ambling across the square toward the street where they lived, her movements sedate and gentle, indicative of a state of profound well-being.

She must have been seven or eight months pregnant and appeared to be blooming; Kristín had almost forgotten how beautiful she was. They hadn't met since January.

She did not go back to the studio that day and called in sick the next morning. The pain, searing at first, quickly gave way to anger. She gathered strength from it. Without it she would have broken down.

Not that she ever used the word "revenge"—it seemed inappropriate. Yet it kept surfacing in her mind, perhaps because she could never articulate to herself exactly what her intentions were. There was no hiding the fact that she intended to teach him a lesson and even humiliate him, but she assured herself that she never meant to put him in danger. His own greed was responsible for that.

She decided to keep silent about seeing Flora, knowing

that the time must come when he would have to tell her that his wife was pregnant. That was an experience she would not spare him. He had clearly been at some pains to hide the situation from her, making sure that she and Flora did not meet. He must also have forbidden Signorina Pirandello to say a word, she realized; otherwise she would not have been able to keep the news to herself. Kristín was disgusted and had to force herself not to show it, but she managed, turning up to work as if nothing had happened two days after spotting Flora on the Corso, and telling Signorina Pirandello that she'd had a stomach bug but was fine now.

She had been restoring a painting by Masaccio for the past few weeks, a *Madonna and Child*, and now resumed her work. Marshall had sent Signorina Pirandello's nephew to fetch it from somewhere south of the city, a monastery from what she could gather, though nothing had been said openly and the account of the trip had been vague. This did not surprise her since Marshall's collaboration with Berenson had been growing ever more dubious. Berenson, for example, had put his signature to the report about the picture alongside her master's, although she was fairly sure he had not seen it.

Marshall's activities had even picked up since the Germans captured Rome in September 1943. Verrocchio and Giorgione were succeeded by Ghirlandaio, Filippo Lippi, and finally Masaccio. Marshall sold the Ghirlandaio and the Lippi to Count Contini Bonacossi, who had visited the studio and spoken openly about his dealings with Walter Hofer, Hermann Göring's adviser. She never discussed these transactions with Marshall because she knew how he would react. They were so anxious to avoid accusations of selling these works of art to the Germans that Marshall was prepared to slip Contini Bonacossi a fee merely for acting as go-between. But it rankled with him to have to pay the Count, and Kristín thought it was probably only a matter of time before greed overcame his caution.

She saw him only briefly on the day she returned to work and not much more during the rest of the week. This was a great relief and she focused her attention on the painting, which was in such bad condition that apart from a few brushstrokes, only the outlines of the *Madonna and Child* remained once she had cleaned off the earlier attempts at restoration. But he turned up at the studio on the Monday and stood for some time in front of the picture before commenting.

"Time hasn't been kind to it, but the master's touch is unmistakable. I have complete faith in your ability to bring it back to life."

He laid a hand on her shoulder and was poised to say something more but she eased herself out from under his fingers in order to wipe some imperceptible fluff from the picture.

She proved adept at forestalling his visits over the following weeks. She surprised herself with her ingenuity in reacting to his overtures, how easy she found it to smile at him when appropriate, how satisfying to hold back her knowledge. Her strength redoubled when she saw that she could deceive him, throw dust in those eyes that she had believed to be all-seeing. Yet she did not overdo it, being cautious by nature. She avoided him as much as she could but she made sure he wouldn't sense it.

She expected his confession any day but it never came. Every time she sensed that he was on the verge of telling her the truth, she was disappointed. He was either incapable of doing so or unwilling, and gradually it seemed as if he had started avoiding her too. She took it as a sign that Flora's due date was approaching.

One Wednesday late in November she arrived at work to find Signorina Pirandello in a state of excitement, though she refrained at first from saying anything to Kristín. At last, however, unable to hold back any longer, she poured out the happy news on the landing outside the office—a son had been born.

Although the news did not come as a surprise to Kristín, she found herself at a loss. Trying not to let it show, she asked Signorina Pirandello the sort of questions people ask when they receive news of this kind, then went into the studio, shut the door, and stood there without moving. Frightened of the thoughts that assailed her, she tried to suppress them.

What sort of person is incapable of summoning up any happiness about the birth of a healthy baby? she asked herself. What's happened to me?

The *Madonna and Child* was waiting, but she did not return to the easel or switch on the light. The morning sunshine streamed white through the windows and she gazed at the shafts of light in the air between herself and the painting, before finally walking up to the sunbeam closest to her and stopping a foot away. She stretched out her hand with its pale skin and white fingers and studied them. Could they do it? She had asked herself the same question before but not as bluntly. But she did not answer herself because the idea was nothing but fantasy, a fantasy she could still snuff out. Am I right in the head? she asked herself, before turning on her heel and leaving.

She bought a present for the boy, a little teddy bear, and asked Signorina Pirandello to pass it on to his parents, as she was apparently going to see them later that day. Kristín couldn't help wondering how her master would react.

He came to the studio two days later. She was at the easel, and he walked over and inspected the painting.

"You're getting on well," he said, although she had only just started. His tone was neutral.

She did not speak.

"I've booked an exhibition space for you. You should go and see it when you've got a moment."

She did not put down her brush as he talked but carried on working with undisturbed concentration.

He straightened up, hesitated before leaving, then said, "I've got myself into a difficult position. A very difficult position. I've no one to blame but myself."

He left. From the window she watched him walk down the street. She sensed no remorse in his movements, only self-satisfaction.

THOSE LAST WEEKS IN COPENHAGEN HAD BEEN A torment. She stood in front of the canvas, unable even to make a start. She wanted to paint a picture of the pond and the swan taking off into the air and the girl in the yellow dress who had waded out into the pond and was watching the swan, but she couldn't do it. It was the picture she had always meant to paint. But now she couldn't see the girl or her mother half-running down the slope or the people gathered on the mound. The colors faded before her brush even touched the canvas.

She gave up. This was a week before she was supposed to hand in her final assignment, an oil painting. Her grandparents had given her a small picture by the Icelandic painter Thórarinn B. Thorláksson when she left to go abroad, taking it down from the parlor wall at home and presenting it to her with their good wishes, and now she reached for it—without apparent pause for thought—and set it up opposite the window in her room. She moved the easel, keeping the window to the left behind her and the picture before her in the white spring light. Then she began to paint.

She was amazed at how easy she found it. The glacier rose up into the sky, casting its radiance on the barren waste— black gravel, patches of moss, and a stream flowing among the stones. She had no need of rest, no wish to put down her brush because she was happy while she worked. She handed in the picture by the deadline, a Friday morning in May, as the birds were cheerful in the blossoming trees. She walked to the Academy relieved and fulfilled, and the feeling continued as she made her way resolutely along the corridors carrying her work. After leaving it in her teacher Jensen's office, she reemerged into the spring sunlight where the mood of well-being slowly drained away, to be replaced by doubt and shame.

"However, it is above all in the technical area that Kristín excels . . . although it should be noted that her graduation picture of an Icelandic landscape was both outstanding and unexpected . . . It is to be hoped that the talent Kristín evinces in this picture is a sign that she is maturing from a first-rate technician into a promising artist . . ."

She knows the report by heart, yet she fetches the piece of paper and reads it in the dim light of the lamp. It's a mystery to her why she should have brought it with her from Rome instead of taking the opportunity to get rid of it once and for all. She lets it fall onto the dressing table as darkness fills the valley and intermittent flashes light up the slopes of Monte Amiata. The war has reached them, its horrors are looming, but this document continues to pursue her. Will she never be rid of it?

The pictures she exhibited in the little gallery just off Piazza Popolo were of the fjord and marsh by the farm, the mountains by the fjord, the sky above the mountains. And the ocean that lurked beyond the mouth of the fjord, with its godlike power to give and to take away. Marshall couldn't see it; perhaps no one could see it but her. She didn't care. The pictures were dark, their imagery abstract. Marshall said they alluded to impressions and feelings rather than to external reality. She heard him explaining this to guests at the opening and found it uncomfortable.

There were around forty people at the exhibition, all invited by her master. She felt like an outsider at the opening; the guests knew one another and chatted during the brief time they lingered to view her work. Fortunately, few of them made any attempt to approach her; those who did merely mouthed some polite sentiments about the pictures, then turned back to one another.

His wife attended the opening. She was as charming as ever to Kristín, kissing her on the cheek and congratulating her.

"I don't know the first thing about art," she said, "but I think the pictures are beautiful. I couldn't do anything like this."

There was a downpour during the opening and the square outside emptied of everybody except the soldiers who took refuge under the walls of the buildings. She was standing at the window, watching the rain, when Marshall came over and told her that two of the paintings had been sold, one of them to Count Bonacossi. She did not reply, and he hesitated a moment before turning back to the guests.

For the first time, he was at a loss as to how to deal with her. Although he didn't like it, he had to restrain himself, for he couldn't risk turning her against him.

He didn't know she had overheard him talking on the phone the day before when he was issuing the last invitations to the opening. She had been passing his office on her way in to work, and his voice was clearly audible through the closed door.

"A first attempt," she heard him say, "but one must support the younger generation. No masterpieces but quite pretty in their way."

She watched the rain. People began to drift away. The soldiers stood against the walls, gray as the stone, one or two with cigarettes in their mouths. She thought about the picture she was going to paint for him. Would he describe it the same way?

IT TOOK HER A LONG TIME TO REMOVE ALL THE paint. Solvent was ineffectual; only pumice stone, a scraper, and tweezers made any impact on the hardened paint, and she had to take great care not to tear the linen canvas. The painting she used dated from around 1600 and had been lying among a pile of other inferior works in a storeroom off the studio. It still had the original strainer, and the canvas was well preserved, attached to the frame by the type of tacks Caravaggio had used.

She chose him on purpose. She could have picked Verrocchio or Ghirlandaio, Titian or Giorgione—painters she was more familiar with, but she didn't. She chose him. Caravaggio. Hothead, thug, genius. The murderer to whom God gave the gifts for which others longed and would have sacrificed everything. For which *she* would have sacrificed everything.

Her plan crystallized as she stood in a quiet corner of the church of San Luigi dei Francesi, not far from Piazza Navona, studying Caravaggio's paintings of Saint Matthew. It came to her in the light entering through the dirty glass of the arched windows, fully formed as if it had been lurking in her brain, waiting to present itself. It sent shivers through her, not of fear but of excitement. She could do it. She knew she had the talent. She would find an insignificant painting from the period, clean the canvas completely, and use it to paint her own Caravaggio. She would find a way to get it to her master, incomplete and damaged. He wouldn't suspect anything. He would ask her to restore and repaint it. No, not ask, beg. He would beg her, and she would agree reluctantly, only to complete his humiliation. Then she would tell him. After she had completed the restoration but before he could sell it. That would be the most painful moment.

Madness, she said to herself as she turned away from Saint Matthew and looked at the light coming in through the windows. Sheer madness.

But she was determined and the word only increased her anticipation. Madness.

The ground layer favored by the rogue genius was different from that used by other painters of the period. Dark, reddish-brown, composed of calcite, minerals, and lead, it is left visible here and there in his pictures, sometimes with a translucent quality owing to the calcite. She brought the materials and tools home from the studio in the evenings and labored on the picture early in the mornings before going to work.

Unlike his contemporaries, Caravaggio did not prepare his paintings with sketches but painted directly onto the ground, sometimes incising the outlines of his model with the handle of his brush while the ground was still wet. Therefore Kristín had to be ready with her composition as soon as she started on the preliminary layer. She decided on her subject before she left the church of San Luigi dei Francesi, staring at Caravaggio's portrayal of the calling of the tax collector, feeling the heat emanating from it. The following morning she approached Maria, who worked in the canteen where Kristín took her meals. Maria accepted the invitation eagerly and did not complain about having to wake up early; it suited her well.

Kristín based her work on Caravaggio's painting of the penitent Mary Magdalene but decided to dress her model in simpler attire, choosing a white nightgown of her own for the purpose. She found the jewelry in the drawer of a desk belonging to the old man who owned the flat: a pearl necklace, bracelet, and hairpin. Assuming that they must have belonged to his wife, she took great care of them.

Marshall had more than once disrobed her from this nightgown. It gave her great pleasure wondering whether it would stir any recollection in his mind.

She began every morning by preparing her pigments just as Caravaggio and his assistants had done. She mixed lead oxide with walnut oil and heated it so that the paint would dry faster. She ground the pigments one by one before adding them to the oil—malachite, cinnabar, and azurite; madder root; kermes and cochineal; indigo and weld; umber and ocher. She went about everything as if she were restoring a painting for him, never deviating from the strict rule of using only materials that had been employed in the original picture, as he would always detect any aberration.

The girl posed on a low chair in the living room, with the jewelry on the floor beside her. Kristín had pulled back the curtain nearest the wall so that the light fell on her shoulders and head but everything below was in shadow. The girl had wet hair when she arrived the first day, and thinking how pretty it looked, Kristín decided to paint her like that. She made her turn away from the light, with one cheek hidden, the other in blue shadow. The girl liked to chatter but quickly learnt to keep quiet.

In Kristín's "damaged" picture, the shoulders and neck were intact, the hands too, the hairpin and part of the bracelet, but only the outline of the pearl necklace could be seen. The background and face were damaged, but it had never been Kristín's intention to use the model's face if she was given the opportunity to restore this picture. She had another in mind.

Kristín told the girl that she would be allowed to see the picture when it was finished. Not before. The girl did not object. She regarded it as an honor to sit for her, and moreover Kristín drew a small portrait of her, which she gave her in parting.

"Will I be famous?" she asked once. She was only half joking and Kristín was embarrassed. She didn't like having to deceive her.

Kristín left her damaged Caravaggio to dry for several weeks before resuming work on it. Removing the canvas from the strainer, she put it on the kitchen table and dragged it back and forth over the edge to break up the paint and produce cracks in it, which she then filled with dust and dirt that she had cleaned off various old works. The canvas tore in two places where it had been stretched over the strainer. She was pleased with this and did not repair it when she fastened it back onto the mount.

Over the next weeks hardly a day passed when she didn't fiddle with the picture in some way. There were always minor adjustments to make—or acts of vandalism, rather—which she knew in her heart of hearts no one but she would notice. But she did not tire of them: with each she grew increasingly convinced that she had achieved the upper hand.

THERE IS A MESSAGE FROM SIGNORINA HARRIS ON MY breakfast tray. I sit up in bed to read it; my eyes haven't yet adjusted to the daylight and I feel terribly weary. I cannot get the events Melchiorre and I witnessed in Montepulciano out of my mind. In my dreams, the German officer walks up to the man lying on a stretcher, points his gun at his temple, and pulls the trigger. At first I cannot see the man's face; it's only when I hear the shot that it becomes visible. It's you. In my dreams, it's always you.

The maid finishes pulling the curtains and when I fold the note again and put it aside, she turns to me to await orders. I gaze at the sunlight streaming in through the east window and follow a ray that lights up the floor where Pritchett loosened the tiles so that I could hide my diary. I watch the sunbeam shimmering on the tiles as if stirred by a gentle breeze.

"Bruno is here. He's been shot in the shoulder," says the note from Signorina Harris. "What shall I do with him?"

I leave the breakfast tray on the bedside table: coffee, fruit, and a slice of lemon cake. I haven't been eating much recently and it's starting to show, or so I gather from Pritchett, who is unnecessarily concerned about me.

On my way downstairs I see Kristín and Signor Grandinetti

heading out to the garden with the children; pausing halfway down, I watch them shepherd their flock along the passage to the back door.

Signorina Harris is tending to Bruno's wounds when I enter the clinic. I haven't encountered him since I mistook him for you and don't look forward to seeing him now. He's always been a troublemaker, harmless but immature, and now belongs to a rowdy band of partisans. His comrades are standing guard at the door but are quick to step aside when they see me approaching. A girl from one of the farms is lying in one of the beds with pneumonia; another is occupied by a laborer who broke his leg at the quarry. Bruno is sitting on the third bed. Signorina Harris has peeled off the rag his friends had used to bandage the wound and has begun to clean it.

"The Fascists wounded me," Bruno says, "but I killed two of them."

"The nurse will tend to your injury but then you must go," I say. "We can't risk the Germans finding you here."

"The bullet is still in the wound," he says.

I look at Harris who confirms this.

"Do you think you'll be up to leaving as soon as she's taken it out?" I ask, repeating, "You can't stay here."

He grimaces and looks at the nurse in hope of support but her face is impassive and she says in a neutral tone, "I'm afraid this is going to hurt."

He turns his gaze back to me to see if her words have brought about a change of heart and grimaces again when he sees that they haven't. Slowly, he nods.

As I leave, my legs feel heavier than usual. It's already hot and sultry; the sun is beating down on the courtyard. I see the children sitting under the linden tree in the garden, listening to Signor Grandinetti read, and I can't help thinking how ir-responsible I've been. I've allowed the partisans to waltz in and out of the place as if they own it, seeking shelter and medi-cal attention, and sleeping in the forest and outlying farms. I've fed them, tended their wounds, clothed them. All in good faith. All guided by a sense of righteousness. At least I try to convince myself of this, though I have begun to have doubts about everything.

Yesterday Pritchett stopped me as I was coming back from the cemetery. I had been smoothing the earth on Giovanni's grave and hadn't yet washed my hands but he took hold of them anyway and was about to say something when a group of partisans suddenly appeared descending the slope and turned in the direction of the *fattoria*.

"Is it possible that you believe the painting will protect you?" Pritchett asked as we watched them go.

Taken aback, I jerked away my hands. We never spoke of the painting, never mentioned it, and I instinctively glanced around, though he had almost whispered the words and no one could hear us. I knew the answer to his question although I may not actually have put it to myself, not aloud at any rate, and he knew it too, so I didn't need to answer. I expected him to press me but he didn't. Nor did he mention the trouble we'll be in if the Allies discover that we've been collaborating with the Germans.

"Have you seen it?" he asked me instead.

I shook my head. I had more than once been on the verge of going down into the vault but had restrained myself.

"Don't you think we should know something about it?"

Perhaps it didn't matter what was in the crate, but I under-stood his point.

"It might be safer to check," I agreed.

"We'll go up there this evening," he replied.

We parted and I went inside to wash my hands. I stood with my hands under the flow longer than necessary, turning them so the water sluiced my palms and the backs of my hands in turn. Pritchett was right: I'd been convinced that the painting was of great importance to the Germans. What if this turned out to be wrong? Would its protective power turn out to be purely illusory, now that they've become less forgiving than ever?

Pritchett was unusually quiet at the supper table. I was uneasy. The fattore kept up a conversation about potatoes. "They can take endless rain," he said. "The harvest has never been better than it was in the summer of '36 when it rained constantly and the garden was ruined. Everything except the potatoes. They were huge, a beautiful crop. Remember, Pritchett?"

I had no appetite and couldn't wait to get going. The priest noticed that I wasn't eating and kept pushing food in my direction, but I asked him gently to stop.

We went to the mill after darkness had fallen. It was still hot and the cicadas were noisy in the quiet evening. Pritchett was carrying a bag of tools in one hand and a lantern in the other, but he didn't light it on the way for fear of being seen. I walked on ahead of him, taking the long way around, heading farther over the hillside before starting to climb. There was a faint light from the new moon and I felt my way between the bushes and undergrowth, across a dried-up stream and up an old path, out of sight of the buildings. I had become very nervous and almost fearful of what we might discover and was on the verge of suggesting to Pritchett that we turn back. But I kept moving up the steep hill and didn't stop until we reached the mill.

We found the trapdoor to the underground vault after some difficulty. It was well hidden, covered by a thicker layer of earth and vegetation than I remembered. We didn't exchange words but hesitated before kneeling down and pushing it aside. What good can come of this? I asked myself. What good?

Pritchett descended the stone steps first, lighting the lantern when he was halfway down, and turned with the glow on his face to light my way. It was damp in the vault and smelt of earth, and we looked around before going over to the crate that stood by the wall where we had left it on that snowy spring evening. Pritchett handed me the lantern in silence, laid the crate on the floor, removed the tarpaulin, and began to pry off the lid with a claw hammer and screwdriver. I had difficulty keeping the lantern steady in my hand and he turned around to see if I was all right. He worked slowly, taking care not to damage the crate so that he would be able to close it again without leaving any sign that it had been opened.

Neither of us could see the painting properly at first. I had put down the lantern and knelt to help Pritchett unwrap the paper that it was packed in, but now I reached for the light again and held it over the crate. Then we saw her, the girl in the white shift, looking away from us, light and shadow on her cheeks. And I said to myself—or rather to her: "So you're the one I've been relying on."

"Caravaggio," Pritchett said in a low voice. "I wonder how they got it."

Maybe he didn't mean to be accusatory, maybe it was all in my head.

"I didn't have a choice," I said.

"So they're planning to take the art with them. They've been planning it for months. And Marshall is helping them. Why am I not surprised?"

At first sight there seemed to be an aura of peace and calm about the girl in the picture, but the longer I looked, that all changed. To my surprise I began to sense not only sadness but profound loneliness.

"Who are you?" I asked under my breath and was on the point of putting out my hand to touch her when I stopped myself. Pritchett knelt down on the cold stone floor and started to wrap the paper around the picture again but then stopped. I looked at him. He was staring at the girl as if something of great significance had caught his eye.

"What?" I asked.

He didn't answer. Lost in his thoughts, he took the lantern out of my hands and held it up to the painting, leaning so close to it that I thought he would touch it. It wasn't until I asked him again that he shook his head and said, "My mind's playing a trick on me." Then he finished wrapping the picture, stuffed the straw back into the crate, closed the lid, and replaced it under the tarpaulin by the wall.

We shoveled the earth back over the trapdoor and then picked our way down the beaten-earth path, our shadows so faint that they were barely visible. When we got back, I sensed that Pritchett wanted to talk but I was in a strange mood and, saying good night, went straight up to my room.

THE GERMANS CAN NO LONGER AVOID TRAVELING BY daylight. The Allies have taken Viterbo, Vetralla, and Tarquinia, and the front has moved up into the hills to the north of them. Pritchett and the fattore wondered over breakfast how the Germans were getting supplies to their retreating forces and agreed that it would be practically impossible given the sheer numbers involved. So they will have to forage for themselves and we all know what that means. According to the fattore, the Allies dropped firearms to the partisans in the forest to the west of San Martino yesterday evening so we can expect more bloodshed. I ask Signorina Harris if Bruno has left the clinic. She says yes and the fattore glances up from his plate. I make no attempt to hide my opinion that the partisans ought to realize their presence is putting everyone here in danger.

"Has something changed?" he asks.

"Yes," I say, "the valley is filling with Germans. Perhaps you haven't noticed?"

This comes out more sharply than intended, as I'm exhausted from lack of sleep. The fattore doesn't answer, and Pritchett and Signorina Harris sit with lowered eyes, unused to my speaking in such a tone. Of course, the fattore didn't deserve it and I am about to say something conciliatory when

Melchiorre appears in the doorway with the news that there are military vehicles on their way up the road to the house.

Pritchett and I go out to meet them. We have been expecting them to requisition the buildings here on the hill, but I didn't think it would be until later when the front had moved closer. There are three vehicles, a jeep and two trucks. The colonel who emerges from the jeep is polite. Instead of announcing his business immediately, he looks around, walks out onto the veranda and takes in the view of the valley—the wet fields, the garden nearest the house. He has not put on his cap since stepping out of the car; his hair is thinning and the rain runs down his face but he doesn't bother to wipe it away.

"It must be very beautiful here in good weather," he says.

We nod.

"We can thank God that it's overcast and raining," he continues, his eyes on the armored column in the valley. "And so can you, because we will have to take shelter once the skies clear and then we will come here."

The trucks are still halfway up the slope, driving with extraordinary caution.

"I advise you to put up a sign, both at the bottom of your road and also here by the villa, stating that this is an orphanage. I have also drawn up a certificate that you can show for confirmation. I don't know when the front line will reach you—it depends on the weather—but I can't see us holding out much longer. Two, maybe three days. We have delayed them at Lake Bolsena but they have got past Orbetello and are making for Grosseto. The troops are exhausted and this affects their behavior toward civilians. I don't expect you to understand."

Pritchett and I exchanged glances. Everything about this visit was odd, his soliloquy not least, and the purpose remained unclear until the trucks finally rattled up to the house.

There were eight children in one truck, six in the other.

"I have three children myself," the colonel said. "Two boys and a girl. It is a long time since I last saw them."

The soldiers helped the children down from the trucks. They had been chattering and singing but stopped when they saw us and stood uncertainly by the vehicles.

"They are from an orphanage outside Chiusi," he said. "It was hit by a bomb yesterday. These children were outside playing. The staff and all the children inside were killed."

"How many are there?" was the only thing I could think of asking, although I could have counted them for myself.

He answered, adding, "I had heard about you. That is why we came here."

"How?" I meant to ask, but instead said more to myself than him, "Where are we going to put them?"

His expression hardened when he looked at me.

"You have room," he said, quietly but firmly.

I was ashamed and could say nothing but Pritchett came to my aid.

"There's no point letting them stand out here in the rain," he said. "Let's get them into the kitchen."

The soldiers escorted the children around the back of the house, through the garden and past the fountain. One of the boys stopped beside it and pointed out the dolphins to his companions who said something to one another and laughed. It was strange to see these children laughing in the rain after their horrible ordeal; perhaps they felt they had nothing more to fear; perhaps they were simply too young to understand.

There was a commotion in the kitchen when we appeared with the group of children and soldiers. I called Schwester Marie, and she and two maids took the little ones under their wing, and washed and dressed them before they were fed. The soldiers sat down at the table and accepted some breakfast; with the exception of the colonel they seemed so young and vulnerable that I felt sorry for them. I expected the colonel to carry on talking but he didn't, simply ate in silence, then signaled to his men that it was time to go. The children were sitting at the table in the dining room, but all stood up when the soldiers came to the door to say good-bye, and went over to them. They took the soldiers' hands and one of them, a boy of about five, began to cry. The officer bent down, patted the boy on the head and gave him an encouraging smile. I won't deny that this sight ignited in my breast a spark of hope that we might in time succeed in patching up this world that for years now we have been so intent on destroying.

I watched the vehicles heading away down the drive. The rain fell unrelentingly and the water collected in the ruts left by the tires in the mud.

THERE WAS NO ROOM FOR THE CHILDREN TO SLEEP in the house with us, so we sent Melchiorre and Fosco by oxcart with mattresses and blankets to one of the outlying farms. It lies highest up the hill and we have made plans to send all the children there when the hostilities intensify, since the fighting is likely to be fiercest down here. They set off in the afternoon; the rain was no longer falling as heavily. We had started to hear explosions in the distance where the weather had probably begun to clear up, and from time to time there was a roar of planes from somewhere in the clouds.

They had not come back by suppertime. Pritchett said the journey had probably been difficult in the mud, since the cart was heavy and the road was bad even in normal conditions, so there was really no need to worry about them. The children all ate together; the two groups had been a little shy of each other at first but that soon passed. Kristín read them a story after their meal and the new children, unused to her accent, asked her where she was from. She told them and showed them Iceland on the map. This led to other questions about her, but she changed the subject and shortly afterward began to read to them again. This didn't surprise me because she seems keen to avoid talking about herself. No doubt she has her reasons, and she's not alone in that.

Dusk was falling when they finally showed up. Hearing the heavy tread of the oxen on the gravel, I went down to meet them. It was still raining and the air smelt of sulfur.

I was taken aback to see that the mattresses were still in the cart. Fosco was walking beside it while Melchiorre sat in the driver's seat, keeping a tight hold on the reins. Both were soaked to the skin and the oxen were stumbling. The mattresses kept sliding off the cart, and Fosco was continually having to push them back on.

They said that the farm where we had intended to send the children was packed with partisans who had taken refuge from the forest when the rain set in. They refused to leave and had, moreover, taken three German soldiers hostage when their car drove off the road in the valley. Bruno was the band's leader, back on his feet after being treated by Signorina Harris. He had declared that since we were no longer sympathetic to their cause, it would be risky to let Fosco and Melchiorre return home.

"They'll betray us," Bruno said. "You can count on it. Little Melchiorre in particular. He's weak."

However, not all his comrades agreed with him. They had argued back and forth, openly discussing their options. Bruno had been unusually erratic and threatening. At the end our boys were allowed to leave but only after Bruno managed to hit Melchiorre in the face for no reason at all.

"What are they planning to do with the hostages?" I asked.

"I think they want to exchange them for some of their comrades who are being held by the Germans."

I shook my head but said nothing. We seemed to be under attack from every side now. God, how I wished you were here.

They were weary and I told them to change into dry clothes and get themselves something to eat; someone else could unload the mattresses from the cart and put them to dry.

The children were worn-out and some had nodded off in the dining room. We discussed with Schwester Marie where to put them, and I went upstairs and looked into the rooms where the refugee children have been sleeping since the Germans requisitioned the buildings in the valley. If we were resourceful, it might be possible to squeeze in another five children. I told this to Marie and Pritchett when I returned downstairs and asked them and myself at the same time where on earth we were to accommodate the other nine.

They exchanged glances and it was obvious that they had been discussing the matter in my absence. Schwester Marie spoke for both of them, as arranged.

"Marchesa," she said, "what about Giovanni's room?"

I wasn't expecting this and I flinched.

"We wouldn't touch anything," she added hastily, "we'll just put some mattresses on the floor by the door. I'll sleep in there with them."

I knew this was the only sensible solution but I couldn't bring myself to agree, however much I tried to reason with myself as I stood there before them.

"No," I said, "they can sleep on the floor in here tonight."

I had disappointed them. Myself too. I left, feeling their eyes on the back of my neck as I walked out of the room.

It was dark in Giovanni's room when I opened the door. I switched on the lamp in the corner but the light was dim and illuminated only a small patch of floor. I sat down on the bed, meaning to talk to him as usual but I couldn't. The words wouldn't come and for the first time I was unable to sense his presence.

I stood up and went over to the open window for some fresh air. The rain disappeared into the sea of leaves outside. Two farmhands trudged across the courtyard with mattresses on their backs.

I went downstairs. Pritchett, Kristín, and Schwester Marie had started moving the table and chairs in the dining room to make room for the children, but I stopped them and asked the farmhands to take the blankets and pillows.

Ten children were easily accommodated in Giovanni's room once we had moved the bookcase closer to the bed. They fell asleep immediately and I told Marie there was no need for her to sleep in there with them. We could both listen out for them if we left our doors open—she from her room farther down the corridor, I from mine next door.

At three o'clock in the morning I went in to check on them. The rain had stopped and the moon was gleaming over the peak of Monte Amiata, its light shining into the house. The fog over the valley was beginning to disperse, and I caught a glimpse of a long line of trucks on the road, carrying an aura of defeat through the darkness.

When I finally fell asleep, I dreamed of our son. The children are in his room and he wakes up and gets out of bed to take a closer look at them. I can't see his face but I watch him as he climbs back into bed. Then I suddenly notice that he has left his footprints in the moonlight on the floor.

WHILE KRISTÍN WORKED ON HER CARAVAGGIO AT home in the morning, making the final adjustments after the paint had dried, she finished the restoration of Masaccio's *Madonna and Child* at the studio. Unwavering in her determination, she avoided her master as much as she could, afraid that he might find words that would change her mind.

It was a cold winter, and life in Rome became increasingly difficult. Food shortages were chronic as the Allies advanced from the south and the Germans tightened their grip on the city. Those who supported the Allies had gone into hiding, many of them in monasteries outside the city, and the canteen where she took her meals was half empty. There were daily skirmishes in the streets and bus and tram services were suspended at night. At the canteen, she would hear stories about the increasing cruelty with which the Germans treated their enemies, but she did her best to keep fear and worry from her mind.

No one knew how long the Germans could hold Rome, but few believed it would be much beyond the autumn. Kristín assumed that Marshall would now be more careful and give up all his dealings with the Germans, indirect as they were. But on the contrary he seemed to despair when he sensed that the boom might soon be over, with nothing to look forward to but uncertainty. He had already sold the Masaccio and put pressure on her to finish it—as good-naturedly as possible—because he was in a hurry to start on the next job. He was vague about when it would arrive and who the artist was, but he talked as if he was expecting it any day and even hinted that there might be two works.

It was early in the morning when she decided she was ready to take her Caravaggio to the studio. She tidied up the tools she had brought home, fingering each in turn—the pumice, the brushes, the spatula—before wrapping them in a cloth and placing the bundle in a small bag along with what was left of the walnut oil, pigments, and lead oxide. She worked slowly and methodically, thinking of the day ahead of her and the weeks behind her, the hours in front of the canvas, her accomplishment. As she studied her forgery in the faint morning light, her perfect representation of the master's technique and, more important, his brilliant but troubled mind, she was sure that Marshall would be incapable of seeing through her deception. She took it off the easel, wrapped it in a white blanket, and placed it more carefully than necessary by the front door.

She made sure she would get to the studio before Signorina Pirandello. The streets were empty, but she was on edge and walked as fast as she could. She looked left and right before entering the building and climbed the stairs quickly. She was alone but she still locked the door to the studio behind her before putting the picture away in the back of the storeroom where she had prepared a perfect spot the previous day. Then she placed the tools and materials in the drawers against the wall and waited for her heart to stop racing before unlocking the door and forcing herself to turn her attention to the *Madonna and Child*.

She had no idea how long she would have to wait for an opportunity to introduce her Caravaggio. At first she felt the rush of anticipation but soon that was replaced by tension and restlessness. She kept her schedule and tried to concentrate on her work, racing to complete the restoration of *Madonna and Child*, arriving early and not leaving until dusk. Never had she been guided by such a powerful impulse, a current that pushed her forward and didn't allow her a moment to reconsider, let alone turn back. At night she stayed home, often sitting in the dark, waiting for the night to pass. And then, a fortnight later, when she had begun to doubt and despair, her prayers were finally answered.

It was a clear morning with birdsong and a light southerly breeze. Signorina Pirandello greeted her excitedly as she entered the building and informed her that Marshall had purchased two paintings that her nephew had set off to collect an hour ago.

"They come from the same monastery as the *Madonna and Child*," she said. "The abbot has no choice but to sell them in order to support all the people who are seeking refuge with the monks."

"What are they?" asked Kristín, unsuccessfully trying to conceal her enthusiasm. "Do you know what they are?"

Signorina Pirandello said she knew very little since neither Marshall nor Berenson had seen them yet.

"But Berenson has spoken to the abbot and is convinced that one of them may be a real gem. At any rate, you'll see for yourself when my nephew brings them this afternoon. Before Marshall does. He won't get back from his travels till tonight."

She waited, pacing back and forth in the studio, cleaning, dusting, examining the *Madonna and Child* once again to make sure there was nothing more to be done. She didn't go out for lunch; she had no appetite and didn't want to risk not being there when the paintings arrived. She stopped herself when she was about to go into the storeroom for the fifteenth time, telling herself to calm down. The sun was now shining through the south window and there was a smell of salt on the breeze when she opened it and looked down the street. Marshall had not yet come back when Signorina Pirandello's nephew arrived with two mediocre works from the monastery that afternoon. Kristín carried them up to the studio while Signorina Pirandello waited in the street with her nephew. Once upstairs she unwrapped them from the blanket, took the more damaged of the two works into the storeroom and replaced it with her unfinished picture of Maria from the canteen. She laid it together with the other painting from the monastery on the worktable before returning the blanket to the young man.

At first she thought she would wait for Marshall. She pictured him coming running up the stairs, stopping in front of the two paintings, quickly pushing the inferior one aside. She saw the excitement in his eyes as he leaned forward and adjusted the table light, staring at the faceless girl and her jewelry. She saw him running his finger over the paint, smelling it, even breaking off a small flake and putting it in his mouth, examining every crack, noticing the dark ground layer visible in the wall behind the girl and in the shadow under her chair. Smiling to himself, hardly able to believe his good fortune.

When she imagined him fixing his eyes on the girl's nightgown, she realized she had to leave before he arrived.

It rained that night. She lay in bed, listening to the drops on the window, unable to sleep. At dawn she got up and waited for the clock to strike nine. Then she put on her coat and, shaking with trepidation, forced herself to walk down the stairs and out into the morning.

I WAS AWAKE WHEN THEY HAMMERED ON THE DOOR
at five in the morning. I had been keeping vigil since the children from Chiusi arrived earlier in the week, checking on
them several times a night although there is no need, as they
do not stir. I put on my dressing gown and went downstairs
where I encountered Fosco, who had been standing guard that
night and now came rushing down the passage from the back
door. He told me the Germans were on the property; they had
broken into the corn store and the *fattoria*, but he hadn't dared
to draw attention to himself, let alone try to stop them.

"I must have nodded off," he said rather shamefaced, but
there was no time now to comfort him and tell him that it
would have made no difference if he had been awake.

I opened the front door. It was still dark and the only light
outside came from the headlights of the vehicles that lit up the
drive. Not even bothering to introduce himself, their captain
asked bluntly where the partisans were. I said I didn't know.

"They've taken three of my men captive," he said, "so I
wouldn't dream of putting on an act if I were you."

"They're not here," I said, handing him the certificate of
immunity that I had been given by the German lieutenant who
brought the orphans.

He scarcely glanced at it.

"I'm telling you the truth," I added. "I wouldn't risk putting the children in danger."

"Come outside with me," he said.

I followed him. He walked around the villa, not stopping until we had reached the courtyard behind it.

"Where is the road to the farms?" he asked.

I told him.

"Is that the only way?"

I hesitated for a second, then not daring to try deceiving him, I shook my head and said quietly, "No, you can also go straight up over there, but the road is bad."

He regarded me in the faint illumination of the headlights; it was dim behind the villa and I could see nothing but the silhouette of his face under his cap. Then he turned on his heel and immediately started issuing orders to his men.

Pritchett was awake and had come out to join me, with Fosco at his side.

"Should we try to warn them?" Fosco asked.

I felt so powerless—so compromised—that I didn't even have the strength to pretend.

Pritchett saved me the effort.

"It's too late. They will get there before us. We'd be risking our lives for nothing."

We watched their progress up the hill. They drove their vehicles along the better road, but took their horses up the track I had pointed out to the captain. The headlights grew distant, vanishing and reappearing as they drove in and out of thickets of trees. Dawn was turning the sky gray and we had long since ceased to hear the rumbling and backfiring of the engines by the time we finally lost sight of them.

We walked slowly across the courtyard. Fosco stayed in the

kitchen but Pritchett and I went upstairs. I felt numb and sat down on my bed.

"There was nothing we could have done," he said.

"I should have seen it coming. I should have gone up there. I should have tried to reason with Bruno."

"It wouldn't have done any good," he said.

"But I didn't even try."

"We cannot be responsible for everyone, Alice. We have more than enough on our plates."

Of course he was right, but it didn't make me feel any better.

"They won't necessarily find them," he said then. "They might have gone."

"Yes," I said. "Maybe they've gone."

He went into his room and I remained sitting on my bed, repeating those words in a feeble attempt to keep my fear away.

It was light when the Germans returned. They did not stop by the buildings but continued on down to the valley. I was relieved to see the back of them and convinced myself that they had been out of luck, that the partisans had gone, taking their hostages with them.

I went downstairs. Pritchett was already outside with Fosco and Melchiorre.

"They're going up the hill," he said. "In case help is needed . . . In case someone is injured . . ."

"Be careful," I said.

In the kitchen, breakfast was being prepared for the children who were now waking up, one after another, their voices chiming merrily from inside the house.

I sat with them while they ate, dreading Fosco and Melchiorre's return. In the middle of the meal, there was a droning roar overhead and when I went to the window I saw two Allied aircraft heading down the valley. The children carried on eating as if nothing had happened and I sat down again, asking myself whether I would let them down as I had Bruno and his flock.

They had gone off to the classroom by the time Fosco and Melchiorre came back. I could tell what had happened from their faces; they didn't need to say a word.

"How many did they get?" Pritchett asked.

"All eight," Fosco replied, his voice a whisper.

"Where are they?"

"We carried the guards into the house. They're all there now. Some were shot in their sleep . . ."

"And the hostages?"

"Gone."

There was silence. I felt I had failed them all. Not only Bruno and the partisans but Fosco and Melchiorre as well. Everyone.

"There was nothing you could do," said Pritchett finally. "Nothing."

There was a strange urgency in his voice so I assumed he was addressing me rather than Fosco and Melchiorre although he didn't look at me.

The farmhands fetched the bodies. Signor Grandinetti and Kristín made sure the children were nowhere near when they brought them. The priest was in Montepulciano, but we couldn't postpone their burial, not in this heat, and not when the Germans might come back any minute. We couldn't risk them catching us with the bodies.

Signor Grandinetti read a passage from the Bible, but I couldn't take my eyes off Bruno in your green sweater, which was now torn and bloody. We should have cleaned them, I said to myself, at least their faces. Of course that wouldn't have changed anything, but still I regretted it and kept torturing myself for the rest of the day, overcome with unbearable sadness.

HE WAS WAITING FOR HER AT THE STUDIO WHEN SHE arrived. He had put the new arrival on an easel and was sitting in front of it, but got up as soon as she came in. She sensed that he'd been thinking about this moment, wondering what to say to her when she walked through the door.

"Kristín," he said. "It's a Caravaggio."

She took off her coat.

"I know. I was here to receive it."

"An unknown Caravaggio." His voice was solemn but quivered with excitement.

"Are you sure about that?"

He controlled himself, didn't scold her for questioning him, answering in the most sincere way possible, "Yes, I'm sure. There is only a record of about sixty of his works. Who knows how many have been lost to time or lie forgotten in a monastery or a palazzo somewhere? This is a godsend, Kristín. This one we can save."

She walked over to the easel.

"It's in bad shape," she said.

"But you can restore it. You are capable of it."

"I was planning to leave when I completed the *Madonna and Child*. I'm almost done."

He cleared his throat. She knew he was now ready to deliver the speech he had practiced.

"Kristín, I owe you an apology. My feelings for you . . . I don't have to tell you. I never intended to deceive you, but I never found the courage either to sort things out. I don't blame you for being angry and disappointed . . . You're young. You've got your whole life ahead of you. Only time will tell whether you'll become a great artist—I'm being completely honest with you now—but you're already a remarkable restorer. That is a rare gift that you shouldn't discount. If not for me, then for history, Kristín. For art, for posterity, for Caravaggio himself. There is no one I can ask but you."

She didn't say anything. For what seemed like a long time, she stood still looking at her painting, listening to the echo of his words in her mind. Only time will tell . . .

He walked to the easel and pointed at the painting, almost touching it.

"Look at this. The light falling on her shoulders, the shadows touching her face, the unmistakable genius in every stroke . . . Come, look . . ."

She didn't move.

"How much will you get for it?"

He was taken by surprise. She had never discussed money with him.

"Kristín . . ."

"How much?"

"If you don't want to work on it, I'll do it myself."

"No, you won't. There is too much repainting involved."

He looked at her. This time she didn't look away.

"I'll pay you 10 percent," he said finally, forcing a smile.

"You will be able to concentrate on your art without worrying about finances for a long, long time."

As she nodded, she saw his relief. He took a step toward her, stopping when she raised her hand.

"On condition that you stay away from me until I've finished."

She worked tirelessly for weeks, immersing herself in her own masterpiece of deception. What a joy it was to get reacquainted with the tools and the colors, the brushes, the spatula, the pumice, what a triumph to have gotten this far and know she was in full control. She worked as winter maintained its hold on the city, as the war escalated, and the end drew near. She tried to ignore anything that might distract her, waging her own war with brush, palette, and hatred. The Allies were approaching from the south, and hundreds of thousands of refugees poured into the city from the war zones and the coastal towns to the west and the east. Conditions grew more wretched by the day. The water supply to people's homes was turned off and the citizens stood in long queues at the city's fountains with containers of all shapes and sizes, while street vendors pushed handcarts through the residential areas, selling jugs of water at extortionate prices. Coal was unobtainable, the gas supply ran out, and power cuts were threatened. When the air-raid sirens blared their warning, she stayed put. When the people in the canteen talked of executions and German atrocities, she tried to close her ears. She had to stay on course, whatever the cost.

He kept his promise and did not come to the studio during the day while she was working but she assumed that Signorina Pirandello informed him the moment she left in the evening. She sometimes caught the scent of him in the morning when she came to work, and once she had the impression that the picture had been moved on the easel.

She started with the damaged background before moving to the bracelet and the pearl necklace of which only the outlines were visible. She hadn't thought she had to do much repair on the lower half of the body but she had no choice since the cracks she had produced were too severe. That was also the case in the shaft of light high up on the wall as well as in the hands and the hairpin. She painted the face last of all, slowly summoning her courage and focusing her energy before mixing her colors and picking up her brush.

The photograph Kristín used for the face had been taken of her in Copenhagen. She had her hair tied back and was turning away from the camera. She had made Maria, her model, turn her head in just the same way, repeatedly consulting the photograph to make sure the young woman's composure was right. Kristín wasn't easily recognizable in the photograph. One cheek was invisible, the other in half shadow, her hair lighter and longer. A student at the Academy had taken the picture on a rainy day; Kristín had just come in from the street after having spent the morning trying to start her final assignment, desperately wanting to paint the pond and the swan taking off into the air and the girl in the yellow dress wading into the pond, but having no success. She didn't want to pose but her friend grabbed her and begged her to do him a favor. In the photograph she was thinking of the swan and the pond and the sky above the pond and the bird disappearing into the sky. She must have opened her mouth when she thought of the cold water touching her legs.

He should be able to recognize her. That's what she told herself. He should if he had thought about her half as much as she had thought about him, his image constantly in her mind, every expression, a record of every mood. He should be paying special attention to the face since there hadn't been one for her to restore, he should be searching for her solution, looking through the shadows, feeling the presence of the face he had held so often in his palms.

What would he say? Smile perhaps and take the opportunity to establish a bond? "Brilliant, Kristín. So subtle, so perfectly executed. This will be our little secret."

She didn't really have much left to do when the painting vanished. Nothing essential, only minor improvements around the head, a subtle touching-up of the shaft of light on the wall and one of the pearls in the necklace. Nothing that anyone but she would notice. She had turned on the light and hung her coat in the closet when she noticed the empty easel. She searched frantically around the studio, running into the storeroom, pulling one canvas after another from the racks before running down the stairs to the office.

Signorina Pirandello must have expected her but still was not prepared. She stammered, fidgeting with the pen in her hands, avoiding Kristín's gaze. Kristín lost her temper. It was as if she was standing outside herself, watching from a distance as she yelled at Signorina Pirandello who, in the end, did not dare withhold the information.

"They came earlier this morning," she blurted out. "The soldiers waited outside in the car. Mr. Hofer carried the painting down himself. Mr. Marshall didn't have a choice . . ."

"Hofer? He sold it to Walter Hofer? Hermann Göring's agent?"

Signorina Pirandello looked inadvertently at her desk. The document was still fresh, the signatures newly dried at the bottom of the page. Kristín picked it up.

"The Count wanted too much money. He's a very unreasonable man . . ."

Kristín didn't reply. She was reading the sales agreement and Marshall's letter of authentication that was attached to it.

"And they have a copy too?"

"Yes, of course. They insisted that everything be put in writing."

Kristín ran out and didn't even bother fetching her coat. It was cold but she didn't feel it, not stopping till she got to Marshall's house. She didn't greet the maid who opened the door, simply insisted that she needed to talk to Marshall, who appeared a moment later. He took her arm and led her into his office where he offered her a seat. She would not sit but took a step toward him and demanded he bring the painting back.

"The buyer was in a hurry. There is nothing I can do."

"You sold it to Hofer."

He was taken aback that Signorina Pirandello had revealed this information and responded carefully after a brief hesitation.

"The work has been sold. Your restoration was first-rate. I was just about to walk over to tell you that. You deserve your full 10 percent for this effort, Kristín. It was absolutely first-rate. I will settle up with you tomorrow."

"You have to get it back," she said. "Or . . ."

She broke off. He waited.

"You can't work on it forever," he said at last. "Your restoration is a work of art, but all artists have to let go eventually. Even Caravaggio himself . . ."

She was not ready for a lecture, not now.

"You sold it to the Germans," she interrupted. "You didn't even use a middleman."

"I sold it to an art lover who happens to be German."

"We both know what you did and now there is documentation to prove it both in your hands and theirs. The Allies will find out. What do you think they'll do to an Englishman who's collaborating with the Germans? Or the partisans to someone who's been selling national treasures to the enemy?"

"The Germans may be retreating, but the war is far from over, Kristín. This isn't something you need to concern yourself with."

"I want to see it."

"Pardon me?"

"One last time. That's the least you can do for me."

"I'll try."

"When?"

Later she tried to imagine how the conversation might have ended if there hadn't been a knock on the door. She could never make up her mind.

"Kristín," Flora said, "it's ages since I last saw you. Is everything all right?"

"Kristín's just finished an important assignment," Marshall said. "Very important."

Flora smiled.

"May I offer you something?"

"She was just leaving," Marshall said.

They escorted her to the door. The sound of children's voices carried from inside the apartment, happy and carefree.

Flora took her hand. Her smile had vanished, and her expression was unreadable.

"Good-bye, Kristín."

Halfway down the steps Kristín stopped and looked back. Marshall had gone inside, but Flora was standing on the landing, watching her. It suddenly dawned on Kristín that she knew.

Flora's eyes followed her outside. Down the street, across the square, home. They stayed with her for the rest of the day, followed her into the evening and her restless dreams. She had never seen such contempt.

How long had she known? How long had she been pretending?

TWO DAYS LATER SIGNORINA PIRANDELLO INFORMED Kristín that the Marshalls were gone. She was frantic when she knocked on Kristín's door at nine in the morning, tears streaming down her face as she repeated again and again, "He didn't even tell me." They had fled in the night with suitcases and artwork, leaving everything else behind. She was crushed that he hadn't taken her into his confidence, the man around whom her world had revolved for so many years, crushed and terribly alone. She also maintained that she knew nothing about the painting's whereabouts, but in that regard Kristín was skeptical. She kept pressing her, pleading with her at first but when that didn't work threatening her and her nephew with exposure. Signorina Pirandello was shocked ("How could you after everything I've done for you . . .") but, seeing how upset and determined Kristín was, she couldn't take the chance. There was news of the Allies attacking the German defense line south of Rome, and some said it was only a matter of time before they would liberate the city.

"Mr. Hofer insisted. Mr. Marshall had no choice. His concern was for the painting. Mr. Hofer wanted him to persuade his friend to store other works as well but Mr. Marshall said this was all he could ask her. I told him he should have paid the Count. I told him . . ."

"Where is it?"

"With Marchesa Orsini at San Martino. Between Siena and Lake Trasimeno. The Germans have been moving their art north, out of harm's way."

On her way out, Kristín turned around.

"Did he say anything about the face?"

"Pardon me?"

"The face. Did he say anything about it?"

"No."

She didn't leave immediately. She had the impulse from the moment Signorina Pirandello gave up the location but not the strength. Maybe he would return, she said to herself, maybe the Allies wouldn't succeed, maybe the painting wasn't even at San Martino any longer.

She was at her wit's end, unable to sleep at night, a shadow of herself by day. She would go regularly to the studio to see if there was any news of him, only to listen to Signorina Pirandello's desperate complaints and disappointments. Twice she walked over to his house and stood outside, looking up at the darkened windows. He was gone. She sensed that she would never see him again.

At the end of May, she couldn't bear it anymore. The Allies had finally fought through the Winter Line south of Rome and were advancing toward the city. She didn't know what she would do once she got to San Martino, but she told herself that anything was better than the crippling guilt and anxiety. She packed in a hurry before she would change her mind yet again and ran to the train station.

It was hot and airless in the carriage and their progress was slow. She was exhausted but couldn't get a seat until she had been traveling for two hours. She fell asleep with her suitcase in her arms. Opposite her sat a man in a dark suit with a cigarette in one hand and a soft drink in the other.

She didn't notice his eyes until after the explosion when he was lying on the floor with the cigarette burning beside him. His eyes were large and colorless and looked as if they were staring at her through a thin, watery film. His hand was still clamped on the bottle and for some reason she grabbed it as she fled the burning carriage.

She has now looked for her Caravaggio all over the villa and in the neighboring buildings. In the *fattoria*, the corn store, the greenhouses, the sheds, the clinic. In the old mill and the chapel. She steals the opportunity to search during the day when she is alone, or wakes up in the night and wanders about while the others are sleeping. She is careful and so far no one has spotted her except Melchiorre one night when he was standing guard. She told him she couldn't sleep and needed some fresh air. He didn't ask any questions and she stayed with him for a while outside the back door, both silently gazing out into the night. Pointing up at the sky, he named a few stars and their hands touched. Nothing more.

She has looked all over the house, even in Alice's and Pritchett's bedrooms. And she searched Giovanni's room before the children from Chiusi arrived; twice, in fact, because she felt so uncomfortable about being there that she had to give up in midsearch the first time.

She has begun to despair and sometimes when she is lying awake at night, pursuing her unruly thoughts, she worries that Signorina Pirandello has either lied to her or been misinformed. But then she comes to her senses and ponders yet again all the places where the painting might be hidden, telling herself yet again that she has to find it before the Allies arrive and discover it or the Germans take it with them on their retreat, making it impossible for her ever to get her hands on it. The booms of explosions sound from beyond Monte Amiata but in the valley the fog is lit by the moon. The whirring of the cicadas is loud and frantic, and there is no breath of wind.

She intends to search the barn again and also the sheds at the bottom of the slope. She mustn't give up hope. Leaving the courtyard, she picks her way along the track toward the greenhouse. The gravel crunches underfoot and the cypresses cast long, thin shadows across the path in the moonlight. Doubt dogs her heels, whispering that her search is futile, that her journey from Rome has been in vain, that she can't save Marshall, who will inevitably be prosecuted. She counters with the usual objections: if she destroys the painting, the only proof that it ever existed will be the documents, the sales agreement and authentication, which they may never find. "Unlikely," that's the word she uses: which they are unlikely to ever find. The voice that used to whisper that he didn't deserve her efforts to save him from disaster has fallen silent.

She opens the door to the greenhouse where the lemon trees are stored in winter and lights the lantern. Her leg is aching but she ignores it. The backdrop that the children made for the play has been taken down but is still stored in the corner along with the empty flowerpots and gardening tools. The building smells of earth and stone, and all the windows are open to the night air. Although she searches the storeroom again and peers around for new hiding places, she knows it is pointless. Yet she persists in her search, going from the greenhouse to the shed beside the chapel, from the shed to the stables, pursuing her despair until eventually she gives up and sinks down in the hay with the horses. She is still sitting there in the soft hay next to the animals when she hears the Germans arrive, and she does not even try to get up.

WE LEAPT OUT OF BED, OUR HEADS STILL FULL OF unfinished dreams, as if a bomb had fallen or a storm had struck. Everything happened at once—the night watchman yelled, the back door was flung open, the roar of engines filled the house. Melchiorre, who had been on guard, was standing in the hall, impotently watching two soldiers who had forced their way in through the back door and were now opening the front door for their comrades.

"*Entschuldigung*," I said, but they didn't give me so much as a glance. Perhaps they didn't even hear me.

First to arrive were the paratroopers, followed by the artillery, with the sappers bringing up the rear. We had been warned about the paratroopers and not without reason: they are brutes. The majority of them bear the marks of having spent months at the front, though perhaps it is the glow from the acetylene lamps that makes them appear even more menacing. Their clothes are torn and filthy, their faces dirty, their eyes sunken with exhaustion. We stand at the foot of the stairs, not daring to go any closer. I try to attract their attention but when no one answers, Pritchett eventually steps forward to ask who's in charge. He is shoved aside, however, because they have just brought a field telephone into the house, and some of the soldiers go straight into the drawing room and slam the apparatus down on the first table they come across. They start pouring into the house in groups, yelling and shouting, charging around and completely ignoring us. The front door is open, and outside in the darkness I can see one vehicle after another coming up the hill. I go outside.

What a sight! The house is surrounded by cars and trucks, some so battered that I can't understand how they made it up the hill. One of them is on fire and when the soldiers drive Melchiorre off to fetch a hose, he doesn't dare refuse. There are two tanks beside the villa; they have been driven into the garden, over flower beds and shrubs, and the soldiers are standing up inside them, apparently lacking the presence of mind to climb out. The moon dips in and out of the clouds and the whole scene is like a bad dream.

When I finally spot the officers, I hurry over to them. There are two; one from a parachute regiment, I find out later, the other artillery. They are quarreling fiercely and don't stop until I'm right beside them.

"*Entschuldigung*," I say again, but get no further because the parachute officer interrupts.

"We need the buildings. You must leave."

I'm speechless but somehow manage to stammer: "Where can we go?"

"You see to her," he says to the artillery officer and stalks off.

"There are children here," I begin. "Orphans. We can't go . . ."

He takes off his cap and rubs his forehead. He's of medium height, neither fat nor thin; his expression is blank.

"There will be fighting here," he says. "Have you made any plans for moving the children?"

"Where can we take them?" I ask.

"You have two choices," he says. "Neither of them good. You can either take them down to the cellar and hope it will hold or else dig trenches in the forest. In my view the forest is safer but of course that could change like everything else."

"Where is the front line now?" I ask.

He looks at me as if I'm completely ignorant.

"This is it."

Total chaos reigns inside the villa. The soldiers are charging around, and the children are terrified. Signor Grandinetti and a maid are trying to comfort those who are in tears. Pritchett is standing by the door to the room where they sleep, denying the soldiers access. Some of them look as if they are ready to lay hands on him but something holds them back, at least for the moment. I go up to my room and dress in frantic haste. I'm in the bathroom when I hear someone come in. Returning to the bedroom, I see that one of the soldiers is halfway across the room. I ask what he wants and he leaves without answering. After watching him retreat downstairs, I lock the door to my room.

The harbinger of dawn is visible in the east, a faint gray luster. Some of the soldiers have flung themselves down on the floor and fallen asleep despite the hubbub. The air is thick with cigarette smoke, the floor muddy from all the tramping feet, and there is a stench of men who have not washed for days, if not weeks.

Pritchett is facing a tricky situation in the kitchen where the soldiers are demanding food. I call the artillery officer and after some wrangling we persuade him that the children should be fed first. Then we will see what we can do for the soldiers.

"We don't have food for all these men," I say. "You must understand that."

"I can't be answerable for them if they don't get something to eat," he says, and it is clear that this is neither an exaggeration nor a threat.

The artillery men make their preparations for the day. The guns have been set up under the trees in the garden, and the soldiers are hard at it chopping down young cypresses to camouflage the trucks and tanks. I wander around the buildings, watching the countryside emerge from the darkness of night, crawling with troops. They have taken over the garden and are still streaming up the hill from the road in the valley or down the slopes from the east, some on foot, others on horseback. Signorina Harris approaches across the courtyard accompanied by two men she's been caring for in the clinic and takes them into the kitchen. Apart from this, our people stay indoors.

I make my way to the chapel. The doors are half open and I am of two minds about whether to lock them. When I approach, I hear the muffled sound of voices and see two soldiers praying before the altar. They don't notice me and, turning away, I walk across the courtyard and in through the back door.

The morning passes swiftly. We give the children breakfast, then hand over an agreed ration of food to the Germans—bread, eggs, and shoulders of pork. An army chaplain who arrived in one of the last trucks has been ordered to liaise with us, to my great relief. He is a Franciscan missionary, Father Augusto, and does not seem the fanatical type. He advises us not to leave any valuables lying around and to make sure that the girls and women do not go anywhere unaccompanied. He also urges us to bake as much bread as possible as this will reduce the soldiers' need for food that is harder for us to spare. We take him at his word and the aroma of baking bread now wafts through the courtyard from the ovens in the *fattoria*, utterly at odds with the surrounding scenes of turmoil.

There is fighting farther down the valley; we see the planes descending from the clouds over the slopes of Monte Amiata and hear the distant booming of guns and the crackle of machine-gun fire. It won't be long before the fighting reaches us. The Germans are everywhere on the retreat, and the army chaplain says that they have suffered heavy losses. The clouds continue to gather, forming a gray roof over the valley; we can only see halfway up the hills above the buildings, and ribbons of fog, torn from the base of the clouds, hang in the trees. As the morning passes, people from the tenant farms and properties to the east of us start coming down the slope, materializing out of the clouds, some on horseback but most on foot with their children in their arms and packs on their backs, bewildered and frightened. A crowd has formed in the courtyard by the back door and is growing by the minute. We give the people bread and something to drink but advise them to turn around and go home because there is no room for any more here and we are more likely to come under attack than are the outlying farms. Few object, not in front of the crowd, not until they get a chance to talk to us privately. Pritchett and I listen and try to comfort them, but this is not easy.

The farmer from one of the outlying farms says that the Germans have taken both his cows and emptied his pantry; another complains that they have stolen his donkey, his cart, and his food. We nod, then urge them to return home with their families and keep their heads down for the next few days. It is not until we begin to walk away that those who have suffered the worst losses step forward.

The farmer from Fontalgozzo, a small property highest up

the hill, speaks so quietly that we have to strain to hear the
words. As he begins to weep, I feel the strength sapping from
my body and my stomach shrinking inside me.

His son was engaged to his neighbor's daughter. I've known
them since they were children; they were going to be married
in the autumn. This morning the boy encountered two soldiers
who had dragged the girl off with the intention of raping her.
When he tried to come to her rescue, they shot him. His father
carried his body into the house where he is still lying, and his
mother refuses to leave him. His fiancée is here with the crowd
in the courtyard, he explains when we ask after her, along with
her mother and two younger sisters.

"Can we bury him in your cemetery?"

The request catches me unprepared. They still have to fetch
the body and bring it down here. By then it will be midday, if
they are not held up, and the fighting will have started. But I
can't refuse him, although I explain that they will have to take
care of it themselves, as we have neither the manpower nor the
time to help them.

He leaves him, and Pritchett and I watch them go. We do
not speak and are still standing there after he has disappeared
from sight; it is not until Signor Grandinetti comes running up
that we recover our senses.

"Kristín's missing," he says.

"What?" I exclaim.

"No one's seen her this morning."

We follow him into the house, slipping past the soldiers,
climbing over discarded clothes, ammunition, and rubbish,
hurrying as fast as we can to the dining room where Schwester
Marie and the farmhands are waiting for us with the children.
Schwester Marie tries to keep them amused while we discuss

what to do and, strange as it may seem, she succeeds in holding their attention.

Melchiorre and Giorgio go in search of Kristín, while Fosco, Signor Grandinetti, and Schwester Marie lead the children down to the cellar since the bombs are now falling close enough to rattle the windowpanes.

"We're going to play hide-and-seek!" they cry.

Just as Pritchett is about to leave the room, I hear myself say, "Do you think he's ever coming back?"

He comes over and puts his arms around me, laying his right hand against my cheek and pulling me against him. We are standing like this in the middle of the dining room, both exhausted although the day has hardly begun, when the first bomb falls on our hill.

A WARNING, NO MORE FOR THE MOMENT. ONE BOMB, of medium size, that fell on the uncultivated land halfway up the slope, leaving behind a crater a meter deep in the ground and terror in people's hearts. The Germans respond with a barrage of counterfire, but the plane has disappeared. The cloud cover sinks lower and lower, turning the world gray: buildings and sky, soldiers and vehicles. We are out in the forest, racing to dig a trench ten meters long in which we can take refuge with the children if the cellar fails to hold. Two soldiers help us, both artillerymen. The trees too are gray, the ground dry and hard. The sky is lit up with flashes in the distance and the air is heavy, humid, and still. Progress is slow. Pritchett tells me to go inside and rest, but physical labor does me good. I enjoy sweating and feeling my muscles grow tired; it provides a respite from thought.

I take a break at noon and go back to the house. It's a ten-minute walk and Pritchett insists that one of the workmen accompany me. As I approach the buildings, I see Melchiorre and Giorgio crossing the courtyard with Kristín between them. I hurry over, imagining the worst when they say they found her lying in the stable. She seems distracted and doesn't look me in the eye. She says nothing until I suggest that she go and take a rest, at which point she shakes her head and apologizes repeatedly, so quietly that the words are barely audible, and for what I don't know.

"I want to go to the children," she says, but instead of answering her, I ask the farmhands to go and help with digging the trench. Then I lead her to the back door.

My own hand is not large but hers is lost in my palm. It is cold and when I ask her what she was doing in the stable, her hand begins to tremble.

"I failed," she says. "I gave up."

Not understanding what she means, I hastily try to comfort her.

"They'll be happy to see you," I say, taking her arm and leading her up to her room. "You must rest. I'll ask Signorina Harris to look in on you."

But she won't lie down. Instead, she stands in the middle of the room with an anguished expression on her face, clenching and releasing her fingers and staring into space.

"I'll ask her to look in on you," I repeat on my way out.

"Alice," she says again, "I failed . . . I did a terrible thing . . ."

I pity her but I can't stay with her any longer.

"Rest," I say. "It'll get better."

Signorina Harris is in the clinic and I ask one of the maids to fetch her before heading down to the cellar to check on the children. They are busy putting on another performance of *Snow White;* the set and costumes have been brought in from the greenhouse and Signor Grandinetti has dug out the script and started to rehearse the group again. A little girl comes up to me as I stand at the bottom of the stairs and says, "There'll be more people to watch than last time."

Dear children. Whatever is to come, we mustn't let anything happen to them.

On my way up from the cellar I come face-to-face with Kristín. The nurse can't possibly have seen her yet; Kristín hasn't even waited for her. She doesn't look at me as she slips past, but I notice that she pauses for an instant on the bottom step before joining the group. Then I hear their cries of joy and understand why she didn't wait for the nurse but hurried straight down to the children in the cellar, to their healing innocence.

In the afternoon it rains. At first it is only a fine mist, but then it grows heavier and soon it is falling in a dense, unchanging curtain. The German soldiers are waiting either beside the guns they have set up under the trees in the garden or in the trucks; there is condensation on the cab windows and from time to time a hand emerges to tap the ash from a cigarette. The rain drums on the hoods of the vehicles and on the paving stones of the terrace, or vanishes into the sea of leaves with a low hiss. Our world shrinks; visibility is now down to the middle of the hillside, the fields are lost in the gloom, and the road is far beyond our horizon. The rain gushes from the eaves of the buildings, runs in rivulets along the walls, and collects in large puddles that reflect the gray sky. The soldiers wait.

They have finished digging the trench and at intervals have inserted pieces of wood onto which they have fastened a waterproof awning. Not that it helps much in this rain; water pours into the trench and the thought of huddling there with the children is terrible. Melchiorre takes a cow into the forest and tethers her to a tree beside the trench so that we won't run short of milk.

The fighting has drawn closer. We have lost contact with the outside world, but Father Augusto tells me that the Allied infantry is now approaching Contignano on the other side of the valley and a little farther down. The Germans need reinforcement, so it comes as no surprise when half the artillery starts preparing for departure. I am relieved to see the guns dragged out of the garden and the trucks starting up, the tanks crawling down the hill.

I am just about to go in the back door to talk to the cook about supper when I see them coming down the slope above the chapel. Although I can only make out vague shadows, I know immediately that it is the family from Fontalgozzo and their neighbors who have come to bury the young man. I hurry across the courtyard toward them. My shoes squelch and I can't get the noise out of my ears when I come to a halt beside them.

The farmers lead the way, their womenfolk follow, and three young men bring up the rear with the body. They stare at me without saying a word, drenched, shoulders bowed, and in the end I am the one to break the silence.

"Won't you come inside while the grave is being dug?"

I direct my words to the women, and they glance at one another but then his fiancée answers, "No thank you, I want to stay with him."

And then neither the mothers nor the sisters will budge either, so I say, "All right, I'll ask the farmhands to help you."

The fathers have brought their own spades; they've carried them all the way here.

"Will you show us where can we bury him?" his father asks.

I fetch Fosco, seizing some lanterns on the way, and then head up to the cemetery with the families. We move slowly to avoid slipping in the mud; the rain has grown heavier, if anything, and the twilight has now deepened into darkness that presses in on the feeble gleam of the lanterns. They have dressed the dead man in his Sunday best and wrapped him in a blanket that is now soaking wet and heavy. The young men pause, wring out the blanket, then lay it over the body again. They catch their breath and their fathers look back to ask if they need help. They shake their heads and carry on. The light flickers, casting our shadows into the gloom; the cemetery lies ahead, beyond it the forest and endless darkness.

Close to Giovanni's grave is an empty plot under a large olive tree. I often sit there on hot afternoons. It is a beautiful plot, with a view that is just as fine as the one from my son's grave—between the tall cypress trees and over the fields and the river down in the valley. I show them the way there and the men start digging; Fosco and the fathers first while the young men lay the body on the stone wall. I move closer to my son, talking to him in silence as I watch them dig, the young men taking the spades from their fathers. I tell him everything will be all right, repeating those words again and again, terribly afraid that it's a lie. The women move over to the body, the mother holding a lantern, the fiancée drawing the blanket off his face. His eyes are closed and she brushes his hair from his brow and the rainwater from his cheeks and then starts shaking. Unable to watch, I walk into the darkness.

Our priest has not been seen for two days. Pritchett has heard that he is trapped in Montepulciano; I hope that's right and that he will stay there. I fetch Father Augusto and ask him to accompany me to the cemetery, telling him what's happened on the way.

They are just finishing the digging when we arrive. Fosco has fetched Melchiorre and they have brought a coffin from the workshop and placed it on the path by the grave. The boys lift the body from the wall, unwrap it from the blanket, and lay it in the coffin. The young man's mother kneels on the ground and tidies his jacket and shirt, saying something I can't hear. Is it different losing your son to violence rather than illness? I ask myself. Is it different losing him when he's grown? Or is the pain always the same? The never-ending, unbearable pain.

They stand in a tight knot while the army chaplain performs the last rites. His words briefly interrupt the noise of the rain, which enfolds us again as soon as he falls silent.

I walk back to the buildings with him once the ceremony is over. The families remain behind by the grave. I offered them lodging but I don't know if they will accept. Looking back, I see in the glow of the lanterns that they have not moved.

EVERYTHING HAS BEEN TURNED UPSIDE DOWN IN the rooms occupied by the Germans. There are scraps of food all over the place, and the floors and furniture are filthy. Wet overcoats lie in heaps on the floor and tables, underwear hangs from washing lines rigged between a bookcase and window in one instance and two light fittings in another. The air is filled with the sour odor of our guests and the cigarettes they smoke. My stomach turns as I hurry from the kitchen to the stairs, trying to look neither right nor left.

My room has been broken into. The few pieces of jewelry I kept there have vanished, along with two silver bowls, a vase my mother gave me, and the picture frames on my dressing table. The photographs lie on the floor, having been torn from their frames with little ceremony. I pick them up; one is of you and me just after we had moved here, taken by the front door; the other is of our newborn son. I'm wiping the dust off them when I see out of the corner of my eye something lying on the floor near where I hide my diary. I panic, thinking for a moment that the loose tiles have been discovered but to my relief, when I walk closer, I see that it's only a piece of paper.

My diary is still in its hiding place, but when I pick up the tiles, I realize how insanely risky it is to keep it there. People have been executed in the past few days for far more trivial crimes than those the Germans would accuse me of if they got hold of it. And not only me but everyone in this household and many of the farmers. How can I have been so irresponsible?

I picture the parachute commander with the book in his hands, see him turning the pages attentively, reading not only about our assistance to the partisans and the Allied soldiers but also about you and me, Giovanni and Connor. I pick it up, shove it in my pocket, and hurry downstairs, past the living rooms and through the kitchen, not answering when Pritchett asks where I'm going, not stopping until I'm out in the courtyard. It's still raining and I stand momentarily at a loss, then cross the courtyard in the direction of the cemetery. I don't have a lantern with me and can hardly see the hand in front of my face, but I keep going until I reach Giovanni's grave.

The ground is wet and I pick up a spade along the way and dig a deep hole by my son's headstone and place the book in the hole, having wrapped it in a thick cloth. I stand over the hole once I've finished filling it in and ask myself whether it's in any way justifiable to hide my secrets in the ground with him. Then I pull myself together and leave, not even realizing that I'm still carrying the spade until I reach the gate, where I put it down.

When I return, I see a crowd of German soldiers walking up the slope to the house. A whole platoon of thirty or forty men, leading a goat and two donkeys they have stolen. The donkeys are loaded with plunder, and the sight would be ridiculous if the men didn't look so threatening. The artillery officer comes out into the drive and addresses them brusquely, whereupon their ringleader answers with a distinct lack of respect. There is an angry exchange after which the soldier falls silent while the officer reprimands him. To my disbelief, the altercation ends with the officer inviting them inside.

The crowd in the kitchen has grown. The people from the outlying farms whom we told to go home have returned and now tell us that they have been hiding in caves on the western boundary of the property. They are wet, hungry, and exhausted, men and women, children and babies, and Pritchett is at his wit's end. He no longer tries to hide his distress, none of us do, and he asks over the heads of the crowd as I come in, "Alice, what are we to do?"

He doesn't usually address me by my Christian name in the presence of other people and his plaintiveness immediately spurs me to action. I tell the people that we will open both the chapel and the parts of the *fattoria* that are habitable—the garage, the corn store beside the bakery, and the cellar under the olive press. I take part of the crowd to the chapel while Pritchett takes the rest to the *fattoria*, leaving the youngest children and their mothers to go down to the cellar with the other children. The farmhands take the remaining blankets and rugs, as well as some bread and water, to the chapel and the *fattoria*.

The night passes slowly. The children are all in the cellar with Schwester Marie, Signor Grandinetti, Kristín, and the mothers from the tenant farms. I had planned to sleep in my own room but lose my nerve. There's a tremendous racket from the living rooms and endless comings and goings, and when I knock on Pritchett's door, it turns out that he hasn't gone to bed either. We go down to the cellar, taking along pillows and quilts, and try to get some sleep there.

I must have dropped off for a few minutes, no more. My head feels boiling hot and my mind won't stop racing. I think about you and Giovanni and my mistakes and Marshall's painting and the diary I have buried with our son. I know I should have burned it, but it's all I have left of our son and possibly of you as well. For I've begun to doubt that I will ever see you again.

Giovanni's face appears to me again and again in my dreams. When I come to, I discover that I've reached out a hand to touch him. I am slow to pull it back; it's still dark and I can't hear the same racket as earlier from upstairs. But I can hear something else, a buzzing, and I can't work out where it's coming from at first. I strain my ears, trying to empty my mind and concentrate, then rise up a little and sit quite still until the buzzing separates out and the words become distinguishable.

He is lying against the wall a short way from me, rattling off verses from *Snow White and the Seven Dwarfs*. Again and again, though he does not stumble over the lines and seems to have no need of further practice, his voice soft and expressionless.

> *The bird sings merrily for you,*
> *Fair Snow White.*
> *The sun shines gaily on your cheek,*
> *The south wind kisses you,*
> *Fair Snow White,*
> *Snow White good and fair . . .*

Over and over again in the darkness, never raising his voice, never pausing before beginning again. I recognize the voice; he is six years old, his name is Mario and he's an orphan from Turin. I want to go over and take him in my arms but I refrain because the floor is covered with sleeping bodies and there would be no hope of crossing it without waking the others. The voice contains no hint of fear, no hint of anything but conscientiousness. He doesn't want to fail his fellow actors, doesn't want to see disappointment on Kristín's or Signor Grandinetti's face. "Fair Snow White, Snow White good and fair . . ."

I get up while it is still dark. Melchiorre and Fosco are both asleep on the kitchen floor, having pushed the chest of drawers against the door so the soldiers can't get in. The kettle on the stove is hot, so at least one of them must have been up recently, but now they are both sleeping as soundly as the children in the cellar. Dawn comes slowly; a reluctant gray light descends on the courtyard and enters diffidently through the windows. The clouds are departing, and there is a glimpse of blue sky above the *fattoria*. I turn up the heat under the kettle and make myself a cup of tea, at which point the men wake up and clamber to their feet. Still worn-out, they take a seat at the table and are sitting there when the plane flies over and the bomb lands in the garden.

The soldiers spring from their sleeping places, grab their weapons, and fire wildly after the plane even though it has vanished from sight. Everything is in turmoil. There are screams of terror and whimpers from the cellar and Pritchett suddenly emerges into the kitchen with the whole crowd on his heels. Those who were sleeping in the *fattoria* and chapel rush over the courtyard and in the back door, some only half-dressed. I try to calm them, but it is easier said than done while the soldiers keep up their futile counterfire; gradually, they lose heart and the guns fall silent.

We try to get our bearings. Standing up on a chair, I tell the people to stay where they slept while the cook and the maids prepare breakfast. They obey in the end but it takes some effort to persuade the children back down into the cellar.

I track down Father Augusto. He tells me that the Allies are no more than a mile away and are now trying to force their way down the hillside from Sarteano, but the Germans are still holding them for the moment. While we are talking, some soldiers arrive with the first prisoner of war, a turbaned Moroccan with a thick mustache who got separated from his troops. They have no sooner locked him in the shed than we hear an explosion from the forest to the west of the villa and shortly afterward a group of paratroopers appear, supporting two wounded comrades. They have trodden on a land mine that they themselves had planted. The army chaplain says that they started laying them yesterday and throws up his hands when I ask if it didn't occur to them to let us know.

"How are we to do our work?" I ask.

"There will be fighting here later today," he says. "The cellar is not safe and you can't go to the trench. There are land mines all around it. You'll have to get out of here."

"Where to?"

"The way I see it, you have no other choice than to try to get to Montepulciano since Radicofani and Contignano are in ruins like the other hill towns closest to the road."

"How are we to do that?"

"On foot. All vehicles will be targets."

"We'll talk to the officer," I say. "He said we'd be safe in the cellar."

"It's a waste of time," he replies.

I'm about to object when I see the officer coming out of the house. He peers down the road and shortly afterward the first tank appears, rattling and chugging up the drive. They have turned back and soon the vehicles that left yesterday reappear—some of them, at least. They are in an even worse state than before and I'm surprised they still work.

I don't spot the plane until it dives over the trucks. The crazy noise of the machine guns paralyzes me; unable to move my legs, or raise my hands to protect my head, I stand rooted to the spot as the bullets tear up the ground in front of me and smack into the vehicles at the top of the drive. The soldiers are no better; they remain frozen until the plane has gone. Then they leap into action, dragging their wounded comrades out of the vehicles and firing pointlessly into the air as seems to be their habit when they are panicked.

Father Augusto grabs my arm as Pritchett comes running to us.

"You have an hour, maybe less, before everything goes up in smoke here. Are you going to waste time running around in circles?"

I'm shocked. He sounds exactly like you.

"We must leave now," Pritchett insists. "I'll go over to the *fattoria*. You see to the children."

With that, he's gone.

"What will you do?" I ask the chaplain.

"I must stay here," he says.

He lays a hand on my shoulder and pushes me gently toward the kitchen.

"You must stick to the road," he says, "to avoid mines. Spread out so you don't attract the attention of the planes. Everyone looks the same from the air."

The orders we issued were clear, although we had to repeat them again and again: "Take nothing with you but the clothes you are wearing, water, and a bag of food. All adults must carry either food or a child. The bigger children are to carry blankets. Those who wish to remain behind must keep to the *fattoria*."

I myself fetch a bag and pack it with underwear, shoes, a bar of soap, and a photograph of you and Giovanni. Schwester Marie, Signor Grandinetti, and Kristín see to getting the children ready for the journey. More people want to come with us than I anticipated, but Pritchett decides in consultation with the fattore who should stay behind with him. I'm glad not to have to make that decision although I don't know whether it is better to go or stay.

Melchiorre and Giorgio are staying as is Kristín, whose leg isn't up to the trip. The cook too and three of the maids. The younger people from the farms want to leave but the older people do not trust themselves to make the journey. In the end around eighty of us set off down the drive with Signor Grandinetti in the lead, me in the middle, and Schwester Marie bringing up the rear.

Pritchett and Kristín escort us halfway down our road. He hugs me good-bye, his weary smile reassuring.

"The painting," I say, pulling him aside. "You can't let the Allies get it."

He's taken aback but doesn't say anything. I know what he's thinking.

"He's not the only one who's at risk," I add. "We cannot take any chances . . ."

He hugs me again, quickly this time, before letting me go.

"I'll take care of it," he says quietly.

The clouds are breaking up, and the sun dries the earth after the rain. A smell of baking bread wafts from the bakery, contrasting with the reek of cordite in the air and the stench of petrol that hits us as we walk past the tanks and armored vehicles in front of the buildings. The garden and forest beside the road are teeming with troops, but I notice that they haven't bothered to camouflage the vehicles with branches, as it is probably pointless at this stage.

It grows hotter as we descend into the valley. We no longer enjoy the shade of the trees that overhang the drive, and the clouds have now mostly disappeared, leaving the sky as blue and clear as if it had just been created during the night. We stop to rest before taking the valley road; I gaze up the slope at my home and find myself saying good-bye to it as if for the last time.

THE ROAD WAS HARD AND DUSTY, THE GRASS BY THE roadside dry and brittle, and the heat was merciless. After the first stretch, which was flat, the road began to climb a long slope and soon some of the children began to wilt. The road was widely pitted with craters and in the first hour I counted eight wrecked vehicles beside it. The bodies of German soldiers lay scattered at the foot of the hill; their numbers increased as we climbed higher, but here they had been gathered together and laid facedown, side by side. The shelling grew closer behind us and the crash of explosions tore the silence.

Some of the bodies were badly mutilated, and I ordered the children to keep their eyes down as we passed them. Most obeyed but some had begun to whimper when little Mario suddenly picked up where he had left off last night and began to recite his lines from *Snow White and the Seven Dwarfs*. The girl holding his hand chimed in, followed by the children next to them and so on until all the actors had joined in the recital. Seizing the opportunity, Signor Grandinetti started from the beginning, slipping in some songs that they all knew.

So we walked for the last hour up the slope and along the ridge until the road divided, one fork leading to Chianciano, the other to Montepulciano. Those who had friends or relatives in Chianciano headed that way, but the rest of us carried on, fifty in all, including some thirty children.

We hadn't been walking long when we heard rumbling behind us and shortly afterward some military transport vehicles came racing along the road. We retreated to the side but didn't dare go any farther for fear of land mines. The four trucks overtook us without slowing down and after they had gone past, we saw the mouths of the guns pointing out the back and the soldiers aiming them at the sky. A moment later a plane appeared in pursuit and we flung ourselves to the ground, pulling the children down with us as the shooting began, both from the plane and from the vehicles that drove for their lives off the road toward a farm at the foot of the hillside ahead. We were still lying motionless, not daring to move hand or foot, when the bomb dropped and almost simultaneously the plane was hit. We didn't see the plane until later when we had climbed the hill in front of us; it lay burning in the middle of the field a short way from the farm, while all the trucks were parked in the yard, except for one that lay overturned beside the road with no sign of life around it.

We didn't stop, but a dog came running toward us from the farm and pursued us a little way before turning back. It was a small mongrel that rubbed itself against the legs of one traveler after another, children and adults alike. There was no mistaking the fact that the thud of explosions was coming from the direction of San Martino. I thought about the people who had stayed behind and my son in the cemetery and the cow tethered to a tree in the forest. Strange as it may seem, when I suddenly remembered her plight, my heart lurched no less than it did at the thought of the people.

The road ahead undulated in the mirage. The heat was

unbearable, most of the children were complaining, and the youngest were all now being carried by adults. Some of the men were carrying two children; progress was slow and no one had the energy to sing anymore.

We decided to take the old track at the bottom of the hill instead of the new road that runs through a broad cornfield. It was not an easy decision because the old road is both steeper and stonier, as well as being a little longer. But we didn't regret it when a convoy of armored vehicles appeared shortly afterward in the valley, pursued by two planes that bombed the road and field incessantly until the vehicles were either in flames or careered into the cornfield where they soon came to a halt. The soldiers fled into the sea of corn in an attempt to hide, but they were plainly visible to us and we knew they would be to the pilots too. It was a terrible sight; they crawled, trying to save their lives, inching along as slowly and carefully as they could so as not to move the corn, in the belief that they were invisible. The planes flew in a great arc up the valley, metal gleaming in the sun, and for a moment it looked as if they would be swallowed up in the blueness. Then they returned, gradually lowering their altitude before releasing a hail of machine-gun fire into the corn. They repeated the maneuver twice, then vanished in the direction of San Martino, sunlight flashing on their wings.

We stood motionless in the hush after the attack, gazing over the field. I didn't have the presence of mind to cover the eyes of the children whose hands I was holding, or to instruct them to look away, but it probably wouldn't have helped even if I had. A few of our men set off half-running down the slope to the trucks. After trying to start some of them without success, they finally managed to get two going and drove up onto the road. They were about to turn around in order to drive up to us when a soldier crawled out of the corn and staggered into their path.

Only two of his comrades followed. Both were wounded, one apparently worse than the other. They were hurriedly helped into the back of the leading truck, which then set off toward us. We waited, watching the dust whirling up in the still air, floating over the road and drifting out over the field, until the vehicles came to a stop beside us.

Of course there was a risk that the planes would return and attack the trucks, but temptation overrode our fear because we were all on the point of collapse.

I made my way over to the soldiers as soon as we were moving, supporting myself on the iron frame that held up the canvas, and waited for my eyes to grow accustomed to the gloom. The injured men were lying down, and their comrade had torn up his jacket to bandage their wounds. One of them was fatally injured, a very young man, his eyes rolled back in his head, his thin lips trembling ceaselessly.

"Montepulciano?" He groaned, so faintly that it was barely audible.

"Yes," I said.

"We were on our way there," his comrade said, wiping his forehead with his torn jacket.

The trucks rattled along. Some of the children had fallen asleep as soon as we set off, and others were singing tunes from *Snow White*. One by one they fell silent, to be replaced by the jolting, the groans of the engine, and our fears. The badly wounded man beckoned to his companion to come closer and whispered something in his ear. His comrade didn't under-stand at first so he had to repeat his request. Then the other straightened up and said to me, "He asks if the children could sing some more."

We had taught those who spent Christmas with us to sing "O Tannenbaum" and "Stille Nacht," among other favorites, so now we reminded them of these carols and soon they were singing them as if nothing were more natural.

So we drove up the valley and over the hill to Montepulciano, in the heat and burning sunlight, with the soldier dying on the floor and the roar of explosions behind us, singing the same Christmas carols over and over again. We continued after he died. None of us stopped, neither his companions nor our party. His eyes were open and his lips were parted. From his expression you would have thought he was still listening.

WE'VE NOW BEEN IN MONTEPULCIANO FOR TWO days. The Allies have taken Castiglione and Rocca d'Orcia and are heading this way. From the veranda we can see the clouds of smoke over the valley and hear endless explosions, both nearby and in the distance. The Germans still control the village but are preparing to leave. They go around plundering and pillaging, forcing people out of their homes and grabbing everything of value that they can find.

I have been put up with Mayor Bracci, his wife, Margherita, together with four of our children. Our group has been dispersed around the village—three here, four there—and I check on them all twice a day. We are comfortable enough, despite the chronic food shortages and the lack of light or running water.

We have received no reliable news from San Martino. The uncertainty is driving me mad. There are rumors, of course, but none of them firsthand and all of them contradictory. We know that the fighting began the day we left but not whether it is still going on. We've had no news of our people. If I climb onto the veranda wall, I can just make out the hill above our house in the distance. It is blue and hazy in the heat and the longer I stare, the more it seems to recede. Sometimes I think I can see smoke rising from it.

In the afternoon the Germans blow up several houses in the village to make the streets inaccessible. They also destroy the magnificent gate that has greeted locals and travelers since the days of Lorenzo Medici, but the German army is in such disarray that they get their vehicles stuck in the rubble and can't get back into the village. From the veranda, we watch them, as well as their comrades down in the valley who plant dynamite on the bridge over the river before tramping back up the hill in the afternoon sun.

At dusk, retreating soldiers start pouring into the village. The last rays of the sun fade on the rooftops, and below in the narrow streets the shadows swiftly deepen and intensify. The soldiers' footsteps are heavy; they pass in silence. During the night the explosions come closer. I cannot sleep; the moon shines uninterruptedly through my window, and when I get up to pull the curtains, I end up staring forever into the distance. Are my people safe? Have they been spared? Are the houses still standing? Will they have bombed my son's grave?

Just before five there is a huge explosion outside. The house shivers and quakes and there are crashing noises from the kitchen as crockery and glasses tumble to the floor. I hurry in to the children to comfort them but by then all is quiet and the silence is so deep that you would have thought we were underwater. Bracci comes into our room and tells us that the Germans have left, blowing up the bridge behind them. We go out onto the veranda and watch the troops receding into the distance in the moonlight.

In the morning, bursts of firing can be heard some way off but we hardly notice them. People move slowly, not daring to celebrate, not until after midday when the first Allied troops appear by the river. They are British and South Africans who climb the hill warily for fear of land mines. We can hardly believe our eyes when they march up the streets and the people run to greet them, flinging their arms around them; they smile awkwardly, detached and weary. The shutters that have covered the windows since we arrived are thrown back and shopowners bring out the goods that they have been hiding from the Germans. I ask the British commanding officer about San Martino, but he knows little, as his unit came here straight from Chiusi.

I watch the celebrations but am too anxious to take part in them. Instead, I go out onto the veranda, climb onto the surrounding wall, and peer in the direction of my home. But now there is a mist in the air so I can only make out the faint outline of the hill above the houses for an instant—then it is gone.

I hasten to pack the little I brought with me. Bracci tries to dissuade me but eventually gives up and has some food prepared for my journey. He offers to send a man with me but I won't hear of it and also forbid Signor Grandinetti to accompany me.

I set off at three. I've borrowed a horse, a dark beast with a beautiful eye. It's hot. The river is tepid when we ford it just below the ruins of the bridge, and I find the purling music of the water soothing. I listen as the sound fades, gripping the reins tighter than necessary.

～

PRITCHETT AND KRISTÍN WATCHED IN SILENCE UNTIL Alice and the group had disappeared. When they got back to the house, Father Augusto was closing the eyes of one of the soldiers who had stepped on a land mine.

"It's not too late for you to leave," he said as he looked up from the corpse.

He didn't expect an answer and Pritchett didn't say anything.

"Have you decided where you're taking your people?"

Pritchett nodded.

"Good. Keep it to yourself."

They heard a plane overhead and jumped. There was shouting and firing but the plane kept going without dropping a bomb.

"You should get a move on," said the chaplain, adding without much conviction: "God be with you."

Melchiorre and the cook were waiting in the kitchen when Pritchett and Kristín arrived. Pritchett gave them quick orders: Melchiorre was to round everyone up, Kristín to help the cook pack food and water.

"Where are we going?" asked Melchiorre.

"There is a vault," Pritchett answered in a low voice. "Up by the mill."

They didn't leave till late afternoon. The fighting got worse; one armored German column after another descended on the houses, seeking refuge from the Allied planes that were hunting them on their retreat. They waited in the cellar for an opportunity to leave, keeping to themselves. There was constant shouting and confusion, soldiers coming and going, and the noise from the planes and the artillery was deafening.

They left during a brief lull, as quietly as they could. They hurried away from the buildings to the far side of the slope before setting off up the old path. They were very careful, Pritchett walking slowly ahead looking for land mines and Melchiorre helping the cook, who was quickly out of breath. Dusk was falling when they made it to the mill; flashes lit up the darkness and the bombing was unrelenting. It did not lessen as the evening passed and the planes left, since the Allied forces were drawing closer, keeping up a constant bombardment.

They hurried to the vault, Pritchett holding the trapdoor open and, together with Melchiorre, helping one after another climb down into the moist darkness. They sat on the floor with their backs to the walls and their legs straight out in front of them, so tightly packed that they were touching, listening to the booming in total silence. There was a tiny gap around the trapdoor and during the first half of the night, flashes were visible from time to time, but later there was nothing but moonlight. They gazed at the light because there was nothing else to see in the darkness, except when Pritchett lit the lantern. Then they looked around, at the gray walls, the steps up to the trapdoor, the suitcases containing Alice's valuables, and the crate by the wall farthest from the entrance.

Kristín stared at the crate. Even when the lantern was extinguished, she thought she could see it in the darkness, thought she could see through it, see the girl with her face turned away from the brightness, in blue shadow. She imagined the smell of paint, her fingers remembered the texture of the canvas, and Marshall's voice echoed in her head, remote and unfamiliar.

She was shaking as she drew both knees up to her chin and clasped them tightly. Her breathing became shallow and rapid, and Melchiorre, who was sitting beside her, touched her gently. She groped for his hand in the darkness and held it.

She didn't sleep that night. There was a short lull around midnight, but apart from that the fighting was constant. They could have been blown up or buried alive at any moment, but no one showed fear. They were all quiet, all alone in their thoughts.

The following day, the ground shook from dawn to dusk. Stone crumbled from the walls, the trapdoor vibrated, and the booming echoed in the vault. It occurred to Pritchett to raise the trapdoor and let in some air but, in the end, he didn't dare. The fighting carried on a second night, only diminishing at daybreak. They heard engines start up, and the rattling and firing grew distant. Yet they were too afraid to show themselves until around noon when the birds began to sing. Only then did Pritchett rise to his feet, inch his way up the steps, and raise the trapdoor off the vault.

Kristín was the last one to go up the steps. Melchiorre waited for her briefly, but she motioned to him to go. She had seen no more than the bottom of the crate because the tarpaulin covered the top half, but now she lifted the cloth a little and took hold of the box to check how heavy it was. Realizing that she would never be able to carry it on her own, she concluded that she would have to bring the appropriate tools to open it. A hammer. A screwdriver. And a knife to cut the canvas from the strainer. Almost forgetting herself, she didn't move until she saw Melchiorre get ready to climb down again. Then she turned quickly and hurried toward the light.

Gradually her eyes adjusted to the brightness. There was no movement by the buildings; everyone was gone. They retraced their steps, making their way slowly. The sky was cloudless and silent, the roads empty: the Allied units had continued their pursuit up the valley.

The house was still standing, but there was a gaping hole in the facade and two in the roof. The *fattoria* and the clinic had also been hit, and there was a deep crater in the middle of the courtyard with bodies lying in it, though it was difficult to tell how many because they were all half-burnt. The garden had been dug up, and there were still more bodies in and around the trenches and in front of the greenhouses. The tanks had gone but two vehicles lay there on their sides, a *Kübelwagen* by the front door and an army transport truck at the top of the drive. The truck was still burning but the flames were dying down and smoke curled harmlessly into the air above it. For some reason, the Canary Bird Roses and the lemon trees had been removed from their pots and now lay strewn here and there around the buildings, among the mattresses, upholstery stuffing, books, and broken crockery. Clothing hung in the trees by the shed, along with the Moroccan prisoner of war, a noose around his neck, the turban still on his head.

Kristín followed Pritchett and Fosco in through the front door. They stopped in the sitting room and stared out through the hole in the wall, then continued farther inside the villa where everything had been turned upside down. The stuffing was hanging out of the furniture, light fittings had been torn from the ceiling, bookcases knocked over. The floor was littered with leftover food, broken glasses, and empty wine bottles that the soldiers had brought in from the storeroom. Everything of value had been stolen. The drawers of Alice's desk lay strewn around her room, among her summer hats, letters, and photographs. The lavatories were all blocked, the floor was awash with feces and urine, and the stench was so powerful that they had to cover their noses and mouths.

They couldn't enter Giovanni's room because of the wreckage from the ceiling. The door had been torn off its hinges and they could see blue sky through the hole in the roof. They went downstairs and into the kitchen where pots and pans had been flung into the hearth and a bag of flour emptied over the stove. Yet the clock was still ticking on the wall, and each of them glanced at it in turn because it was the only sound in the silence.

Pritchett turned on a tap in the kitchen sink but there was no water. Nor was there any electricity, but he kept flicking the switch on the wall up and down, click-clack, click-clack, until Fosco coughed. Then he came to his senses, silently shook his head and walked out into the courtyard with them.

They waved away the flies that greeted them. They were everywhere, both outside and indoors—buzzing over the food and the excrement and corpses. People from the tenant farms had begun to trickle out of the forest into the courtyard, quiet and dejected. Instead of going to meet them, Pritchett walked off. He had a good idea what kind of tales people would have to tell, but he couldn't face listening to them. Not yet. Not until he had got his bearings.

He walked a little way along the hillside to be alone and when he came back, he had recovered his composure. He knew he had to show strength and, despite feeling sick to his stomach, was able to gather everyone and say a few words of encouragement.

"We are fortunate. We're alive. Everything here can be repaired. Now is the time to start."

They were all hungry, and he instructed the women to clean the kitchen and the men to start carrying the corpses out of the building so they could eat. While the kitchen was being tidied, Melchiorre and Fosco fetched ham, eggs, olives, and vegetables that they had hidden before escaping to the vault, carried water from the well, lit a fire to heat the water, and helped the women wash the floor and tables. Finally they crowded around the table, eating in silence at first, but then someone felt the need to say something and soon everyone was talking. The people from the farms had all lost something, either a loved one or a home, some both, and Pritchett was ashamed as they described the events of the last days and nights, and told himself he had failed them. He knew he couldn't have done anything, couldn't have changed anything, yet he was ashamed. He had escaped. He had hidden in a hole while others suffered.

He started when someone asked after Alice and the children.

"No," he said, "no news."

He had wondered whether he or someone else should go to Montepulciano to try to track them down but decided it was a bad idea. Booming still sounded from farther up the valley and the roads were hazardous—a man from one of the farms reported that a group of partisans had that very morning come across some German soldiers who had been separated from their unit and were hiding in the valley. Pritchett did not ask how their encounter had ended.

They worked all day long. Some who had shoveled earth

over the bodies of their loved ones out in the forest, not knowing how long the battle would last, now went to dig them up
and bring them down the hill. It was unclear how many bodies
there would be by the end, and there were no open graves
in the cemetery, so Pritchett had them kept until just before
sunset in the shed behind the chapel, which was shaded by
trees. The corpses of the soldiers were dragged out of the crater
in the courtyard and the trenches in the garden and taken to
the shed as well. Pritchett and Fosco cut the Moroccan down
from the tree and laid him with the rest, then spread a canvas
over the bodies to protect them from the flies.

Daylight was fading when they saw a vehicle down in the
valley. Pritchett raised a hand to his brow and watched it maneuver around holes and craters in the road until it finally
stopped at the turning and continued up to the house.

THERE WAS AN OVERTURNED GERMAN TRUCK AT THE top of the drive, and the two soldiers, both American, one in his early forties, the other in his midtwenties, got out of the open jeep and walked the last stretch to the house. Seeing Pritchett and Kristin coming toward them, they waved and quickened their step.

"We thought we'd never make it up here. The road is a disaster."

"There was fighting here till this morning."

"We know. You British?"

Pritchett nodded, introducing himself.

"Captain Duane Heller, US Fifth Army, Monuments, Fine Arts, and Archives. This is my partner, Lieutenant Hart."

They shook hands.

"What is that?" asked Pritchett. "Monuments, Fine Arts, and Archives?"

"Yes, sorry. Let me explain," said Captain Heller. "The Monuments, Fine Arts, and Archives program was established last year. We're mostly art historians, museum directors, and curators. We follow the troops, try to protect cultural property, and recover art stolen by the Germans."

"There is nothing here," Pritchett said before he could stop himself.

Kristín looked at him. She was relieved by his answer but tried not to show it. The sooner these men left, the better.

Captain Duane smiled. He was neat for someone who'd been on the front for weeks but he looked tired.

"We're on our way to Montepulciano and were asked to look in on you. The troops didn't see anyone here this morning. They thought it was strange."

Pritchett explained that all but a few of the household had left for Montepulciano two days before.

"The rest of us have been hiding."

"And the Germans are all gone?"

"As far as we can tell."

The afternoon sun bathed the hills, but down in the valley a light-blue haze was spreading over the cornfields. All was quiet nearby but in the distance they could hear explosions every now and then. Sour-smelling smoke rose from the bonfire they had built in the crater in the courtyard and drifted to them in long, thin veils.

"It's beautiful here," the captain said, looking over the valley. "Despite all the destruction. You got off lightly compared to some of the other farms and villages we've seen."

Pritchett asked them about Montepulciano.

"The Germans are still holding it but we're closing in on them. It's only a matter of hours."

They walked to the back of the villa. The number of arrivals from the farms had grown; they stood gloomily in groups in the courtyard waiting for Pritchett to talk to them. He asked Kristín to take the Americans into the kitchen and make sure they were properly fed before they continued their journey, then turned his attention to the group from the farms.

Kristín led them inside. There was no one in the kitchen but the cook. The Americans sat down but Kristín went into the pantry and helped the cook fetch a loaf of bread, eggs, and ham.

"Where are you from?" asked Lieutenant Hart, the younger of the two.

She told them.

"Really? Not too many of you around here."

She tried to smile and then, in as neutral a tone as she could muster, she asked them about their work.

They both liked to talk. Not least Lieutenant Hart.

"Are you interested in art?" he asked.

"Yes," she said, hesitantly.

He was her age. Tall and slim, narrow across the shoulders, a bit hunched. His fingers, long and delicate, had a tendency to touch his face, which was recovering from sunburn.

"There aren't many of us," he said. "Not yet. We're on the front lines and go into the villages as soon as they've been liberated to see what can be done to save anything of cultural value. Frescoes, monuments, churches . . . Sometimes there's nothing we can do. Everything has been destroyed. But more often than not we have some success."

The cook asked Kristín whether she thought Pritchett would want her to offer them wine, then put two glasses on the table and poured. They thanked her in poor Italian. Kristín watched the lieutenant cut up his ham, the movements of his lean, elegant fingers measured and precise.

"Have you been here long?"

"No," she said. "Not long," adding after a brief silence, "I had an injury. My train was bombed."

Uneasy talking about herself, she stood up and looked out the window. Pritchett was trying to organize the groups, pointing toward the *fattoria*. Fosco and Melchiorre carried a dead soldier across the courtyard, disappearing into the smoke from the bonfire.

"Yesterday we found a Giovanni Bellini in a villa south of Chiusi," Lieutenant Hart said. "The Germans had hidden it in an empty barrel in the wine cellar. It was an early tempera; the most beautiful Pietà. The colors soft and . . ."

He stopped himself.

"Sorry, I get carried away."

"How did you find it?" she asked.

They both smiled.

"Pure luck," said the Captain. "Our soldiers were thirsty and broke the barrel . . ."

"But we knew the Germans had it," added Lieutenant Hart. "They kept such accurate accounts of everything they stole or bought. There were file cabinets full of information in the Gestapo headquarters on Via Tasso. Some of it they burned with other documents, some they must have taken with them, some we got. I guess it never occurred to them that they'd lose the war."

Her mind was turning. Did they have the signed contract between Hofer and Marshall? Did they have Marshall's letter of authentication? Or was it all ashes now?

She couldn't sit still. She had to get to the painting and destroy it. There was constant ringing in her ears, voices that tried to outdo one another, voices of fear and hope and guilt. Why did she care anymore about what happened to him? What did she owe him? Nothing, she said to herself. I owe him nothing. Then, a breath later: but no matter how much I despise him, I cannot have this on my conscience.

*This.* What did she think *this* might be? Her mind was racing, but she tried to slow it down and get control of it. She had gone through this a thousand times, even in her sleep. If the Allies found the painting and connected him to the sale of it, he would be prosecuted as a traitor. If the partisans found out about his involvement, they might execute him as they had so many others who had aided the Nazis. And as before, when she pondered all the possible outcomes, every permutation, she concluded that she had no choice but to destroy her own forgery.

"It's getting late," Captain Duane said. "We don't want to travel in the dark."

They stood up and walked outside. Pritchett saw them and hurried over.

"Is there anything we can help with before we leave?"

"We'll manage. If you see Marchesa Orsini, please let her know we're all right."

Captain Duane pointed at the chapel.

"Anything of value there? Anything that might be compromised?"

"No, there is nothing. But you're welcome to take a look."

The captain said there was no reason. They shook hands.

"By the way," said the captain, "you may expect the French troops of the Fifth Army later today or tomorrow. I hate to tell you this, but the Moroccan Goums who fight alongside them consider loot the just reward for battle. They leave no stone unturned."

Pritchett and Kristín watched the two men climb into the jeep and make their way down the hill. The sunlight now illuminated only the tops of the hills, and the haze in the valley had darkened, except by the river where the reflected rays undulated in the gentle breeze.

They were about to turn back when the jeep stopped. Pritchett's heart jumped a little, but then Lieutenant Hart turned around with a smile, raised his hand, and quickly waved good-bye.

THE EVENING DARKNESS WAS WARM, AND THE MOON was out when Pritchett headed up to the mill. In the cemetery the farmhands and the men from the tenant farms had begun digging graves by the light of a fire they had lit; when the smell of burning kindling reached Pritchett halfway up the slope, he paused for a moment.

The Goums had not yet arrived. There had been no traffic down in the valley after the Monuments men left, but the bombing in the distance had grown more persistent. Outside the open doors to the *fattoria*, people stood in silence watching the ovens being fired up, waiting for the aroma of baking bread to start drifting out through the courtyard. All remaining blankets and rugs had been gathered and Kristín had supervised the cleaning of the new sleeping quarters, the chapel, and the corn store, before helping Signorina Harris find morphine bottles that had been hidden in the back of the greenhouse. There were two men from the farms in the clinic; one had stepped on a land mine and was badly injured, the other had been shot in the arm as he tried to prevent the Germans from leaving with his horse.

Pritchett continued up the slope, Captain Duane's warning echoing in his mind: they leave no stone unturned. He had tried to leave sooner but never got the chance; everything was now on his shoulders. He had never wanted to be the one in charge, had always been content to defer to Claudio and Alice and play the role of a trusted friend; with responsibility came nothing but anxiety. This was his nature but he didn't realize it till he was in his thirties, chafing under the pressure of running a small architectural business in Florence. That's why he had left for the countryside, that's why he had fled a life so many of his countrymen in the city had coveted.

He stopped, wiping the sweat from his brow. There were fires burning in the distance, but the night had muted the sounds of battle. Where was she? Where were the children? Had they made it to Montepulciano unharmed? Were they safe? He wasn't a religious man, but as he continued up the hill, he found himself mouthing the same prayer that had been on his lips since they left. It was banal, he knew that, the words of a child, but it didn't matter.

He had promised her that he would take care of the painting. Saving Robert Marshall was not what he had bargained for, but for her he would do anything. And she was right: they would not want the Allies to find out that they had been hiding a cultural treasure for the Germans. Neither the Allies nor the partisans who had never fully appreciated everything they had done for them could be allowed to know that. But that wasn't the whole story. He knew that, more than anything, Alice did not wish to explain the reason why she had agreed to assist Robert Marshall in the first place.

She had made that clear to him the day the Germans brought the painting, and he had never asked her again. He didn't need to; details aside, he could envision what had happened. He just hoped it hadn't been with Marshall himself. The thought alone made him sick to his stomach.

He loved them both dearly, but he was disappointed in Alice and Claudio. No, that wasn't the right word. He was angry with them. How could they have let this happen? After all they had been through together, everything they had accomplished, hand in glove. Why?

He was upset with himself. He should have sensed how much had gone wrong between them. He, who thought he knew them better than they knew themselves, had been caught off guard. There were signs, he saw that now, but he had ignored them, perhaps in the hope that they were nothing more than a passing cloud. He had once asked Claudio if everything was all right, but Claudio had only made light of it.

"My friend," he had said. "Marriage can be complicated. You Brits are a strange bunch . . ."

That was all. A wry smile, then a change of subject.

It came as a complete shock to him when Claudio disappeared. He hadn't been himself since Giovanni's death, and the arrival of the evacuee children from Genoa had only made things worse. But that he would pick up and leave without a word to anyone? Disappear a few days after the first bomb fell in the valley? That was unfathomable.

He had made some discreet inquiries but to no avail. At first he had expected Claudio's return any day, believing more than once that he'd heard his voice or even seen him in the distance. But that had just been his overactive mind at work. By now he feared the worst.

He had brought along a hammer and a crowbar. He lifted the trapdoor and descended the stone steps slowly, lighting his lantern when he was down. He put it carefully on the floor before opening the crate and unwrapping the painting. Then he knelt down in front of it and reached for the lantern.

In the feeble light, the girl in the white shift avoided his gaze, tilting her head slightly. He moved closer, staring at her delicate shoulders, wet hair, parted lips. Reaching out a finger, he raised it to the painting, allowing it to lightly touch her cheek. Then he slowly withdrew it.

Where had he seen her before? The answer was in his mind somewhere, and he leant forward instinctively in anticipation of its arrival, his eyes glued to the painting. The light flickered and for a moment it was as if the girl was about to turn toward him, the shadow on her cheek disappearing, her eyes still avoiding contact. He brought the lantern closer, but the answer had slipped away; the girl receded into darkness and refused to reemerge, no matter how hard he tried.

He was tired. He could feel it now after this unexpected rush, the sudden burst of energy gradually dissipating, leaving him deflated. Was his mind playing tricks on him? He had immediately detected the turbulence beneath the beautifully textured surface when he saw the painting with Alice, the sharp contrast between light and shadow, the alliance of guilt and innocence. He had immediately had the strangest sensation that he knew this young woman.

He eased the canvas off the strainer. His hands were shaky, his eyelids ready to close. He dismantled the strainer and wrapped the canvas carefully around the pieces of wood, the image of the girl floating in and out of the shadows of his mind.

He retraced his steps down the hill in the pale moonlight, and from there along the edge of the forest, not stopping until he was halfway down the drive, in the rough where no one ever had a reason to go. There he put the bundle in a bag, tied it up, and buried it under a bush before making his way back to the house.

I'VE BEEN TALKING TO YOU INCESSANTLY EVER SINCE I left Montepulciano. The horse picks its way along the path, the sun shines on our progress, and I talk to you to try to dispel my anxiety. I'm scared. I tell you everything and you listen but I notice that you lower your head when I ask for forgiveness. It's as if you are ashamed too. I'm not trying to make excuses but as I recall my mistakes, it's like talking about a woman I don't know except by reputation. I'm not saying this to throw dust in your eyes, you know that. I lost my way. Maybe you did as well. I thought you had when I saw you visiting the young widow. But that's not an excuse either. And neither is your silence nor your occasional distance. How did we let this happen to us? How could we be so reckless? How could I be so selfish? One can find faults with everything; our marriage was no exception. But our problems were trivial in the scheme of things. We can see that now that the world lies in ruins.

I haven't thought about Connor for a long time. When I stopped seeing him, whatever feelings I had quickly evaporated. I suppose that says it all. He wrote to me, but I didn't answer his letters. He even wrote to Pritchett on some pretext, though they hardly knew each other, and asked after me. I suspect that Pritchett saw through him, though he was careful not to imply any impropriety when he brought up Connor's name. I asked him not to mention me in his reply.

I haven't spoken to my mother in two months. She's more self-centered than ever, and besides, I cannot bear listening to her questions about you. She's always been so unfair to you and while I can only blame myself for my mistakes, she certainly didn't help. I tell myself that maybe I should try to get a message to her that I'm all right, knowing full well that I'm unlikely to make that a priority.

I'm nearing our home now. The horse is lathered in sweat; I stroke his neck and turn him down to the river where he drinks. I have no idea what awaits me. I imagine that you've come home; I picture you in front of the buildings like the first time we went there. Do you remember running up the stairs and calling down to us from the glassless window in the master bedroom: "This is paradise!" Do you remember? Do you remember how happy we were?

When I reach for my water bottle, I see a horseman on the road ahead. He's far off and appears to be hardly moving. I narrow the distance between us and see as I draw closer that it is the priest. He sits stooping on his horse, which is walking slowly in the heat.

The priest lifts his head when he hears me ride up.

"I looked for you in Montepulciano," I say. "Where were you?"

He tells me he didn't reach Montepulciano but was forced to seek shelter in a Franciscan monastery on the way. He looks like a crow sitting there on his horse, so terribly small and hunched, and I have to pull up my horse and strain my ears to hear what he says. When we carry on again, I tell him how afraid I am, how terribly afraid that something bad has happened to our people.

"Do you want to pray?" he says.

"Yes," I answer without hesitation. We pray together for the rest of the way, my voice as low as his, a whisper that the gentle breeze carries across the cornfields.

My heart starts pounding when I see the roof of the villa emerge from behind the last hill. Paralyzed by fear, I sit motionless in the saddle and stare into the distance as if waiting for a sign that I should continue. The priest stops and waits patiently until I gather the will to face what awaits us. Finally, I urge my horse on and the priest follows a little way behind, his lips continuing to move in a silent prayer.

Halfway up the slope, I see smoke curling into the air. The road is so badly cratered that I get off the horse and continue up the hill on foot.

The villa is just coming into view when I see someone running toward me. For a moment, I'm convinced it's you. But my sudden euphoria evaporates when I wipe the sweat from my eyes and see Pritchett's smiling face and outstretched arms. He calls my name and, hearing the sound of his voice, I start to cry. We embrace for a long time, and when we finally let go, I am completely exhausted.

It's evening now. We're sitting at the kitchen table in the glow of the candles. We've buried the dead, those from the storehouse and others whom we found today in the forest. It's a terrible thing to witness, all these young men disappearing into the ground. The trees conceal even more bodies but we can't look for them until tomorrow when the postmaster from Chianciano is due. He knows how to handle explosives; apparently he's already deactivated innumerable mines in the village. The Germans were generous with their parting gifts; the forest is teeming with mines, though fortunately most lie on the surface. There's an unexploded bomb lying outside the garden door and another by the door to the cellar, both hastily constructed but no less powerful for that.

In the face of so much death, the priest seemed to revive suddenly. His voice rang out clearly in the chapel, and his gaze was sharp as if he could see something that had been hidden from him for a long time. But now he is silent as he sits hunched over the table beside Kristín and opposite me, and his shadow lies on the wall, unobtrusive and still.

Before we go to bed, I ask Pritchett about the painting. We're standing outside, by the large crater in the courtyard where the fire is still burning.

"Don't worry," he says. "I've taken care of it."

I know I should feel relief, but there is something in his voice that troubles me.

"What did you do with it?" I ask, lowering my voice.

He looks at me, surprised.

"Sorry," I say. "I'm just nervous."

He takes my hand.

"You don't have to know that," he says. "You just have to trust me."

IT IS THE PRIEST WHO COMES TO SEE ME WITH PRITCH-
ett just before noon. It is two days since I came back, and I've
decided to tidy my room a bit. I'm not making much progress,
feeling disjointed and tired. It is the priest who speaks for both
of them, who takes my hands and looks into my eyes with his
own clouded ones, who says:

"They found him."

Pritchett is standing behind him with head lowered, clasping and releasing his fingers, slowly, as if performing an intri-
cate task. I stare at them while the priest's words echo in my
head, those three words that turn the world upside down. The
priest's hands are cold, but his grip is surprisingly strong. I jerk;
he doesn't want to release me, but I take a step backward and
hear myself ask, "Where is he?"

They exchange glances, and I repeat my question, louder
this time.

"Where? I want to see him."

It is then that Pritchett looks up and says with difficulty,
"Better not to."

Before I know what I'm doing, I've grabbed Pritchett's shirt
with both hands.

"Where is he?"

Shocked, he blurts out the answer.

I set off at a run. He follows, calling repeatedly, "Alice, wait, Alice, don't go . . ." But I don't listen, I run as fast as I can, unaware of my legs, unaware of anything but the ache in my breast and the despair that has paralyzed everything but my feet.

I don't stop until I am east of the gardens, where no one ever has any reason to go. That's where they found you, in the hollow at the foot of the wall we built when we decided to cultivate the area around the buildings. The hollow is overgrown with twisted bushes that give way farther east to stony ground, after which the land rises again toward the quarry. They found you lying facedown in the bushes and recognized your jacket and, when they drew closer, your watch and wedding ring.

I can't see you at first. Pritchett has reached my side. I can hear his breathing. He's panting.

"Alice," he gasps, "Alice . . ."

"Where is he?" I ask.

"You don't want to see him. Not in the state he's in. It's not a good idea."

I climb over the wall and he follows me. Once I am down in the hollow, I spot your jacket under the bushes. It looks as if you have fallen off the wall and rolled down the slope. Your legs are turned toward me, I can see right to the bone. I start to run, meaning to take you in my arms, crush you against me, but Pritchett grabs me and holds me back. I struggle in his arms, fighting frantically until I run out of strength.

You have been lying there a long time and the animals have got at you. But your jacket removes all doubt; the jacket I gave you for your birthday the year before last. I tell Pritchett as much. I say, "I gave him that jacket for his birthday," repeating it over and over again. And he strokes my cheek, holding me tight and saying, "I know. I remember him wearing it the day he disappeared."

He led me home. I don't remember which way we went, don't remember anything. I lay down in my room and Signorina Harris came and gave me some pills. As she was leaving my room, I sat up.

"Can you check if he killed himself?" I asked.

She paused for an instant and I thought she nodded. Then she was gone.

When I wake up, the priest is sitting by my bed. The room is sunny and I raise a hand to my eyes because the light from the window is unbearably bright.

On the bedside table is the picture Giovanni painted for you. It's of our house. We are standing in front of it with him between us. You had it in your jacket pocket.

"He didn't take his own life," I hear the priest say as I put down the picture. "He was shot."

"Shot?"

"There was fighting in the hills that day. Pritchett remembers it clearly. A sudden flare-up. Claudio must've got hit by a stray bullet."

"But I hear his voice . . . When I speak with him, I can hear it . . ."

"In your mind," he says. "Where he'll always be."

I feel detached, as if I'm watching the scene from a distance. My thoughts stray to the cleft in your chin, and all of a sudden I'm filled with such a longing to touch it that I begin to tremble.

Then I close my eyes again.

THE CHURCH HAD BEEN BOMBED AND THE CHAPEL
could not hold more than a fraction of those who came to
pay their last respects to you. The doors were left open to the
courtyard so that the crowd outside could listen to the echo of
the sermon. Some of these people had lost everything but the
clothes on their backs and were ashamed of turning up in such
a state, but I believe that Pritchett and I managed by our combined efforts to reassure them. I'm not sure, though, because
these are proud people, proud, dependable and kindhearted.
They are my people, my dependents, and I draw strength from
them, although they don't know it.

Now you lie buried beside our son, with a small plot between the two of you where I will rest when my turn comes.
Next spring I'm going to plant bluebells on both your graves
and a tall shrub or low tree in the middle to provide me with a
little shade when I tend to them.

I dug up my diary yesterday morning. I had considered
leaving it there, saying to myself that the graveyard was
where it belonged. But I can't bury my sins and I need my
memories, all the little details of our daily lives, the good
and the bad, our joys and sorrows. I read it into the night and
when I finally put it away, I saw the first sign of day in the

east, a shy ray of light, barely penetrating the veil of darkness.

I keep talking to you, keep asking you for forgiveness. I do not hold anything back, let alone try to justify my actions. We both know how wrong I was. I picture you sitting on Giovanni's bed. I'm with you and I take your hand as I begin my confession. There is a pained look on your face and for a moment I sense that you're about to leave. But you stay and, for whatever reason, I become more hopeful as I continue.

I busy myself from morning to night and am pleased to say that we've largely escaped mishaps so far. One of the oxen trod on a mine down in the field but the driver was not hurt. Every able-bodied person lent a hand with the reaping, and it looks as if we're going to save the harvest.

Pritchett and I rode to the outlying farms the day before yesterday and did not return home until late. Most of them are in a bad way, some lie in ruins, the roof has collapsed in others; all have been plundered. Unfortunately, the Germans were not alone in that; some of the Allied units were as bad. At one farm there are thirteen people sleeping in two beds; in another, eleven have to sleep on the floor. Kitchen utensils, blankets, and furniture that people either made themselves or acquired over many years have been spirited away. Mice, now with a free run of the place, eat the few worldly goods that remain.

We must raise a roof over the houses before winter, but the oven in which we fire bricks and tiles runs on lignite, which cannot be had for love or money. Yet we'll find a way, I'm sure of that. We'll have to.

When we came back from doing the rounds, Pritchett and I went down to the vault by the old mill and fetched the belongings I've been hiding there for months, jewelry and various personal items with sentimental value, as well as important documents and the title deeds to our land. The crate with the painting was gone, but when I kept looking at the spot where it had been, he reassured me again that I would not have to worry about it.

I took his hand and squeezed it. That morning the partisans had shot the barber in Chianciano after accusing him of collaborating with the Germans. I'm afraid his only crime was that he didn't close his door to them.

Repairs have begun on the top floor of the villa; today Giovanni's room was cleared and they have started work on the roof. We are still without electricity but we now have running water and are scrubbing the place from top to bottom for the second time. The chickens that we hid are back in their coop and have started laying, and the rabbits and geese that survived are fattening up in their cages. Signorina Harris is run off her feet by the injured who flock to her with their wounds, some of them days old. For the moment we are free of disease, and there are fewer flies since we buried the bodies that we found on the property and burnt the animals that died, including the poor cow that was tethered to a tree beside our trench. But we've heard that elsewhere in the valley paratyphoid fever has broken out, which is a great worry.

Last night Kristín came to see me. She never says much, but it was obvious that she had something on her mind. I was folding the laundry. She started to help me, and we worked silently for a while until she announced that she was leaving. I replied that she could stay as long as she liked, and she thanked me, saying she could never repay me for all I had done for her. I changed the subject, asking her instead where she was headed. She said she intended to go first to Rome to fetch her belongings but did not expect to stay there long.

I knew she had come from Rome where she had been studying art but that was the extent of my knowledge. She's very
reserved and, besides, we haven't had much time for chitchats
this summer. But, as I said, I sensed that she wanted to talk, so
I asked her if she intended perhaps to go back home to Iceland.

"I don't know."

I was stunned at how lost she suddenly seemed.

"Where were you going when your train got hit?"

Maybe someone had told me when she arrived, but I
couldn't remember. People have found their way to our door
from every direction over the last few months, sometimes because they had heard that we offered a refuge for those who
had nowhere else to turn, sometimes by chance. I suppose I'd
always assumed that she belonged to the latter group. Now it
occurred to me that she might need help in getting to her des-
tination but didn't like to ask for it. Her reaction took me by
surprise, however. She didn't answer immediately but looked
away, her fingers gripping the garment she had been folding.

When she finally tried to open her mouth, I saw that her
eyes were full of tears.

"Would you mind if I didn't answer that?" she asked.

"Kristín dear . . . ," I said.

"I'd be very grateful if I didn't have to," she continued, and
I sensed that her voice was on the point of breaking.

Shocked to see her in such a state, I glanced down at her
hands, which were still clenched on the piece of clothing, a
light-colored shirt belonging to one of the girls. Before I knew
it, I had taken her hands in mine.

"Kristín dear," I said, "do take care. Whatever you do, take
care. Don't be too hard on yourself; I sense you have a tendency to. Perhaps we're not so very different in that respect."

She didn't answer, but I felt her hands relaxing in my grasp. She didn't move them though, and it was not until I let go that she withdrew them, then hugged me.

We stood like that for a long time. She wept in silence at first, and her slender body shook in my arms, but then she grew calmer. After she had released me, she dried her eyes and tried to smile.

She got a lift down the valley with Melchiorre this morning. He was supposed to be working on the repairs to the roof, but I hadn't the heart to refuse him permission to take her. I watched them drive down the road until Signor Grandinetti came to me with a question. I realized that they had long since vanished from sight, and I couldn't understand why I was still standing there.

The harvest is exceeding all expectations, and I'm confident that we will be able to stock up the farms for the winter. We need oil, sugar, salt, and soap, but it looks as if the wool from the sheep that survived will be sufficient for clothing essentials. If not, we'll find a way somehow.

I don't sleep much at night, yet I'm not tired. I lie awake with a little light on, thinking about you, our life together, our son. There are so many good memories despite everything, so much that I can be grateful for. Hopefully I gave you some happiness. Hopefully you weren't angry when you died.

Then I turn off the light, rest my head against the pillow, and wait for sleep to take me in its arms.

MORE THAN TWO HUNDRED GUESTS ARE GATHERING in the National Gallery in Trafalgar Square—press, patrons, trustees, scholars, and staff. The ceremony is to take place in the Central Hall where the painting has been placed on a high easel and veiled with a white cloth. There is a lectern with a microphone next to it, and the area has been cordoned off with a red velvet rope. Black-clad waiters bearing trays of glasses and canapés move skillfully through the growing crowd, which has deposited umbrellas and coats in the cloakroom and is quickly shaking off the afternoon gloom.

She walks slowly up the steps to the portico entrance, one hand holding the rail, the other an umbrella. She has a slight limp—it has worsened over the years—but in other respects she has mostly been spared the afflictions of old age. During the four decades that she worked in the museum's conservation department, she seldom had a reason to use the main entrance, and then, as now, she found the long flight of steps from the square somewhat overwhelming.

She stops midway up the steps and looks back. The pigeons are in their place, fluttering down by the fountains where tourists gather, poring over their maps and guides. In the summer she used to go for walks during her lunch break and sometimes in winter too, weather permitting. She would feed the pigeons before making her way to St. James's Park, where she always found the peace and quiet she was looking for. She has not visited her old workplace for years but feels as if she never left—as if she's coming back from a lunch break in the park, having enjoyed the company of squirrels, moorhens, and tufted ducks.

For the first few years after she retired, her opinion was occasionally sought on problematic restoration jobs, but she made every effort to train her successors to the best of her ability. The museum director had mentioned this especially in his speech at her farewell party; she had tried to get out of attending but was given no choice. He had described her as generous.

She doesn't want to arrive too early, doesn't want to have to talk to anyone, doesn't trust herself when confronted with the painting after all this time. During her first years at the museum, hardly a day passed when she didn't check to see whether an undocumented Caravaggio had been unearthed somewhere in the world, but gradually she did so less and less. And then she received this invitation in the mail one Tuesday just over a week ago, when she was coming home with some tulips she had bought from the florist on the corner. She opened it walking into the kitchen but had to support herself against the doorframe with both hands when she had read it; the strength left her legs, and before she knew it, she had slumped to the floor with an unbearable ringing in her ears.

The guests are moving closer to the easel, waiting for the ceremony to begin. There is a loud buzz coming from the room; she hears it after giving her umbrella to the young man in the cloakroom, senses anticipation in the din of voices, and hesitates before making her way to the Central Hall where she takes her place in the back.

She tries to make herself invisible as she watches her former colleagues enter the room—the museum director, the head of the conservation department and his counterpart from the scientific department, the press secretary and her two young assistants. But she doesn't have to worry: they're too busy to notice her hiding in the back. The press secretary, who is very dedicated but always a little nervous, goes over the final arrangements with the director, who nods politely but is quickly distracted by guests he has to greet on his way to the lectern.

The press secretary helps him turn on the microphone, and he calls for quiet with a soft "Ladies and gentlemen . . ." A fidgety silence descends on the room, but even then she can only hear the echo of his speech. She moves closer, slowly, stopping when she reaches the photographers who have lined up against the wall, waiting to be invited to come forward after the unveiling.

"Although closely related to his picture of Mary Magdalene, this is a more mature work," she hears him say. "The hints of sorrow and remorse are more subtle, the revelation of the most intimate sentiments not quite as forthcoming. Whereas Mary Magdalene, in her determination to leave her past behind, has unequivocally discarded her coins and pearls, symbols of the material world, the young woman in our painting has one hand closed, possibly holding on to a connection to her past or concealing an important secret . . . The model may be the same, the prostitute Anna Bianchini, though this is only conjecture . . ."

There is a buzzing in her ears and the words blur, becoming nothing but a distant reverberation. She is no longer standing in the Central Hall of the National Gallery but in the damp vault the night after the visit from Captain Duane and Lieutenant Hart, holding a lantern, looking at the open crate on the floor. She had not dared set off with the tools she had gathered until everyone had gone to bed, guided by the moonlight up the slope that Pritchett had climbed only a few hours earlier. She is looking at the crate and the straw that is scattered on the floor when she spots a splinter that broke off the strainer when Pritchett took it apart. She picks it up and raises it to her nose. The lantern is behind her, halfway up the steps, but she doesn't have to hold the wood up to the light, needs no confirmation, immediately recognizes its texture and smell. For a while she stands still, then puts the splinter in her pocket, reaches for the tools, blows out the lantern, and climbs back up the steps into the moonlight.

She retreats from the memories, from the vault and the moonlight and the despair that gripped her and wouldn't let go as she made her way down the hill. Why had she come here? Why hadn't she thrown the invitation in the bin and carried on with her painting of tulips, a modest still life that she had been amusing herself with for the past few days? Why had she allowed the shadows to emerge once more, the sleepless nights to return, the fear and helplessness to gain the upper hand?

Why?

"Integrated physical-chemical and analytical methodologies have further confirmed the authenticity of the painting," she hears the director say. "The ground layer, characteristically left visible in more than one place, is Caravaggio's typical red-brown mixture of calcite, minerals, and lead . . ."

She can picture her former colleagues, so dedicated and thorough, so diligent and patient, applying their tools—X-radiography, infrared reflectography, pyrolysis, gas chromatography—to analyze pigments and layers in minute detail, only to reach the wrong conclusion. She can predict almost every word from the director, which only compounds her feeling of guilt.

"The obtained results indicate that Caravaggio used white lead and natural earths; malachite, cinnabar, kermes, and cochineal; umber and ocher . . . The considerable amount of amorphous particles of copper chlorides found in the green pigment verdigris suggests that it could have been produced according to the ancient recipe of *veride salsum* . . ."

She watches the backs of her former colleagues: the manager of the scientific department, a man in his early fifties, leaning forward a bit when the director details his department's examination, as if to make sure his superior doesn't deviate from the careful script, the press secretary looking around, discreetly reading the audience. There is a spotlight on the covered painting, and the veil ripples gently in the slight draft.

"While it's clear that the painting has undergone significant restoration—particularly the head, the jewelry, and parts of the background—we cannot accurately determine its time or place, partly due to the excellent care taken in using almost exclusively materials employed in the original painting . . . It is quite possible that this expert restoration is the work of Robert Marshall who we know restored paintings by Ghirlandaio and Lippi for Count Contini Bonacossi, a supplier of art to the Germans. There is, however, no evidence of this since much of Mr. Marshall's dealings during the war are still murky, as are the facts surrounding his alleged escape to Berlin in the spring of 1944 where he and his family are believed to have perished a year later . . ."

She's never believed that story. For years after she moved to London she was convinced that he was there, sometimes spotting him in the street, sometimes in a store or even the museum. The first time that happened, she was stunned by her own reaction. Fear mingled with relief and even longing. She started running after him but stopped when she realized how absurd her feelings were, how ridiculous to believe that he was there. But those arguments had all evaporated a few weeks later when she thought she caught sight of him again.

Hope and despair. And then the aching loneliness. Again and again. For years.

"As is the case with several of Caravaggio's paintings, the provenance of this picture is uncertain. The early Caravaggio biographer Giovanni Bellori, writing in 1672, mentions a *Portrait of a Young Woman* sent by the artist to the Grand Master of the Knights of Malta in the hope of regaining favor after having been expelled from the Order in 1608. While we cannot be absolutely certain that Bellori was referring to this particular painting, we know of no better candidate . . ."

The director pauses, reaches for a glass of water before adjusting his glasses slightly on his nose. She had always admired his scholarly enthusiasm, his tireless advocacy for the museum, and his unwavering support of his staff. A decent man, that's how she would describe him, a trustworthy man. He looks at the painting on the easel before continuing, and her eyes follow his.

"In the light of concern that some works of art now in public collections may have been improperly acquired during the period 1933–1945, without restitution having been made, the National Gallery has paid particular attention to the whereabouts of its paintings during those years. While we cannot rule out the possibility that the *Portrait of a Young Woman*, as we have officially termed the painting, may temporarily have been in the possession of the Germans during the war, and while it's also conceivable that they may have hidden it at San Martino on their retreat, this is only speculation, as there is no record of it prior to the war and no claim asserting that it was at any time improperly acquired. Perhaps we will never know more than our donor, Mr. Cecil Pritchett, whose will I quote: 'A portrait of a girl, now on the north wall in my study, shall be donated to the National Gallery in London. Found in 1951 in the attic of the *fattoria* amongst other items.'"

Pritchett. He must have kept it hidden the whole time, she says to herself, for how would she be able to know that some nights, when only he and the cicadas were awake, he would sit in his study and stare at the painting, trying to place the girl. There were times when he felt he was only a corner away from finding her in his mind's labyrinth, but as the years passed, those times became less frequent until, at the end, he had given up. When Alice was still alive, he would only take the painting out when he was alone, leaving it otherwise hidden in a closet. It was only after she passed that he put it on the north wall in the study.

When he lost his sight, he would every now and then ask one of the maids to describe it to him. He would sit in front of it and pepper them with detailed questions in his attempt at piecing it together in his mind's eye. "What do you see?" he would ask again and again. "Tell me what you see," becoming frustrated and even angry as failure visited him once again.

She isn't listening anymore, but the director continues, speculating whether the painting may have been on the property prior to the Orsinis' purchase of San Martino or whether the Germans may have left it there, mentioning Marshall again and making doubly sure it's clear to all that there is no record of the painting prior to the war and no dispute about Mr. Pritchett's rights to it, pointing out the poor documentation of Caravaggio's works ("By 1921 there were only thirty paintings attributed to Caravaggio, according to a catalogue edited by Lionello Venturi"), before finally citing three renowned experts who have concluded that *Portrait of a Young Woman* is without a doubt the work of the troubled master. There is a din in her ears, but when the director finally raises his head, looks at the easel and says, "And now the moment has finally come . . . ," she turns her back on the crowd and hurries out. Her leg aches but in the distance she sees the exit, the gray light entering through the door, accompanied by determined visitors. She gropes her way forward as if in semidarkness, her master's voice loud and merciless in her ears: "You're capable of this . . ."

Suddenly she stops as if someone has caught hold of her. She hears the moment the painting is unveiled, the gasps from the guests, the ensuing noise. She stands without moving, and gradually the shadows retreat and the mist dissolves before her eyes. She stands absolutely still, trying to get her bearings, then slowly looks over her shoulder.

People have moved closer to the painting, which is bathed in bright light. She can see its upper half, the wet hair, the delicate shoulders, the cheek in blue half-shadow. Inadvertently, she raises a hand to her face and gently touches her cheek, then lets it fall to her side.

She forgets to retrieve her umbrella from the cloakroom. The rain has dwindled to a light drizzle, and the sun is trying to break through a gap in the clouds over the buildings across the square. She hesitates, waiting for the ground to stop undulating beneath her feet, then grips the handrail and sets off slowly down the long, broad flight of steps.

# ACKNOWLEDGMENTS

Many books and sources were important to me in my research for this book. I am particularly indebted to a few: the diaries kept by Iris Origo during 1943–44, and later published as *War in Val d'Orcia*; Caroline Moorehead's biography, *Iris Origo: Marchesa of Val d'Orcia*; and *The Rape of Europe* by Lynn H. Nicholas.

Parts of *Restoration* are inspired by and draw on the life of Marchesa Origo who, with her husband, restored La Foce, their Tuscan estate, in the 1920s and sheltered allies and partisans during World War II. While Alice Orsini undoubtedly shares similarities with Iris Origo, it is important to stress that the former is a purely fictional construct. The same applies to other characters and historical figures. They may share their names or certain features with characters in the book but that's where the similarities end. I have treated real places and events in the same cavalier manner, while sticking to "historical fact" to the best of my abilities.

I am also indebted to my agent, Gloria Loomis, for her care and support; Jason Epstein, who read this book in an early draft, for his friendship and wisdom; Dan Halpern and the team at Ecco—in particular my editor, Lee Boudreaux, who worked her magic on these pages with infectious enthusiasm.

And to my wife, Anna, whose patience makes this all possible.